I0653581

THE NASH CRITERION

INTEL 1, BOOK 4

EREC STEBBINS

TWICE PI PRESS

Only one thing is impossible for God: to find any sense in any copyright law on the planet.
—Mark Twain

Cover design by Erec Stebbins © 2017

Edited by Michael Matheson.

ePub ISBN-13: 978-1-942360-22-3

Paperback ISBN-13: 978-1-942360-12-4

Hardcover ISBN-13: 978-1-942360-13-1

Kindle ebook ISBN-13: 978-1-942360-11-7

To Pete and Michelle:
I try to keep an open mind

O Conspiracy,
Sham'st thou to show thy dang'rous brow by night,
When evils are most free?

— William Shakespeare, Julius Cæsar

PART I

OLD WORLD ORDER

"Behind the ostensible government sits enthroned an invisible government owing no allegiance and acknowledging no responsibility to the people."

— THEODORE ROOSEVELT

1

HOTLINE

"Will there be anything else, Elaine?"

Tipping her bifocals down, President York looked up from the mass of papers on her desk in the Oval Office. Before her stood a lanky man in a formal business suit, white hair and blue eyes staring back.

"No, George," she said, rubbing her eyes. "A crazy week. I'm sorry about the Senate vote. It's a slap in the face to me that they held it up as long as they did. In the end it wasn't even close. You deserved better."

George Tooze nodded. "Homeland Security is a macho position. They don't want some academic heading it. But it's done. Onward."

"Onward indeed, George," she said, gesturing to her desk.

Tooze motioned to leave but caught himself, turning back to the president.

"It was something today, Elaine. I remember when Obama was sworn in. First African-American president. Now this. No one will forget your speech. It will be in the history books."

"We've come a long way, baby. But if I hadn't been in boots and fatigues? Wouldn't have scratched that glass ceiling. So much fear out there. They don't care if you've got a law degree from Harvard, served in the Senate ten years, hell, even that your daddy was in that chamber. People need Daddy in the White House. Richard was a genius to use my military photos so much in the campaign. I think I ran mostly as a soldier!"

"You have a large base. A strong one. And we'll use that, don't you worry. We just had to convince enough fence sitters. And we did. Congratulations, Ms. President. You've earned it."

He smiled and closed the door behind him as he left. York watched him exit the White House and step toward a black town car idling in the driveway. It was good to have such loyal supporters early on. If you didn't, when things got rough, you were in trouble. And Elaine York didn't fool herself—in this business, sooner or later, things always got rough.

A large phone at the far end of the desk vibrated.

"You're kidding me."

York stared dumbfounded. The device was a military-grade smartphone, a one-of-a-kind custom gadget with cutting-edge voice and data encryption, designed specifically for one job: to serve as the President's communication device of convenience for hotline calls.

Hotline calls.

More than twenty bilateral hotlines existed between the United States and other nations. The famous Russian hotline was complimented with many spanning allies in Europe to frenemies in Asia and the Middle East. The phone was not supposed to buzz except when the White House Communications Agency had received and was routing a call from one of these nations' leaders. York felt the weight of her office descend like a mountain on her shoulders.

She grabbed the device and keyed in her unique code. "President Elaine York on Direct Link."

Static only. York engaged several additional security clearance codes. Nothing. Her heart began to pound. They checked this line every hour of every day! How could it be malfunctioning?

A pop of static startled her. A man's voice spoke.

"President York. It is so good to finally be able to speak with you."

York felt cold. She had run simulations with the hotline communication system. Procedures were followed, protocols in place. She should be speaking with White House Communications. She should be briefed and transferred to the incoming hotline call. What the hell was happening?

"Please don't be alarmed."

"Who is this? You aren't WHCA."

"No, we are not. We are not a formal part of the US government. Or any government."

York stared slack-jawed for a moment. "How the hell did you get this number? Who are you?"

"The answers to both questions are intertwined. You need to discover those answers before your presidency continues much further."

"Look, I don't know what this—"

"There is someone waiting for you underground. At the new Cogcon Line. I think that he will peak your curiosity."

"How do you know—"

"We know and we have access. Which should tell you all you need to know."

York blinked. "You have access to the train line?"

"Rest assured, Ms. York, your gleaming new railway is still a secret, known only to the proper governmental agencies. And our group."

"Who are you?"

"It is best we explain in a different setting."

"Why should I trust this? You could be luring me into a trap. I'm going to call—"

"Friendly fire, Ms. President!"

Her face paled. Elaine York stared forward wildly and swallowed. "What did you say?"

"Battle of Khafji. Terrible accident. Was it eleven servicemen died? You were assigned to that unit, weren't you?"

"In a non-combat role. Everyone knows that! Women weren't allowed to serve in combat roles then."

"But we both know the truth, don't we, Ms. York? Your actions were noble, truly. But of course it's not me you would have to convince. You and several other soldiers resisted some men in uniform who were out of control. The ensuing firefight was a tragedy." He paused. "And easily misconstrued. It would be terrible for your presidency if certain information were released to the public."

She squeezed her fingertips to her temple. This wasn't happening!

"The Cogcon line, Ms. President. Try at least that far. Someone will be waiting for you."

The connection closed.

In a near panic, York opened the trap door underneath her desk and descended into the Horsepower command post. It was empty. She searched for the Secret Service staff who manned the post, but found no one. Monitors *around her displayed camera footage from inside and outside the building. Communications equipment crackled and blinked. A filled coffee pot steamed beside several unopened sandwiches.*

"What the hell?"

Continuing was insane. This was an attack on the Presidency. Only an idiot would follow the directions from that cipher on the hotline.

Friendly fire.

She couldn't escape it. It would ruin her, strip her presidency of all moral authority and hand her opponents the perfect weapon to discredit her. Whoever had been on the other end of the line, they had terrible knowledge— dangerous knowledge, and the power that came with it. She had nowhere to go but forward, into the trap they had set for her.

She made her way through several of the hidden passageways leading to the classified rail line. Outside the deepest military and governmental circles, the new train was only a distorted rumor. The line served to secrete the president and staff deep underground, away from the White House in the event of a national catastrophe. As she opened the final doorway with a retinal scan, she saw the gleaming metallic surface of the presidential car in front of her, the hum of the electric motor purring softly.

A tall black man in a sweater looked down at her solemnly.

"Hello, Elaine," came his deep voice.

York stared up at the former community organizer, his hair completely grayed, his shoulders stooped and his gait limping. He looked old. He looked defeated. He looked mournful.

"Barack?"

2

SEWERS

"Those were *soldiers!*" said Houston. "We need to go back!"

The three stood in a stairwell, two flights down from Intel 1. The hacker Fawkes had just been killed in the office of John Savas—his head blown open from a sniper shot through the window. Sara Houston and Francisco Lopez had fled along with the remaining FBI agents, only to have Angel Lightfoote pull them to the side and toward a glowing EXIT sign.

"*Trust me!*" she had whispered without further explanation.

For reasons Houston would never fully understand, she had. In a split second decision, she had followed the bald woman into the stairwell, Lopez behind them. They glimpsed at the last moment a group of soldiers pour from the elevators with weapons drawn.

Browning in hand, Houston began to climb the stairs. The muscled arm of Lightfoote held her back.

"We can't!" she said. "There isn't time! They'll be looking for us. They'll know soon we're not with them."

Houston nodded. "We're wanted fugitives, I get it. But they've risked everything with us. I'm not going to abandon them now."

Lightfoote shook her head. "Not for you. For me!" She removed a thumb drive from her pocket and brandished it at Houston. "Fawkes's email and attachment. They want this! We can't let them have it. Not until we know what it is." Houston's pause was all the assent Lightfoote required. "Now, let's move!"

The FBI agent bounded down the stairs like a spider. Houston glared at Lopez who shrugged, and they followed after her, both struggling to keep up.

"Subbasement?" rasped Houston, glancing at the signs over the doorways.

Lightfoote landed heavily from a jump. "Yes."

A door was ajar, the stairway ending in a dank and musty corner. The smell of rotten eggs assaulted them. Lopez grabbed Lightfoote with his good arm, the sling on the other soaked in sweat.

"Where are we going?"

Houston scowled at the dimly lit passageway in front of them. "The goddam sewers. That's where."

Lightfoote nodded. "These huge buildings produce a lot of shit. There's got to be a connection to New York's underground rivers. If we can get access, we can follow it to some of the manhole connections—maybe find one they haven't welded shut. Come up on street level somewhere a little downstream." She turned on the flashlight app of her smartphone. "There has to be an access door down here somewhere."

There was. After several tense minutes of searching around pumps and other machinery, they found an iron hatch opening to the main sewer line. It required all the strength Lopez had left to pry it open, but soon they scrambled into the dark bowels of the city. A knee-high river of waste greeted them.

"Glad we skipped lunch," said Lopez, holding his hand to his mouth.

Houston stopped Lightfoote with her hand.

"Okay, before we go any further, hacker girl, what the hell is going on? Who were those soldiers? What do you know?"

Lightfoote cocked her head to the side. "I don't know. I feel it. Fawkes opened up Pandora's Box, Sara. Bad things came out. The soldiers came out. They're part of it. We have to see what's in this file. That's what they want. That's why he was killed."

"But you don't even know what's in that file!"

"Fawkes was a crazy bastard. That's what I know. But we had a kind of sick relationship." Lightfoote stared down into the darkness of the tunnel. "Whatever's in this, it was everything to him. It's why he did it all, brought the fucking world to its knees. He was trying to kill something. Something in this file."

"This Bilderberg?"

"Maybe," said Lightfoote.

Lopez shook his head. "And you think he's right? You think his death and those soldiers are somehow related to this?"

"Yes," she said. "Let's just give ourselves the chance to find out, get a look at this, okay? Before they whisk us off to some dungeon somewhere."

Houston stared into the green eyes before her. "Some dungeon? So that's what's going to happen to them? We left them to that?"

"I don't know for sure."

"But you feel it." Lopez crossed himself. "God be with them. I know what the monsters do in those dungeons. I've seen the product up close." He passed his finger over the stigmata on his forehead.

"All right," said Houston. "Let's get out of here. Get back to the apartment in Harlem. We've got computers. Internet access—to whatever's left of it. We'll see what we can find out there. And we better find something. Or we abandoned them for nothing."

An old Chinese couple crossing the street jumped backward and scampered away as a manhole cover rocketed into the air and landed several feet away from the dark hole. The iron disk wobbled like a giant coin to a ringing stop.

A bald woman in combat fatigues leapt out of the manhole, landing heavily on her feet. She drew a pistol and scanned around her, body in a tense crouch. Two others followed: a second woman covered in black, giving a hand to a large man in a flowing coat nursing his left shoulder.

Chinatown was empty, the old couple having thought better of continuing their walk. Shops around them were boarded up, many looted, debris and trash littering the roads and sidewalks. As the sun began to dip below the ridge of buildings in lower Manhattan, the three of them raced out of the road and into the alleyways, disappearing like silent shadows into the falling night.

3

RENDERED

The nightmare began as soon as they exited the FBI Jarvits building. Savas glimpsed several black vans and military issue trucks parked outside, armed men lining the perimeter. Soldiers marched them in file to the convoy like prisoners of war, hostile eyes tracking their movements, weapons in plain sight and at the ready.

As they approached the vans they were separated, each directed to a different vehicle. Savas had only an instant to stare into Cohen's eyes before the men jerked fabric over his head, leaving him in claustrophobic darkness. They cuffed his arms behind him, then roughly shoved him forward. He stumbled into the vehicle, smashing his forehead. A foot thrust him tightly into the corner and knocked the wind out of him.

"Shut up and don't move, and I won't have to use this."

Savas could hear the static crackle of a Taser inches from his face.

Several heavy bodies dropped into seats around him before the door slammed shut. The engine turned over and the vehicle lurched forward into the streets of New York.

With no visual input his brain had nothing to offset the choppy movements of the drive. Growing nausea churned his stomach into a painful knot. He tried visualizing images with the movements, always a step behind, the effort hardly compensating. *God help me from getting sick in this bag.*

He tried to guess their direction, the streets taken, hoping to learn where these men were taking them. But he failed. Within minutes, the vehicle's jerky maneuvers had scrambled his sense of direction.

He guessed it had been half an hour when the van stopped abruptly, throwing his face into the chair in front of him. The impact gave him a black eye, and he tasted copper from a busted lip. Unable to wipe his face, the blood dripped through the hood.

"He's a bleeder!" cried a man standing over him.

Laughter erupted. Arms hoisted him roughly to his feet and flung him out of the van. He forced himself not to gasp as his shoulder smacked the concrete. Pulling up slowly, he spit blood. *Focus, John.* He tried to slow his heart rate. He breathed deeply.

The sea.

The thick taste of brine and marine life penetrated the hood. The gull cries and sounds of waves told him all he needed to know. He'd been taken to a port, likely in lower Manhattan given the travel time. Boots rang on thin metal as a massive object thudded gently into the space before him.

A boat.

His other senses were primed, hearing and touch sharpened. He sensed the vessel and its weight rocking on the waves, knocking against the dock.

They're taking me out to sea.

~

THEY STOWED him roughly below deck, his wrists chained to the wall, the pitch of the boat sending another wave of nausea through him. They still hadn't removed the hood, the fabric now glued to his face from clotted blood. He didn't dare show any weakness or ask for aid. Whoever these men worked for, they had been instructed to treat him like the worst terrorist suspect. The implications sent a chill through him as he thought about Cohen and Miller, and what fate awaited them all.

At least he knew they would be together. The three had been split up, either for security or psychological warfare. Perhaps both. But their captors weren't careful enough. He'd heard the high-pitched sounds of a woman's voice—*Rebecca's voice*—as she cried out, an impact sounding from her hitting the deck heavily. *She's on board.* But he couldn't let himself dwell on what had happened to her. He had to focus, keep his wits about him, and discover all he could that might aid in an escape.

But he wasn't fooling himself. He'd known too many rendered terrorists, read too many reports, and could appraise professionally their situation. Statistically, escape was all but impossible. Only a handful had been recorded. As he fought off the bile climbing in his throat, he forced himself to face the truth—any attempts to escape, should they ever present themselves, would almost certainly end in failure. Probably in death.

We'll have to work with them. A recipe for Stockholm Syndrome. But the only hope for freedom, for survival, lay with their captors. Hope depended on meeting the desires of those now controlling their lives. Part of him wanted simply to resist, to find an opportunity to make a last stand and take down as many of them with him as he could.

But I'm not alone. Rebecca's here. Such a selfish death would not only break her heart, but would seriously endanger her life. He had to swallow his pride, his anger, suppress the desire to strike out. He had to act calmly. Shrewdly. He had to find a way to bring his captors to his side and convince them to release them. But without knowing who had taken him or why, it was impossible to know what to do, or how likely such efforts were to succeed.

The boat moved. He felt the random vectors of pitch, roll, and yaw from the waves give way to a clear direction. The sounds of powerful engines vibrated through the walls of the vessel. Kerosene fumes began to choke him.

The ship left the dock, but headed where, or why, he couldn't guess.

4

PANDORA'S BOX

"Holy shit! Look at this!"

Lightfoote leapt across the cluttered floor of the dilapidated brownstone, holding a laptop in the air as she approached Houston and Lopez.

"A second, fly-girl," said Houston, eyes focused on the deep wound in Lopez's shoulder.

Lightfoote stared at the hulking form of the former priest, shaking her head. *Damn.* Even in the middle of everything else, he *was* distracting. His shirt removed, he resembled a bodybuilder more than a former math teacher. His pecs flared and his lats striated as he tensed from the pain. She watched Houston finish applying ointment and seal the wound with taped gauze.

"Healing?" she asked, impressed with the CIA agent's field dressing.

Lopez grabbed his shirt and stood up. Houston exhaled. "Yeah, he heals fast. But it was an ugly gash. High caliber round ran like a spear through the muscle. But it's closing well. Just need to keep it from infection. Couple weeks and he'll be back in the ring."

"Well, if blowing up bad guys gets boring, he's got a career modeling for the Priest Calendar."

Lopez smirked and turned away, slipping his shirt slowly over his head. Lightfoote's gaze followed him as he walked to the window and stared outside.

"So, where's the fire," said Houston.

Lightfoote crouched and placed her laptop on the floor, turning the screen toward Houston. A series of colored strands ran across a map of the world in a diabolically complicated web. *More and more,* my *web.*

"Remember this map?"

Houston nodded. "Yeah, your worm versus Fawkes's. Yours were red? Looks like you've turned the tide."

"Right?" Lightfoote grinned softly. "At this rate, just a few weeks and the danger's gone. Well, millions of computers may still be infected. But my code isn't going anywhere. It'll take down any further attempts of his to spread. Best case scenario: we'll just have a few years of flare ups before we can hunt down the last copies."

"Congratulations, Angel," said Houston, rubbing her temples. "You need a medal or something."

Lightfoote breathed deeply. "Well, that's the good news."

Lopez turned around and walked over to the pair. "Sounded much too positive given current events. What else?"

"World's gone to shit. Communication's spotty from overseas. Media's mostly down and what's up is just broadcasting propaganda."

"Propaganda?" said Lopez, crouching down and looking at the screen.

Lightfoote opened a series of windows. Headlines from newspapers appeared online alongside video from ashen-faced newscasters.

"A presidential *coup?*" said Houston.

Lopez touched a window filled with text. "York claimed emergency powers and dismissed Congress? Nation-wide martial law?"

"I told you it was Pandora's Box," said Lightfoote. "Times article has the most details. York annulled the constitution and suspended civilian courts. Half the military's gone over with her, claiming extraordinary wartime powers. The other half is protecting members of Congress and attempting to end the coup." She leaned back on her hands and looked between the pair. "Basically we're in civil war, if you believe this."

Lopez eyed her sharply. "Do you?"

"There's a war on, that's for sure." She gestured at the screen. "The public opinion damage control is in full swing. But York, a dictator?"

Houston nodded, locking eyes with Lightfoote. "We met her. Only for a few minutes, but you learn a lot about someone when bullets and bombs are blasting around you. I didn't see dictator in her."

"I agree," said Lopez. "But if we're right, how do we explain this?"

"Assume there is a coup," said Lightfoote, "but not led by York. What if in the chaos Fawkes unleashed someone else decided to play Beautiful Leader?"

"Right," said Houston. "They'd need to sell their narrative. Slander York as the rebel, turn the population against her."

"Which means they don't have her," said Lopez.

"Not yet, anyway," said Lightfoote, pleased her new companions were so quick on the uptake. "But one thing's for sure, we're in a bad zone."

Lopez cocked his head at her. "The press slant?"

"If they're being fed this shit, we're in hostile territory." Lightfoote put her hands in her lap. "You said you left York at Mount Weather. That's Virginia?"

Houston nodded. "Seemed safe at the time. Didn't count on our government eating itself."

Lopez laughed. "Maybe it shouldn't surprise us. They sure have been quick to eat their own to cover dirty laundry. We know about that." Houston winced, and he reached out, stroking her hair. Houston cupped his hand.

Lightfoote looked between the two, her voice raw. "Let's hope the battle lines are drawn there."

"And if they aren't?" asked Houston. "If York's inside enemy territory?"

"Then we'd better hope she got the hell out."

The three sat in silence for several minutes. Videos of carnage and chaos looped on the laptop screen. Lightfoote fought to suppress the vague visions percolating within her. What had Savas called it? *Intuition.* Something Kanter and Savas had found useful to the Bureau. For Lightfoote, it was something else entirely. *Hypersensitive.* As painful as it was protective. Once burned, one detected even the slightest heat. And right now, the world was on fire.

"All right, been avoiding this one. There's even more bad news," Lightfoote paused. "I've tracked our friends."

"How?" asked Houston. "Not their phones. We made sure to use phones without GPS."

"Lots of ways to triangulate if enough towers are up. They're coming back online." Lightfoote entered several keystrokes, closed other windows and opened a map of the Eastern seaboard. A white circle blinked in the Atlantic, centered in a triangle of dots. "That's Rebecca's phone. John's and Frank's aren't responding. I assume they were taken, probably destroyed. Maybe Rebecca managed to hide hers, stow it somewhere."

"A bit of luck in a sea of disaster," said Lopez. "And speaking of *sea*— what the hell is her phone signal doing there?"

"Remember Fawkes?" said Houston. "He wanted to base his operations at sea to avoid the chaos he produced. Maybe our coup leader had the same idea."

Lopez leaned back and grunted. "But if they're out there, it's not on an armored yacht. If this is a military coup, our friends are likely secured on a naval destroyer."

"Complicates a rescue mission," said Lightfoote. Her stomach churned.

Houston shook her head. "Makes it *impossible*, Angel." She placed a hand on Lightfoote's shoulder. "I'm sorry."

Lightfoote stood up and removed the thumb drive from her pocket, pushing the conversation from her mind. "So we deal with this, what we can. Maybe it's the key to solving our crises, and finding our friends."

"Assuming you can get into it," said Houston. "Didn't Fawkes taunt you that it was encrypted?"

"I've tried. It's not going to be easy." Lightfoote set her jaw. "But I've got some ideas. In fact, a bunch of people have a bunch of ideas."

5

THE BRIG

The engines shifted to different pitch, the powerful thrust easing as the ship slowed to a stop in the dead of night. Savas remained handcuffed to the wall in the bowels of the boat. He'd seen no one in the hours since they left him there and heard no sounds but the machines churning around him.

The nausea had passed, his body having adapted to the ship's rocking. Exhausted, unable to sleep or relax with his hands chained high on the wall, he stood upright, muscles ceaselessly contracting to keep his balance, his body unable to rest a moment during the journey. His wrists bled from the repeated trauma of rubbing against the cuffs, blood trickling down his arms. Classic protocols designed to strip him of any power to resist.

And it's working.

For the first time in many hours, he heard human sounds. Footsteps clanged along a metal stairwell somewhere near his cell, boots banging down the outside corridor. A door opened with a grating wail. His hood was yanked off, the clotted blood ripping like weak glue. Light assaulted him.

"That's the one," came a voice from the blinding radiance.

Before he could discern more than the blurred outlines of bulky forms in front of him, they slipped the hood tightly over his head again. Strong arms grasped his wrists, unlocked the shackles, and twisted his hands painfully behind his back, cuffing him again.

"Move!"

They shoved him forward harshly through the doorway. And kept shoving him forward until he ran his shoulder into a metal bar. His ankle felt a platform. *A stairway?*

"Climb!"

Awkwardly, blind, he stretched out his foot and planted on the first step. He ascended by sense of touch alone, slipping on several occasions only to find himself shoved upward from behind, once with the barrel of a weapon placed against his neck.

"Stop!"

He'd reached the top of the stairwell. Heavy vibrations on metal accompanied the sounds of more soldiers approaching.

"What the fuck, Harrison? Haven't you ever taken prisoners before? Cuff the hands in front, dumb-ass! How the hell are we going to link the chain?"

They freed his hands and moved them around to his belt buckle, cuffing him again with a heavy chain latched to the restraints. The first tug nearly sent him sprawling, but he stumbled forward, trying to keep slack in the chain.

"Keep up, traitor! Or you're going overboard to the sharks."

The roar of the sea overpowered him—the crash of waves against the hull of the boat. Wind kicked up wildly, spraying sea across his hood. They'd reached the deck.

Denied vision for so long, his other senses began to paint phantom portraits. He sensed something looming over them as they dragged him forward, images of high walls and cliffs forming in his mind. The wind blew from the opposite direction, blocked completely by something massive and tall, a thing so large it seemed to block the sounds of the waves and reflect it back into their faces. He began to perceive a deep throbbing as if building from within his bones themselves—a gigantic motor churning beneath the waves.

A loud crash startled him, and the deck shook.

"Walk!"

Pushed forward, he stepped off the deck of the ship and onto another metallic platform, a gangplank of some sort. It bridged the gap between the boat and something far larger, a sea-going island of metal approaching like the mouth of a cave.

He toppled down, the plank ending without warning and an empty space swallowing his foot. He stumbled onto a much more solid surface, the sound of movement and laughter above him.

"Enough!" came a commanding voice. "Get him to the brig!"

Arms hoisted Savas, then pushed him forward down a secession of stairwells, through a series of heavy doors sealing like airlocks, and finally into a tight space with grill-work for walls.

The brig.

Again they left him cuffed to the wall, the chain hanging heavily along his arms, hood still cloaking his vision and nearly suffocating him. He wondered if the others would be brought here as well, but he knew it unlikely. Protocol isolated terrorist leaders, interrogations conducted without the opportunity to communicate. Standard operating procedure for these types of renditions.

A creaking metal hatch groaned and several pairs of boots tromped toward his cell. Keys unlocked the door in front of him and someone yanked the hood off. He had to turn his face from the light and shut his eyes.

"Well, you son of a bitch, you look about as fucked up as you ought to right now."

A hand grasped his chin and jerked his face forward. Savas squinted into the painful glow, a chiseled jaw and cold blue eyes staring at him.

"And I can tell you right here, right now—it's going to get a hell of a lot worse. Real soon. We're gonna make you wish you'd never been born, never dreamed up in that diseased head of yours to betray your nation. And before we kill you, kill your scumbag friends as well, you're going to tell us every goddamned thing you know about this cybercriminal."

"Fawkes?" muttered Savas.

The man struck him with the back of his hand.

"Fawkes? Who the hell is that? *Lightfoote*, you bastard. Your cyberterrorist whore! The one who let that damn worm loose!"

Lightfoote? It didn't make sense. These men had it all wrong. But he knew better than to try to explain. The tribunal had made it clear—someone had engineered a witch-hunt. He spit blood and ground his teeth.

"Go to hell."

"Oh, sweet Mary Sue, we got ourselves a tough guy." The man snorted. "Well, boys, we're gonna have us a good time breaking this bronco." He leaned in and whispered to Savas. "And we got all the time in the world to explain things to you."

6

AMBUSH

"Three cars have pulled up outside, Francisco!" Houston held the Browning beside her temple, parting the yellowed curtains as she stared through the window. *Things are moving too fast!* Already a noose was closing on them. "Two vans. A black town car. They're pouring out like roaches, heading for the steps." She darted away from the window and ran to the center of the room.

They'd killed the lights. The musty brownstone in Harlem was strobed by headlight beams darting through the windows. She saw the broad form of Lopez drop a laptop into a backpack and drape it stiffly over his shoulders. *He's still in pain.* He picked up a pump-action shotgun from the floor, catching and holding her eyes for an instant. A sheen of pale skin gleamed as it moved through the light streaming through the window. Lightfoote stood beside him with a drawn pistol, bald head and piercings flashing.

"They'll send a few round the back, coordinate the entry," said Houston. "We've got thirty seconds."

Lightfoote checked the display on a smartphone. "Getting a signal from the sensors—back and front. Right on the money, Sara. Let's see if they're ready for this."

"Watch for debris!" cried Houston. *I never get the damn yields right!*

The three crouched behind overturned boxes and furniture. Dust from the long-abandoned building filled the air with fine snow. The front doors rattled violently from a sudden blow. Lopez raised a metallic box in one hand.

"Now!" cried Houston. She ducked as he pressed the button.

Two explosions rocked the building. The front door erupted in a fireball, launching wood and metal in all directions. Several windows near the entrance shattered, exploding outward. Poorly maintained sprinkler systems sputtered, rusty water haphazardly raining across the interior, smoke-stained rivulets running across the floor.

"Go!" yelled Houston. She leapt forward.

The three sprinted, weapons pointed toward the shattered doorway. Mangled bodies were strewn across the brownstone steps, blood black with soot, dripping like molasses to the street below. A driver gawked at them from one of the vans, the door half open, his body tense and frozen in shock.

Use it. Houston set herself, firing two shots before he could react, and he toppled to the ground. The door slammed in the other van. The engine coughed and raced as the driver gunned the accelerator, the gears popping loudly as he shifted. The van lurched forward.

A shotgun blast from Lopez burst the back tire. The van pitched as the driver tried to turn sharply. The right side elevated off the ground and the van flipped violently onto its roof. It landed with a shattering of window glass and crunching metal on the left side. The front end plowed into a lamppost. With a single beat of silence, a fire ignited in the engine.

An empty car waited beside the entrance. Either the driver had fled or been killed in the explosions. Houston waved them to the vehicle. *Did any survive the rear blast?* If so, they had only seconds. "I'll drive. Move!"

The three dashed down the steps and into the car. Houston in the driver's seat, Lopez and Lightfoote aiming their weapons out the rear windows. The car jumped forward with a squeal and raced into the streets of Harlem.

"Damn that was fast!" Houston gunned the engine and aimed for Harlem River Drive. "Backtrace said an hour?"

Lightfoote shouted from the back, the air rushing through the windows mangling her words. "Barely! The NSA is back. Their fingerprints are all over the trace. But that fast? That wasn't a general scan. We're their target—they *know!*" The waterfall of sound stopped as the back windows were shut.

"Jesus!"

Lopez grimaced and placed the shotgun on the floorboard. "That was a strike team. Serious players."

"But not after *you*," said Lightfoote. "They don't even know you two exist."

Houston nodded, steering roughly, the tires screeching as she ran a red light. The relative quiet felt unnatural, adrenaline still coursing through her veins. "I'm getting a little tired of running like this."

Lightfoote swung away from the window and set down her gun. "We're going to have to be a lot more careful. They *really* want this damn file."

"Then it's important," said Houston, darting onto the highway. Tail-lights flashed past her, horns blaring.

"Whatever's in it," said Lopez, "must be bigger than we can imagine. They've taken the FBI team captive. They're tracking us with the full power of the NSA, sending professionals after us. We need to figure out what it is we have."

Lightfoote sighed. "That's what I was trying to do, dammit!"

"Well, your hacker friends are going to have to work faster," said Lopez. "We barely got out of that."

Houston turned toward the Willis Avenue bridge. *I have to think clearly.* "I'm going to avoid the toll stations. Take us on I-87 into the Bronx. Disappear this car as soon as we can. Steal another one. Angel, we need to get you online again. You need to find this hacker collective."

"I've got to warn them," said Lightfoote. "If they tracked us, they can track them. They've got to take measures to prepare. Disappear and arm themselves. They're going to be risking their lives to do this."

"But will they?" asked Lopez.

Houston cursed as a delivery truck weaved in front of them. "Francisco, she's a hero in the hacker underground. You saw those chat rooms, the messages she got."

"People worship a hero from a distance. Not many want to be heroes when the bullets fly."

"We'll see," said Lightfoote. "Maybe not for the good of it, or for me. Maybe for the challenge of Fawkes's encryption. Something Big Brother wants us *not* to see. Maybe they want to see it as much as we do. Maybe they want to be the ones to spill the secret."

"Maybe," Lopez muttered.

"Either way," continued Lightfoote, "we need to come up with a new plan. Digital security for sure. We'll need every anonymous protocol around. We'll need to move frequently. No more than a few hours at any connection. We need decoy stations to mimic our profile, lock those down and have them waste manpower checking them out."

"And we need to distribute the file."

"Yes, get it out to every hacker with a functioning processor. Parallel processing. Together, we can crack it."

"You sound confident," said Houston. "How can you be so sure?"

Lightfoote stared forward into the red taillights in front of them.

"Because we have to."

7

ENHANCED INTERROGATION

Savas felt himself scream again, but his body had been pushed far beyond conscious control. He could only react to the waves of torment and panic. The survival machine encasing his consciousness performed desperate actions shaped by millions of years of evolution.

The cry exploded from his lips without volition, drowned in the waterfall pouring into his lungs. Strapped to a wooden board, a partially permeable fabric tight over his mouth, only a fraction of the liquid penetrated, but it triggered thrashing and an adrenaline response. The rest spilled over his face, completing the illusion of submersion, dying, suffocating, and strangling to a final end. His muscles convulsed as he struggled against the restraints.

It ended and a boot plunged into his left side to cast him face first onto the wet metal. The impact registered as a small gnat in a hurricane of agony. Fabric fell from his mouth and he coughed violently, puttering out small sprays of water. Too little to have actually killed him, the volume still set all his physiology of imminent death into motion. He gasped for air.

"You're just making it harder on yourself. As well as the others," came the cold voice that had begun to haunt his dreams.

Savas coughed roughly. "Others. No. What—"

"How long will you make us work her over, Savas? Just tell us the truth and her pain can stop."

"I've told you everything!" He didn't recognize his own voice. The words were the cries of an asylum inmate.

"*Where* is Angel Lightfoote? Tell us and you can go. She can go. It's that easy."

Savas struggled to hold back tears.

"*Please*. I don't *know*."

"What was in the email? Tell us that then. Was it another worm you would use to attack the country?"

"We didn't *attack*."

Savas cried out as a boot toe speared him in the side. The kick lifted him off the floor, and he moaned.

"Stop insulting us. Do you think that mock tribunal is going to get you out of this? You'll be convicted, I have no doubt. But even if you aren't, there's no way—*no* way—you traitorous scum, that I'll let you leave this place alive. Do you understand? You aren't going to walk out of here after what you've done. Maybe, just maybe if you play ball, and help us track down these terrorists, your precious Rebecca might live."

"Please, don't hurt her. I've told you everything I know."

A hand reached down and pulled his head back by the hair.

"What is the Nash Criterion? What does it *mean?*"

"Don't. Know." He gasped. "Fawkes. Last email. Death trigger. No time."

The hand smashed his head into the metal grating. The room spun. He couldn't focus on the words. Strong arms dragged him from the room and down a short hallway, grated metal cages lining each side. Faceless forms slung him into one and he landed heavily on his shoulder, a stab of pain jolting him conscious.

A broad shape stood silhouetted in the doorway, the outlines of the man's face barely discernible. But the Voice—everything had mutated into a voice now. No eyes, no face, no person. Just a hateful Voice that meant pain and impossible requests. The Voice dragged him and others through hell and back, teasing them with relief that came in the form of unscalable mountains, nonexistent answers, locks that could never be opened, and pain that would never end.

"This is really going nowhere," said the Voice. "It's time you thought carefully about giving us some of those answers, agent Savas. And soon. Your friends don't have much time left."

"I told you *everything.*"

"You can do more. And I know just the ticket. We'll resume our discussions soon and we'll let you in on some of our work with the others. Maybe we'll let you sit in and watch as we work on your sweet Rebecca? Would you like to see her?"

"No, please—"

"I can see it would mean a lot to you. We don't usually have an option like this for difficult prisoners. Can you imagine all the work we put in only to have some motherfucker like you die on us? What a waste of our time! But bring in a child, or lover, and these tough men break like china. I think you're one of those men, Savas. I think when you've seen enough of what we'll do to her, you'll shatter like a plate and tell us what we want to know."

"No, please! I'll tell you now! Everything, I promise. Whatever you want to know." He would lie. He would make up any story. Find one they could accept. Anything to stop them.

"Now, that's very helpful of you, John. But it's just lying desperation. I've seen that, too. No, no—only when you're truly broken will you skip the lies and get to the truth. I just hope that point comes before your dear Rebecca is too damaged to be worth anything to you anymore."

"*No!*"

Another kick to the face cut short his scream. The door slammed shut as he rolled away from it, nauseous and dizzy.

Footsteps and laughter poured like acid over his fading consciousness.

8

MILLER

Frank Miller stood upright, his shirt removed to reveal enormous musculature. Wires were taped to heaving pectorals that dripped with sweat. His arms were pulled out to the sides, clamped tightly. His pants stained with sweat and urine, blood dripping from his lips, teeth marks in the torn flesh. He panted with his head cast down.

A man beside him turned a knob, generating a throbbing hum. Miller screamed, his entire body convulsing. His eyes rolled back involuntarily in his head. The electrical jolt ended quickly, but it demanded a high price. Miller slumped forward heavily, the restraints on his broad arms groaning.

The blue-eyed man stepped beside him and pulled his head back by the hair.

"We've got juice to do this every day for the rest of your life. Right now the damage is minimal, whatever the pain. But the more we fry you, the more cells will burst in your tissues, the more nerves will be damaged. First, you'll lose feeling in your extremities, your fingers and hands. Coordination. Then eyesight. Brain damage is next. Agent Miller, after all you've done, this is hardly the way to end your life."

Miller drooled to the floor, his mouth twitching. Words slurred with spit and blood escaped as a whisper: *"Fuck you."*

The inquisitor sighed and rubbed his temples. He looked toward the man at the controller.

"Call it a day, Rice. The specialist arrived an hour ago. Tell him he's up."

"Yes, sir," said the man, exiting the room quickly.

"I don't have time for heroes, Miller. I need results, and I need them now. Fortunately, technology is on my side."

The soldier Rice returned, the door groaning as he opened it. A bald, thin man followed him with two large duffel bags, his expression detached.

"Ah, here he is. Dr. Kuriyan." The blue-eyed man examined the bags. "That's all you need?"

"Yes," Kuriyan said, removing wires and electrodes, drills, scalpels, and power sources. "Designed for any environment. You already have him immobilized, so I'll just add this."

He removed a metallic skull cap encased in a cage. Sizing up Miller, he nodded.

"He's big, but it will fit."

"You've come highly recommended."

The visitor plugged in power supplies and set his tools along a small table. "I'll need ten minutes to prep him, once he's properly restrained. Once I've located the brain regions and tested the voltages in the tissue, you can proceed. He'll answer truthfully anything you ask. Cognitive function will be minimally impaired." He looked over the wires connected to the prisoner. "Assuming it hasn't already been. I'll need all that disconnected."

"Rice—do what he says."

The soldier nodded, eyes wide. He rushed to remove the wires from Miller's chest and arms, ripping the tape, tearing hair and skin in the process. Miller didn't flinch.

"He's nearly unconscious," muttered Kuriyan as he fiddled with the skull cap. "My technique is far more useful with a prisoner in his right mind."

"Your technique is here to get a job done. We need information yesterday. We expect you to get it."

Kuriyan frowned and continued to adjust the equipment. "All right. I'll need you to hold his head against the board," he said, indicating the metal stand on which Miller was strapped.

The blue-eyed man nodded and the soldier grasped Miller's head and pushed it backward.

"Easy, his muscles are slack. Don't want to break his neck. Keep him facing forward—yes, like that. Good. Now," he stepped forward with the caged skull cap. "I'm going to fit this over his head, clamp it to the metal behind, and then tighten it over his skull." He scanned the room. "I'll need that chair to stand on."

The blue-eyed man pushed a metal chair loudly across the floor. Kuriyan stepped on it, ducking slightly under the low ceiling, and raised the cage over Miller's head.

"Hold him steady. *There.*"

Miller's eyes flashed and his head darted to the right. His forehead smashed Rice, who stumbled against the wall, holding his eye and cursing.

The leather clamp on Miller's right arm groaned and popped, the material failing as he brought his arm around and struck the visitor in the mouth, sending him careening from the chair. Rice had regained his footing and charged, but Miller swung his arm again, connecting violently with the soldier's head. Rice's head jerked backward, eyes empty and unfocused, before he plunged downward. His head struck the side of the metal table, wrenching his neck to the side and he lay unmoving on the ground.

Miller reached out for the blue-eyed man, fighting against the remaining restraints, fingers clawing the air in front of him.

Three shots roared off the small room's metal walls as the interrogator fell away from Miller's grasp, gun in hand. The first shot sent sparks and metal shards flying behind Miller. The other two buried themselves deep in Miller's chest. Blood misted into the air and spilled down Miller's torso.

"Shit!" cried the blue-eyed man.

He moved quickly to the fallen soldier, keeping a careful eye on Miller. He placed his hand at Rice's throat, checking for a pulse. He pulled it away scowling and glared at Miller.

"He's dead, you son of a bitch. Broke his damn neck."

Miller gasped and choked, blood frothing at his mouth, eyes swimming.

"You better not fucking die on me yet."

He kept his weapon trained on Miller and circled around him to the crumpled form of the doctor.

"Doctor Kuriyan," he said. "Are you all right?"

The doctor groaned and stumbled against the wall, bracing one arm against the corner. The other cradled his jaw. He pulled his hand away, tissue and teeth floating in a red pool.

"Jesus," said the interrogator. "Go get cleaned up, and send a medical crew in here." The hatch clanged open, and several soldiers with raised weapons entered.

"Sir, we heard shots!"

The blue-eyed man waved them away. "Get our visitor some attention. And send a crew down here to save this motherfucker." Miller continued to thrash weakly before them. "Tell them I want him alive and conscious long enough so the doc can drill into that stupid skull of his and place his wires."

He turned to them, holstering his gun, eyes frigid.

"I want some fucking answers, goddammit!"

9

HACKER ARMY

A rusted sun set through the clouds over vandalized cars and buses littering the streets of Queens. A lone figure stepped around a corner, a swollen backpack over his shoulders, two heavy bags in each hand. Dark sunglasses and a newsboy hat concealed his features.

Lopez scanned the deserted street in front of him and placed the bags on the ground. Reaching around his oddly flowing robes, he removed a handgun and checked it, replacing the firearm quickly. He took up the heavy duffels again and made his way cautiously across the street.

As he approached a towering apartment complex, he made his way down a tight alley filled with piles of rotting garbage, the reek potent even in the cold December air. Near an overflowing dumpster he walked up to a small door that angled sideways, the hinges ripped from the wall. He kicked softly and it swung from a remaining hinge near the top. He entered.

He moved directly to a dim stairway and descended quickly, breath strained and broad shoulders bowed by the weight he carried. Three flights down the stairwell ended at a door with a shattered EXIT sign, one bulb still flickering. Glass crunched on the ground under his feet. He placed the bags down again and removed the pistol, opened the door quickly, and spun toward a dark hallway with the firearm aimed in front of him.

He saw no one in the corridor. Grabbing the two bags with one hand, he grunted from the pain to his shoulder, but kept his weapon ready, shuffling awkwardly forward. He passed a janitor's closet, the door smashed open, broken items inside strewn haphazardly. He dropped the bags in front of a small door with a faded label reading: TELCOM CLOSET.

He rapped a brief pattern on the door and it opened to reveal Houston's piercing blue eyes.

"Damn, Francisco," Houston said. *Three hours.* You had me scared. We need to find chargers for these phones."

"Tomorrow." He entered quickly, dragged the bags inside, and dropped the backpack on the ground with a loud impact. Houston locked the door behind him.

The three of them repositioned awkwardly in the cramped room, the space hardly larger than a suburban wardrobe closet. A single incandescent bulb lit the space in a soft yellow, revealing a spaghetti of wires spilling from opened pipes above them. Many of the wires ended at several computers placed in a row along a rusted table. Lightfoote danced around the laptops like a grandmaster playing simultaneous games of chess.

"She getting anywhere?" Lopez asked.

"Angel is in the room and can hear gossip about her," said Lightfoote, not taking her eyes from the screens or fingers from the keyboards.

Houston smiled. "Yes. Brief you in a minute. She did get a message out to York. Had to hack through a bunch of defense computers. If she's picking up, York will get the last coordinates from Cohen's phone. A brief message about what we saw."

"She owes us one."

"She does. Meanwhile—what's the loot?"

Lopez grunted. "Just about everything is gone out there. People fled and took out almost every shop. I'll be damned if I know where they all went, or when they're coming back." He opened the duffel bags. Metal disks glinted softly in the dim light. "Cans. Mostly vegetables. Some fruits. Guess people don't like to eat healthy when civilization is collapsing around them."

"It'll do," she said. "I'm famished."

He dragged the backpack beside her.

"But there is *this*."

He unzipped it, and a pile of boxes spilled out of the bursting fabric and slapped heavily on the ground. One opened and numerous bullets rolled across the floor.

"Now we're talking." Houston kissed him and smiled. "How the hell did you find it?"

"They've cleaned out the gun shops—I wonder how many of those idiots end up shooting each other? But they didn't think to look for storage. Or maybe they couldn't get through the locks. Big megastores have shelves of ammunition and some firearms. No weapons we don't have. Lots we wouldn't care for. But the ammunition—we're low after that raid."

Houston pulled a box out of the bag. "Holy shit, Francisco—.45 ACP?"

He smiled. "Yeah, I figured you'd be glad to see those."

"You bet your ass." She removed her Browning. "Mama's got some milk for you, baby boy. Thank God. Now I won't have to be shooting one of those plastic toys people insist on calling guns."

"Hey, Glock's a good friend," muttered Lightfoote, clacking the return key emphatically and looking in their direction. "Might save your life someday."

Houston shook her head. "Maybe. What now, FBI girl?"

"Now, we wait. I've done all I can. We've got more bandwidth here than we can use. The entire complex seems abandoned."

"Those gangs didn't count?" said Lopez.

"Not in my book. Not enough fight. Anyway, no traffic on the inbound cables. So, I've routed the main lines to the laptops. The data is out, the hacker groups have it. I sent it through a maze of servers and TOR networks. The NSA will track it down eventually, but maybe not before we get what we need and can get the hell out of here."

"What we need is that file decrypted," said Lopez.

"Right. Whatever Fawkes did, it's good but not unbreakable. Patronizing bastard wanted it just tough enough to test us. Make sure we're *worthy*."

"What about the NSA? They've got the file presumably?" asked Houston.

Lightfoote nodded. And collapsed on a plastic chair. "Definitely. They just needed to raid my accounts. I didn't have time to wipe anything. And there are ways around that, too."

Houston stared at the rows of numbers running wildly across the screens in front of them. "So how the hell is some group of distributed hackers going to out-muscle the computational power of the NSA?"

"They can't," said Lightfoote. "Our only hope is to be smarter. More clever."

"And if we aren't?"

"Then they're going to get the information first," answered Lightfoote. "It's clear they want it. They're willing to kill for it. Even if we do break the encryption before them, they'll still get there eventually. So, if we get lucky, we're going to have a small window. We'll need to act fast."

Lopez exhaled. "And do what? We have no idea what's in that file. Maybe it's a final, insane joke from Fawkes to troll us once and for all."

Lightfoote shook her head. "I don't think so. I told you: I think I knew him in a way few did, even if we only spoke a few times. His personality stains his code, his worm. He's much too serious about all this. That file has something radioactive. Fawkes was killed for it. Our friends were snatched for it."

Houston smirked. "And we were almost killed for it, too, Francisco. She's right."

Lopez looked over to the computer screens.

"Then I hope these hackers know what they're doing."

10

<hr>

COHEN

The hatch opened and a figure plunged onto the floor. Long brown hair spilled in clumped knots to conceal her face. Her hands were splayed out in front of her and bound, and she struggled to use them to prop herself up. Soiled clothes hung from her frame.

"Get up, Agent Cohen," came a cold voice from behind her.

Several men entered the room alongside a short-cropped older man with ice-blue eyes. He gestured to the floor and the men stooped down and dragged Cohen to her feet. Two women stood in front of her in lab coats, a large flat-screen monitor hanging from the wall to their left. Numerous sharp objects glinted on a table beside them. They looked like surgical tools.

"Put her on the table."

The men did as instructed and tossed her harshly onto a metal slab mounted in the center of the room. Cohen groaned from the impact, hair still obscuring her face.

"We're reaching the limits of our tolerance with you and your people, Agent Cohen," said the cold voice. "We need you to understand that you don't have much more time. The tribunals have been a circus act, a show to convince you and your husband that cooperation is mandated. Those sessions failed. So, you've forced our hand. We can't let your seditious plans continue."

"We aren't traitors." She leaned forward weakly. Her eyes burned through the matted strands of her hair. "We aren't terrorists, either!"

The interrogator nodded and one of the men beside her struck her in the mouth. Cohen rolled hard on the table away from the blow, moaning. The man on the other side shoved her back in position.

"Your tired refrain angers me."

"You're monsters," she gasped.

"Do you think you're being mistreated?"

Fearful eyes stared back from the table.

"Perhaps you don't understand just how serious we are."

He nodded to a man standing guard by the door, who opened the hatch and called down the hallway. A rough scraping echoed outside. Someone was dragging a heavy object across the floor. Two burly men wedged themselves and a third figure through the hatch. They tossed a body to the floor.

Cohen screamed.

"*Oh, God.* No!"

The naked body of Frank Miller lay prone on the metal floor. Clotted and dried blood caked his torso and head. The hair had been shaved from a portion of the scalp, and three large holes had been drilled into the skull. A coating of frost melted along the grayed skin.

"No, Frank. I'm so sorry."

"Agent Miller was most uncooperative. Attacked and killed a good soldier, in fact." The cruel eyes leaned toward her. "This will be your fate soon. It will be the fate of your dear husband, Agent Savas, if we do not learn the whereabouts of your accomplices. There isn't going to be any escape. Your trick with the phone was clever. But it's over. The device destroyed. No one is coming to save you."

Tears ran down and smeared the dirt on her face.

"No. Please. I've told you everything. I'll tell you anything. I'm not holding anything back."

"That may well be true, Agent Cohen. Perhaps you were not privy to all the information. But I can't take that chance. Instead, I have found a way to make you most useful to our efforts."

Cohen blinked as the monitor across from her lit up. "John?" A guttural sound escaped her lips. "What have they done to you?"

The battered visage of Savas blinked in stunned silence, an eye swollen shut, the same side of his face cut and covered with blood. His slurred words poured from split lips.

"Oh God, *no*," came the voice from the screen. "You bastards—no! Don't do this! Please!"

The men alongside Cohen strapped her arms and legs tightly to the table.

"*Stop!*"

"Two bodies, Agent Savas, as you can see from your cell monitor. One dead." He walked up to Cohen and held up a large hunting knife, laying the edge near her throat. "The other still alive for now." He ran the edge slowly down her torso, over her breasts, to her crotch. He smiled at the camera mounted in the flat screen. "And still mostly unsullied."

"They're in Harlem!" screamed Savas, weeping. "It's a safe house. They're hiding out there!"

"John, no. Don't." Tears fell from her eyes.

"Oh, but he has to, Agent Cohen. That's what I'm counting on."

Savas continued in a high pitch. "Please. I'll tell you where it is. Where they're hiding. Everything you need to know. Let her go!"

The man spun the knife in his hand.

"Sadly, Agent Savas, that is not enough."

"*What?* Why?"

"You're too late with that information. We already discovered that lurking place. We nearly had them, but they escaped. Killing, you might want to know, several of our people. We will need more from you. Where else would they go? How can we track them?"

"That's all I know! It's the only place! There isn't any other way to track them! We used burner phones. They'll be in hiding!"

"Oh, this is terribly unfortunate." He shook his head sadly. "I am inclined to believe you. I think the china has shattered. What a tragedy you had not told me this earlier, before they could escape." He frowned. "But you had to be a tough guy."

He nodded to a man next to him, who moved toward Cohen's feet.

"These men are not soldiers, Agent Savas. Do you know why?"

Savas only stared in panic at the man.

"Most of the soldiers aren't good at this. They follow orders, but only up to a point."

"No, wait!"

"But these men," he said, "have no such qualms. They are most useful when we need to go beyond certain points." His blue eyes shown as he rolled the words off his tongue.

"I can work with you. I can help you locate them, serve as bait. *Anything*. Please!"

"Yes, Agent Savas. I'm sure you will. Once you are convinced. When you have watched us hurt her day after day, it will seal your *honest* cooperation."

"I told you already about Harlem! I'll cooperate!"

"A sudden break. Emotional with no time to override." He shook his head. "But tracking them will take time. Weeks, perhaps. During that time, in the hours at night when you can't sleep? When you remember what has happened to you, your friend Miller here, your wife? No, you will devise some trick. We will lose time and more men." He walked up to the screen and stared coldly at it. "No, agent Savas. Too much time for you to plot. Unless you are utterly broken."

The other man reached the top of the table.

Cohen spoke firmly through tears.

"John, just close your eyes. Don't watch. *Please.*"

The blue-eyed man smiled.

"Even the blind can hear."

11

TOOTH FAIRY

"I didn't want to be here," said the rich baritone. "Usually the last president has to make this important transition, but with that unexpected death, well, I'll have to do." He nodded to his reflection in the window. "This way you'll trust them. They've found it smooths things significantly."

The train sped through the underground tunnel, the absence of Secret Service officers only one of many factors unnerving York. She turned toward the former president, his frame slouched and angled in the plush chairs, his gaze unfocused through the window at the blurred stone walls speeding past.

"Trust who, Barack? What the hell is going on?"

"I think we're almost there," said Obama, standing awkwardly as the car swayed. The train decelerated rapidly. He motioned to York. "You'll get off here."

She stared through the window as the brakes hissed, the cabin coming to a complete stop. "Here? We aren't at the terminal point. We're in the middle of the damn tunnel! How do we get off here?"

Obama smiled wanly. "You'll see. Come on."

The doors opened, and she followed him out of the car numbly. A small ledge rose over the tracks, a set of steps rising from it. A metal door gleamed at the top of the stairway.

"This isn't in the maps."

"*Retinal scan will get you in,*" Obama said. "*You're lucky—you should've seen the digs they had when I was sworn in. This is Madison Avenue.*" *Again the weak smile.* "*It's going to seem impossible, Elaine,*" *he said, looking down the length of the train as it curved around the tunnel.* "*It's like growing up, except doing it again later in life. You have to give up a lot of childish ideas that aren't true. Santa Claus. The Tooth Fairy. Of, by, and for the People. You have to accept the adult world and work with what it is, or—well, or you won't make it in that world.*" *He put a hand on her shoulder.* "*The train won't leave until you go in. Good luck.*"

She watched in shock as he turned around and boarded the train, the automatic doors closing behind him. York glanced down the tunnel walls, along the tracks and train cars, and finally back to the doorway before her. She half-believed she was dreaming.

"*Maybe it's a stroke,*" *she whispered, slowly ascending the stairs to the gray metal door.*

A lens with a red light glinted down at her.

"*So, Star Chamber—all this and you weren't prepared for a short woman?*"

She rose on her toes and stared into the glass circle in front of her. Seconds later bolts disengaged with clangs and the door swung inward. York stepped forward into a dim chamber that turned pitch as the outer door slammed shut behind her. The locks sealed loudly.

The walls shuddered, she felt her stomach drop, and the floor plunged downward. As she fell, her eyes adjusted to the chamber, noting metallic walls devoid of instrumentation or insignia. Void of information.

Gravity tugged heavily on her as the lift came to a stop. The door behind her hissed, and she spun around to see an opening into a room glowing with blue light.

Straightening her blouse, she exhaled sharply, staring forward with determination.

She walked through the doorway.

12

COMMANDO RAID

"**N**o!"

Savas lunged forward with all his strength, but the two guards on his right and left held his shoulders down. His arms were tied harshly behind him, lashed to the chair. His feet were bound at the ankles. He could not stop the events in the other room. Forcing him to watch, the men beside him held his chin up to the screen.

Blackness. The screen popped and fell dark. A deep hum dropped through the ship in pitch until it fell out of human detection. Bass notes shook through him.

"What the fuck?" One of the guards beside him cursed, stumbling in the darkness, tripping on a leg of the chair, his body impacting the unseen wall.

"That was the reactor, Burton."

"Nuclear powered ships don't lose power, dumbass! And we've got rows of batteries. Power's cut somewhere."

"Where's the backup?"

"I don't know! Shit! Can't find the damn door. Here!"

A metallic grating screeched and a rush of air entered the room. Savas still could see nothing except the faint afterglow of the monitor. No light entered from the outside corridor. He heard muffled shouts and explosions from above.

"Holy shit! We're under attack!"

A light leapt forward highlighting the barrel of a gun.

"Burton, mount your weapon-light! It's all we have!"

The other soldier followed suit and both rushed down the hallway.

Savas closed his eyes and strained to hear. The sounds of fighting intensified. He felt the boat slowing, yawing clockwise as the engines remained quiet. He yanked at the restraints but got nowhere, and slumped in the chair in frustration. Their one chance of escape and he couldn't take advantage of it!

A thunderous blast shook him. Metal shards flew through the hallway, clanging and slamming against the walls. Acrid smoke spilled into his room, followed by the sound of rushing boots.

A bright light shone into his eyes from the doorway. Completely blinded, Savas turned his face away, squinting.

"They're here! I've got Savas!" cried the voice with the light.

"Found the others!" came a muted voice down the corridor.

The man pulled out a stick and cracked it, and a bright blue light filled the room. He tossed it on the floor in front of Savas and switched off his flashlight.

"What the hell?" asked Savas.

The man dropped to his knee behind the chair. "We're a rescue team. Seal assault squad. We're here to get you *out!*" Savas felt a hard tug on his wrists and heard the restraints tear. His hands were loose. The man bent over to his ankles and cut the ties with a large blade, freeing him.

Savas stood up and almost fell, his knees buckling. The man caught him from behind.

"Can you walk?"

"Hell yes."

He willed himself forward. His muscles screamed, but he forced them to move, the motion and adrenaline quickly loosening the tightness.

Cold metal touched his hand. The soldier had placed a gun there.

"We might be shooting our way out, Agent."

He stumbled into the hallway. Above, the chaos continued: explosions and the sounds of aircraft and heavy guns firing. Two more soldiers stood in front of them. They were dressing a woman.

"Rebecca!"

Her head turned as he limped forward. They embraced and he wept, holding her tightly to him.

"John, no time," she said, pulling back, tears in her eyes. "We've got to move fast."

"FBI man," came the clipped voice of one of the Seals. "Off with the shoes and pull these over you. Now!"

He didn't have time to think or understand. The man handed him an oversized suit. It felt synthetic. A similar dark material covered Cohen and she held swimming flippers under her arm. The men pushed them forward as she zipped up the suit.

"You're going to go straight up the ladders. If we still have it secured, it will take you to a lower deck, near water. SDVs are there waiting with drivers. Don't hesitate. Jump in. We've got only minutes."

Another set of explosions rocked the ship. The soldier speaking to him smiled.

"At least air support is giving them something to chew on."

They reached the ladders. Cohen climbed above him, racing for the top. Savas followed closely behind.

"Rebecca, the men—"

"Not now, John. Please. They're dead."

He heard the strain in her voice. He closed his eyes and climbed.

They stepped onto the deck as salt water sprayed over them. Rough waves battered the hull, the ship no longer under power to steer. Fires flicked above as wounded men screamed over the gunfire.

"My God," Savas whispered. "It's an aircraft carrier."

The enormous expanse of a flight deck loomed several stories above him. A Seal shoved a mask into his hand and helped him fit it over his head, another strapping flippers on his feet. The man shouted through the turmoil.

"Dive in toward the SDV!" he screamed, pointing below at a dark shape. "They'll hook you up. Do what they say! Stay calm!"

The man pushed Savas forward. He saw Cohen leap into the night air and plunge into the water below. Grinding his teeth, he stepped off the deck. The sounds of battle funneled into a point over his head, and a great, wet maw opened below him, wind and waves drowning out the battle above.

His feet smacked the surface and the cold water enveloped him. Arms pulled him against a black hull and he felt someone grab his head and attach something to the back of the mask. Stale air began to flow into it.

A hand pointed to the hull, and Savas saw an opening to a hollow interior. Brown hair billowed from within as Cohen moved inside, out of his sight. He kicked with the powerful flippers and approached what looked like an oversized torpedo. Seals helped him inside and followed behind him.

He floated to the back of the chamber alongside Cohen. Bubbles erupted from behind her as she breathed, her eyes focused intensely into his. He grasped her outstretched hand.

The door lumbered shut, but the water remained, along with two Navy Seals accompanying them. Not a submarine, the interior remained flooded for the duration, air supplied by the tanks hooked up to their masks. The craft's acceleration pushed them backward. Cohen leaned her mask against his and closed her eyes.

13

THE UNDERWORLD

He lost all track of time and sense of direction in the cramped submersible. But he didn't care at that moment. Just to be next to Cohen again, to have escaped that hell-hole—he couldn't process the miracle. He felt grateful. Delivered. They held onto each other.

Part of his mind continued to race. Who had sent these soldiers? Why had they turned on their countrymen? And who had kidnapped them in the first place, whisking them out to sea on an island-sized aircraft carrier?

He had no answers. He began to obsess about pursuit, a panic building that somehow the cold man with the voice would return, strap him down, make him scream. The carrier had seemed badly damaged and incapacitated. Had it remained so? Were small ships sent to hunt them down? He doubted this submersible could stay underwater for prolonged periods of time. Where were they headed? He stumbled from dreamscape to dreamscape.

A soldier in front of him spoke into his mask. The soldier beside him answered silently and looked in their direction, motioning with his hand to the door. Savas glimpsed a communications setup in his suit, but surrendered to fatigue and ignored it. He simply nodded back.

The other Seal engaged the mechanism and the side door opened to blackness. Savas and Cohen followed the two men outside the craft, swimming awkwardly and trying to keep up, beams from their helmet lamps strobing the water. The soldiers often doubled back to help them along.

Above, Savas began to catch a faint glow. A diffuse radiation supplemented the helmet lamps. Perhaps the moon or artificial lights. He couldn't be sure. He began to make out shapes in the water around him.

A wall.

In front of the two soldiers, a sheer rock face loomed. The men took no heed and swam straight for it. Savas and Cohen flailed forward, a dark circle growing in the surface before them.

A tunnel. Broad enough to allow them to swim inside, but too narrow for the submersible. Savas looked behind them. The craft had disappeared. They were on their own and headed into the bowels of a cliff.

As they passed within the opening, Savas saw that it was manmade. Too round, devoid of the growths and imperfections of natural formations, his headlamp revealed telltale evidence of boring machines. Someone had dug these tunnels. For what purpose he could not guess.

The Seals ahead turned in their direction. A flash of light from their headlamps pierced the darkness. The FBI agents had lagged behind, and the soldiers waved them on. A current pushed outward from the tunnel like a tide, dragging like gravity as they tried to continue inward. Their pace was slowing. They were tiring. Savas prayed they did not have far to go.

After some minutes, the soldiers stopped ahead. As Cohen and Savas caught up, he saw that the passage split four-ways. The two men discussed the different tunnels animatedly, gesturing in each direction. *Wonderful.* He saw a blue light flash from each of their helmets and what appeared to be a screen superimposed on the glass. *A frogman's heads-up display?* He hoped they had a map for these tunnels to reference. *How much oxygen is left?*

After several minutes of watching the back and forth, Savas saw them come to an agreement, settling on the rightmost tunnel. Again the soldiers waved them forward. The marathon swim continued, exhaustion beginning to take a severe toll. Cohen struggled, her eyes downcast and unfocused. His own breath filled the inside of his mask like some elephant's gasping. They couldn't go on much more.

Ahead, a shaft of light dove into the water. The soldiers aimed right for it, their pace accelerating. Savas felt his heart leap, adrenaline coursing through his veins. *The last push.*

The tunnel opened into a wide chamber, multiple other passageways underwater embedded around them. But the soldiers ignored the other tunnels and began to swim upward, toward the light. Savas grabbed Cohen's hand. Her face was pale, but her eyes glowed with hope. They kicked upward together, the current gone, the final burst of energy giving them the power to keep pace with the Seals.

The four of them broke through to the surface, artificial light reflecting off the ripples and partially blinding them. An enormous domed roof arched above them. Around the pool of water ran a stone walkway. Doors and passageways opened in different directions away from the chamber.

As his eyes adjusted, he saw figures lining the pool—soldiers, weapons in their hands, aimed in their direction. In the middle of the group of men stood a short woman, her silver hair contrasting with the black body armor she wore.

The Seals urged them forward. They covered the short distance to the water's edge, and with the help of several soldiers above managed to drag their bodies and equipment out of the water. Feeble and nearly helpless on land, others helped them out of the wetsuits, two female soldiers covering Cohen's naked form in a robe. Savas stood with trembling legs, his soiled clothes, suit, mask, and air tank at his feet. Soaked and dripping, he shivered in the crisp air.

The gray-haired woman walked forward, her gaze stern as it assessed them. She placed a hand on Cohen's shoulder as she spoke:

"Agents Savas and Cohen. I'm honored to meet you. I only wish the circumstances had been different."

"Ms. President," whispered Savas, his fatigue nearly overwhelming.

Cohen smiled wanly. "Thank you. I thought we were lost. Worse than lost. How did you find us?"

"We'll explain more soon. Right now let's get you two looked at and off your feet." She paused. "Looks like you missed the luxury accommodations."

Savas stared dumbfounded at the subterranean space, the military men, and the woman before them. *Could I be hallucinating?*

"Ms. President, please. Where are we? What is this?"

She smiled from one side of her mouth.

"Welcome to the Presidency in Exile." Her eyebrows arched. "Seven stories below the streets of New York City."

"Below New York?" he said, his eyes straying upward to the arching supports of the towering ceiling.

"Welcome to the underworld."

14

ENLISTING

Savas sat down next to Cohen outside the medical facility. They were dressed in borrowed fatigues, soldiers donating whatever they had available. For the first time in what felt like years, they were left alone. He stared at her in awe. The quiet and stillness transfigured her familiar form. She dimmed the world around him, infinitely valuable. He reached out and squeezed her hand.

"Always thought you'd look good in gear," she said, smiling.

Self-consciously, he examined the camouflage patterning, the baggy shirt sagging around his midsection. He rubbed the thick stubble on his cheeks.

"I don't get the luxury of making everything I wear look good," he said, raising his eyebrows toward her. "But thanks."

She inhaled sharply, staring into space. "We just left him there."

Savas closed his eyes. He wasn't ready to face the losses. *More losses.* A price for service that now rose beyond anything he could justify. "Yeah. I know."

"Did you see what they did? I mean, why?"

He opened his eyes but was unable to make eye contact. "I don't know, Rebecca."

"And JP? He was wounded in the firefight at the Bureau. Anything?"

"Still no word. Not sure he was even taken to the ship. He would have needed serious medical attention."

Cohen shuddered. "Just so they could torture him later?" She glanced over his bruised and swollen face. "What did they do to you?"

He squeezed her hand again. The guilt that he'd betrayed good people burned inside. *In the end, I was weak.* "Nothing good. But I'm okay. Docs say no lasting damage. The bastards knew how to work it slowly."

She stared off into the distance. "Is there nothing they wouldn't do? How can they be soldiers?"

"I'm not sure all of them were. Some were contractors. That blue-eyed monster, for one." Cohen inhaled sharply. Savas wrapped his arm around her. "What they did to Frank, his head—well, Sara had told me about something like that."

"I remember," Cohen shivered. "The CIA agent. They used some kind of brain stimulation to get him to talk."

"Yeah," said Savas, rolling his pained shoulder. "They found a dead doc. Traced him to some shady military contractors. Apparently it's the new thing. Electrodes in the brain. Turn off free will. Get answers. Less blood."

"Didn't seem like less blood to me. They *butchered* him, John. Threw him down for us to see. To hurt us. Break us. Before they—" She stopped and held her hand to her mouth.

"Stop. Slowly. Not all at once."

She nodded, holding back tears. "Right." She looked around the room. "*Jesus.* Now what?"

A firm voice answered from behind them.

"Now you get to choose." York walked in with several aides and military men.

"Choose what?" asked Cohen.

"Whose side you want to be on in this conflict, and what you want to do about it."

THEY STOOD around a map of the United States. It was displayed on a table in the middle of the subterranean lair's enormous operations center. Soldiers manned computers and communication equipment, tracked troops and intel, and spoke into headsets to contacts unknown. Along the sides of what looked to be a retrofitted subways station, wall-sized flatscreen monitors surrounded them, displaying a bewildering series of images from satellite downlinks to war-game simulations.

On the LCD screen before them, the nation glowed in blue and gray. The East Coast and parts of the Deep South shown with a gray hue. The map was colored blue in the center, a bright star flashing in the state of Colorado.

"General Hastings has most of the Navy under his thumb, except for several contingents of Special Forces that stayed loyal to my office. Fortunately, almost no one knows about this facility. It was scheduled to be decommissioned, a relic of the Cold War."

Savas shook his head. "What is this place then?"

"A local Mount Weather or NORAD. Was once intended as a governmental bunker in case of nuclear attack. A huge network of abandoned tunnels and water stations were converted to the purpose. Telecommunications, arms, food stores. You name it. It's in disrepair, as I said, headed for the chopping block, but we've gotten it up and running. Thank God the air filtration systems still worked or it would have been over before it began."

"Why won't Hastings look for you here?"

"He might eventually. That's why we can't stay long. But it's obscure and buried in archives. All but forgotten. Except for us old timers. Not high on the military priority list either, deemed too vulnerable to attack. Which it is."

"Comforting."

She looked him in the eye. "We're on a knife's edge. Every day we stay here brings the noose closer. But every day rallies more to our cause. We've managed to muster a good part of the 2nd Infantry Division from Fort Lewis. Those that didn't join Hastings's ranks, that is. I have a small army at my disposal."

"Can we trust them? How do we know loyalties?"

York frowned. "We don't. That's the hard truth. But we're doing all the PR we can. Trying to win hearts and minds. But we don't have any problems Hastings doesn't. Going to be brother against brother."

"It doesn't sound real," muttered Savas.

"The fight is up there, too," she said, gesturing toward the ceiling.

"Propaganda wars before the blood is shed in earnest. People are taking sides. But the real battle will be somewhere in the middle," she said, indicating the map. "We have the Rockies, NORAD. They have the coast. Someday soon, we're going to meet up between these points. Before that, we need to get to NORAD. We need to run our campaign from there. And that's where we're headed if we can make it."

"Why risk it?" asked Cohen.

Savas saw that she was in analytical mode, but his mind refused to function when he stared at her. She still wore a blanket from the medical center. Small in the cavernous space, a petite brunette wrapped in layers of fabric, her form called to him. *Vulnerable.* He struggled to process the conversation.

"Because here, I'm just as much a prisoner as you were on that ship. It's a matter of time before they find us. Maybe days. We've secured a lot of machinery, troops. We have air attack options from several locations. We'll move soon."

"Air options," said Cohen. "I heard jets over the ship."

"Not jets. Cruise missiles. Immune to the worm. A great irony— modernizing our aircraft, we left them vulnerable. The best attack and transport craft are either grounded or too unreliable in the air. Each side is racing to fix that, but we don't have the time to wait."

Savas turned to York, the president's words focusing his attention. "Wait? For what?"

"My best strategy would be to hop a transport and fly to Colorado. But my advisors say it's too risky. Too few working planes, too few air traffic systems. There'd be no escort. Some surface-to-air missiles and it's over. Since we can't wait for the air, we move on the ground."

Cohen stared sharply at the President. "Why did you come?"

"Here? I told you. It was the only—"

"No," she interrupted. "The boat. *Us.*" Savas heard the restrained emotions in Cohen's voice as she continued. "You're running for your life while the nation crumbles. Why did you come? How did you find us?"

York smiled and put her arm around Cohen. "Because you have some friends in high places. Actually, I don't know where they are, but they reached me. Hacked into our damn servers." York laughed, moving back to the map. "Hastings's men can't find us yet but your computer girl sure as hell did."

"Angel," said Cohen.

"Don't know her name—or maybe you're being figurative? Anyway, she was with two people that cashed in a debt I owed them—my life."

"Mary and Gabriel," said Savas, using their codenames.

"So *you* sent them? I'd guessed. No coincidences in this game. But it's good to know. And you two have my thanks as well."

"We can call it even, then," said Savas.

"Where are they now?" Cohen asked.

"Don't know. They got into our servers, routed messages directly to me, identified themselves. Sent me your profiles and GPS coordinates. Seals did the rest. Honestly, I didn't think we had a prayer. But Hastings is too confident, didn't count on a lot of things."

"Like what? How did they pull it off?" said Savas, shaking his head. Images of the titanic carrier rushed through his thoughts.

"Wasn't that hard in the end. We had some air *options*, but that wouldn't have done much with the firepower they could have launched our way. But the US military hadn't seriously considered an internal war —same team, suddenly at each other's throats, with all the codes and perfect intel on our targets."

Cohen nodded. "You knew where to hit them."

"Not only, darling," winked York, "but we also knew how to get into their onboard systems and shut everything the hell down. Turned that thing into a hundred-thousand-ton floating hunk of iron."

"They tortured us," said Cohen flatly. "Murdered our friend. They drilled holes in his head."

The President's upper lip twitched. "I've been briefed. I wish I could act surprised. This country's wrestled with some monsters, about how to deal with evil people. Hastings belongs to a wing that sees no road as too dark, no line that can't be crossed. All the more reason we need to find a way to stop him. Which brings me to your choices."

Savas barked a laugh. "I don't think we want to go back to the Hastings side, Ms. President."

"I'm sure. But you don't have to help me. You can flee. Hunker down with your families. I'd understand that. But I know who you are. I know what you've done for this country and what those you sent to help me can do. And if I understand things, it was your department at the FBI that stopped the worm that started this mess. The nation needs you. And I want you by my side."

"By your side?" asked Savas. Cohen's eyes squinted.

"Personal bodyguards and problem solvers. Heavy, I know. But there is one more piece to this puzzle you don't know about. Something that makes everything in this coup secondary."

Cohen shook her head. "What could do that?"

York exhaled. "*Bilderberg.*"

15

STAR CHAMBER

A spartan room devoid of furniture or decoration. Twelve enormous flat screens mounted from the ceiling, forming a circle. In the circle's center stood Elaine York, marveling at the design efficiency, the brutal and humbling focus that centered the occupant in front of twelve titanic faces.

She rotated slowly, examining each of them, feeling dizzy in the process. Eyes bored into her from every direction. God-sized faces. All strangers.

It was impossible. Here she stood, Elaine York, President of the United States, two-time US Senator, political player for most of her adult life and observer before that during her father's career—and she didn't recognize even one of the faces staring back at her. All her connections developed over a lifetime meant nothing in this dark room. People more powerful than she could have imagined surrounded her, making her question the entire world order she had taken for granted. And she knew nothing about any of them.

The door closed behind her.

"Thank you for coming, Elaine," said a voice she remembered.

York stared ahead at an ancient visage, a face from another age with blue eyes and pocked skin.

"You're the one on the phone," she whispered,

The man smiled, revealing yellowed teeth. "Yes."

"Who are you?"

"There won't be any names here, Elaine. Only yours."

A female voice. York turned to her right. Two enormous pools of brandy confronted her, keen eyes of a beautiful woman with dark hair and vaguely Middle Eastern features. Her accented English reflected her appearance.

York scanned once more the ring of faces gazing down on her. Faces from all over the world. Dark and light, old and young, men and women. She returned her eyes to the older man.

"Why am I here?"

He smiled again. "You've read some science fiction in your youth, have you not, Ms. York?"

"Yes," she said, bewildered.

"Your brother's books, I believe. Wasn't so fashionable for a young woman to have such boyish hobbies, no?"

"I'm glad to say things have changed."

*"Indeed. But some things do not change. And that is why you are here."
He held up a dog-eared paperback. The book on the screen loomed at twice her height. "Isaac Asimov—Foundation. Do you remember this book, Elaine?"*

"Yes. One of the first science fiction books I really loved."

"Stilted, clumsy language. But it had a very interesting idea. A brilliant idea. Do you remember it? It was what the series was based on."

York felt lost. "Scientific prediction of society, of the future. Shaping society with mathematical sociology."

"Exactly!" The old man smacked the paperback with his hand. "What if I told you it wasn't science fiction? What if I told you it is possible to predict, and therefore shape, human societies and civilization through quantitative modeling?"

"That's absurd."

"Is it?" said the woman to her right. "Economists use mathematics to predict recessions, bubbles, and investments. Traders do the same to play the markets. Epidemiologists can predict the course of disease and optimal quarantine and vaccination strategies to prevent epidemic spread of pathogens. Are we not shaping our world with mathematical predictions on a constant basis? What could one achieve by integrating all these models, especially if one had the capital resources to alter the inputs?"

"That's different than Asimov's idea."

"Only in a matter of degree," said the older man, pulling her attention forward. "In fact, that's why you're here. Because the course of human events is

being shaped toward a brighter future by such methods. And we are those carrying out this noble task."

York glanced around at the faces. No one smiled. No one laughed. These people appeared utterly serious, spouting nonsense.

"Looks like you're dropping the ball a bit. The world seems pretty FUBAR to me."

"A deceptive illusion, Ms. President. Scored as a percentage of population and cultural dynamics, human civilization has achieved the highest stability ever measured in the historical record."

"How's that possible? We have four major wars ongoing, political chaos in several nations, resource and environmental problems—you name it!"

"It's a matter of perception, Elaine," he said. "Ten billion people with lightning fast tech is very different than one billion and snail mail. Most chaos is minor, blown out of proportion by crisis-driven content in the news media. Local chaos notwithstanding, as a planetary average, we exert unprecedented control."

"Unprecedented?"

The woman spoke again. "Ours is not a new organization. Faces may change over the decades. Tools modernized. But not the purpose. That remains constant. With ultrafast computers, more robust theory and modeling, we can now predict and shape the world to a degree of precision our predecessors could only have dreamed of."

"Predecessors. What the hell is going on here?"

"Very simple," said the man again, "You must accept that your assumptions about the world, how it is governed, where the power lies—they are all wrong. Power does not rest with nations or the individuals leading them. It rests with us. We have held this power for centuries, controlling economies, making kings and presidents, directing conflicts and religions. Clumsily at first, to be sure. Almost to our own extinction at several points. But no longer. The modern age has advanced the modeling of social groups to a point that, like the weather, we are increasingly accurate over longer and longer stretches of time. We have consolidated our power and influence."

York squinted at the screen. "So, you're telling me that behind all the world governments, there's a super group of individuals"—she gestured around her—"these same individuals glaring down at me, who run the world? In secret? Without anyone knowing?"

A man's voice behind her spoke. "I wouldn't say no one knows. It's a ques-

tion of how much *they know and what they might do about it. Rumors of us persist no matter what steps we take to erase them. Sometimes we're Jewish bankers or cultist Illuminati. Hidden extraterrestrials or demonic forces. Vampires." The god-like faces chuckled. "Strange and inaccurate myths concocted to explain anomalies and pieces of data recalcitrant individuals obtain. Sometimes we encourage certain wild ideas to cast doubt on the real truth."*

York shook her head. "How do you expect me to believe this?"

"You've seen what we can do. The power we have over your national system to bring you here. Your own former president playing the role we specified for him."

She felt like crying. It was madness. "Then what do the masters of our universe want with Elaine York?"

"Probably nothing," said the man.

"Nothing?"

"Truly, we do not wish to interfere in your service to your nation. It is likely our direct intervention will be extremely rare. It is increasingly so these days. In fact, you may never hear from us again. Our efforts are so pervasive and thorough, so long-planned, often we can allow the models of behavior for you and your political parties to play out without, shall we say, adjustments. However, should there come a time when reality and our models diverge, should our goals be threatened, we may be required to contact you. It is imperative that you then do as we ask."

"Or what?"

"You risk far more instability and harm by rebelling."

"And if I still refuse?"

The woman spoke. "The consequences will be harsh. We will be forced to remove you from office and replace you with a more cooperative politician."

"Replace me? How?"

The old man frowned. "Consider the fates of presidents throughout history who have rebelled against our requests. Lincoln and Kennedy. William Henry Harrison, Zachary Taylor, William McKinley, Warren Harding, Franklin Roosevelt."

The room felt cold and hostile. York swallowed. "These are all presidents who died in office. Several assassinated."

"Indeed, President York," he said, leaning back in his chair. "As you can see, our reach is centuries old, and we do, as they say, play for keeps."

16

COMING WAR

I'm ranting.

Cohen paced back and forth in the President's private office. Her mind burned. Her arms gesticulating of their own accord. She flicked glances at Savas, desperate for him to intervene, to exorcise this demon in their midst. *Say something, John!* But he sat quietly, looking too stunned by York's revelations to do anything but nurse a cup of steaming coffee.

"Then, *everything,* it's been a lie!" she cried. "For generations! Democracy's been a facade! We took marching orders from these shadows? World events, wars, millions of deaths—all controlled by these ghosts?"

York nodded from behind her desk, her fingertips pressed against each other.

"Why, Ms. President? *Why?* How could you go along with this?"

"They threatened me. They could have ruined me and others. They tried to confuse me with that bullshit about building the perfect world. But the truth was all too clear. They were dictators brutally enforcing their control. I couldn't see a way out."

Cohen swallowed bile. Anger coursed through her, but also pity. This strong woman, *a soldier,* someone Cohen had admired for years, reduced to a lackey for other powers. *Not only York.* Every president for centuries.

The image of former president Obama standing in front of a train made her dizzy. Nothing seemed real. *Who can we trust?*

Cohen placed her fingers to her eyes. "Obama really met you in a secret underground railway station and brought you to them?"

York nodded. "Yes, Rebecca. And it was every bit as devastating to me as it is to you right now. But try to look beyond it. See something important. Whatever damage this Fawkes did, he provided a golden opportunity."

"Which is?" she asked.

York stood up and walked to an American flag tacked to the wall behind her.

"The country's divided. At war. But what we're *really* fighting is an enemy we've never seen before. One that's covertly controlled us for hundreds of years. Presidents cowered before them. Because we believed it was the only option." She spun back around to face them. "But Anonymous changed the ground rules, ripped the carpet out from under all our feet. They've blown the support structures and stripped them of their armor." She walked back to her desk and dropped into the chair, closing her eyes. "But they won't go down without a fight. Right now, the US command structure's in chaos. They've infiltrated every level, all the way to the Joint Chiefs. Military contractors at their right hand. Hastings their current puppet. But we have a loyal core, tough and smart. They've taken Cheyenne Mountain and set up our headquarters for the war."

"War?" asked Cohen.

The president's eyes flashed open. "The war to win our country back. Since you've been imprisoned, I've fanned the chaos created by Anonymous. It's spread. I saw an opportunity. I've rebelled against our *masters*. The first chance in hundreds of years to free the world of their control, to create truly independent nations."

York keyed in several strokes at her computer, and a flatscreen monitor on the wall to their left flashed to the blue-gray image of the US. She drew her finger across it from New York to the Rockies.

"We're not going to hide. We're going to muscle our way straight across interstate 70, and our forces are going to blow out of the sky, water, and into the earth anyone who tries to get in our way. We won't get another chance. We have to get to that mountain."

"But how can we stop Bilderberg?" asked Cohen. "Let's say you make it to the mountain, even end the coup. We're no closer to doing anything about them, knowing who or where they are. What happens after Cheyenne, Ms. President?"

"*Elaine*. Please." York put her hands on her hips. "Look, if I'm going to be first naming you two, I want it reciprocated. I need you as real advisors. People who'll speak their minds, tell me hard truths. I've got enough people to salute me."

"Going to take some getting used to," said Cohen. Discordant images of York fought inside her. Authority figure. Savior. Coward. Revolutionary. *Friend?* "Okay, *Elaine*, how can we do anything about them?"

"Right now, we can't," said York. "My first priority is to get me, what's left of the Constitutional government—the members of Congress, the Judiciary, all we've managed to round up with us—get us all to NORAD. From there we stage a war of ideas and bullets until we crush this coup once and for all. Afterward, we go after the Bilderberg Group."

"Won't it be too late?" Cohen asked, her frustration building. "Isn't it the same chaos that led to the coup that makes them vulnerable? If you win, if you start normalizing things, their power will return. They'll assassinate you like Kennedy."

"Yes, a distinct problem," York said coldly.

Savas stood up, pacing before the map. Cohen sensed his mood before he spoke, felt the rhythm of his movement, smelled the testosterone fomenting action. *Please be back, John, we need you. I need you.* He had seemed so broken.

"You said Angel was following up on the message from Fawkes?" he asked.

York sighed. "She didn't say much, but it sounded like they had discovered something important."

He turned to York. "You said you wanted advice. Well, let's start now. You've got a solid game plan for fighting this coup. God willing, you'll get to Cheyenne Mountain. But we need something else for Bilderberg. Maybe Angel and our other friends are our secret weapon. Can you get us in contact with them? We need to find out what they've discovered."

York nodded. "I can try. We have less than half the satellite networks functioning, but at least we control most of those."

Cohen shook her head. "I can't believe it. He's dead, but Fawkes is still jerking our chain."

"Yeah, maybe," said Savas staring at York. "But until today, I'd never thought to ask where the chains came from."

"Fawkes saw them," said Cohen. The mysterious hacker came into focus for the first time. "He was willing to burn down the world, cause the deaths of billions of people to break them. But no—not like that. We aren't terrorists or mass murderers. There has to be another way." She turned her gaze to York. "We have to find another way."

"Then let's start by finding out what the lunatic was trying to tell us," said York. "We'll reach out to your people. I'll make this a priority."

Cohen exhaled slowly. "And let's hope they escape the net a little longer."

17

ALIEN HIEROGLYPHICS

"I'm hearing more from upstairs. Looks like the neighbors moving back." Houston pressed her ear against the door of the telecommunications closet, straining to filter the muffled sounds. "Someone's bound to come down here at some point. It'll be soon."

"Doesn't matter," said Lightfoote, glancing back from her laptop. "We have to leave anyway. I'm getting hits on my sentries—NSA is poking around. I give us a few more hours before they zero in."

"Packing," said Lopez, dropping food and firearms into bags. "No need to convince me. They aren't messing around. Not another Harlem raid."

Houston walked away from the door and stood over Lightfoote, gazing at the laptop screen. A strange image glowed before her. "Well, at least we got what we came for."

Lopez barked a laugh as he zipped closed one of the duffels. "Sure. And *still* we are no closer to understanding what the Nash Criterion is all about." He gestured toward the screen. "Just look at that chaos!"

Houston frowned. *He has a point.* "Angel, nothing in that image makes sense. Are you sure it's decoded correctly?"

"Sara, if it weren't it would be gibberish."

"It *is* gibberish," said Lopez.

"No! It's an *image*. A clear image. The encryption was broken correctly or it would be total junk—no image, no text, just incomprehensible bytes. We have the contents. It's a very high-resolution TIFF file. That just doesn't pop out randomly. The decoding is correct. We just don't know what it means."

Houston pointed to several regions of the screen. "An image of an image. What is this? Some lunatic's cork artwork? What are these chicken-scratch labels on all these graphs?" She read out loud. "Epsilon-equilibrium, evolutionarily stable strategy, subgame perfect equilibrium, perfect Bayesian, Riemannian manifolds, catenary formulas, n-person games, C1-isometric embeddings—what the hell? What does it all mean?"

Lightfoote looked at the ground. "I don't know."

Houston continued. "And this thing on the edge—gold color, half a circle, a line—looks like alien hieroglyphics."

"No idea."

"I thought you were the genius here," muttered Lopez, leaning back against the wall and closing his eyes. "Two days, no sleep. A hacker underworld. A thousand computers processing and what? This *nonsense*. This is what people want to kill us for?"

"I'm not a mathematician," snapped Lightfoote. "I don't know what this is about. Neither did any of the hacker groups."

"I taught high school math once upon a time," said Lopez. "These aren't any topics I've heard of. We're wasting time we don't have."

We're getting run down, turning on each other. Houston tried to diffuse the tension. "Maybe higher level stuff, Francisco. It reads like a graduate school math course book scribbled all over some wild cork board." She wasn't even convincing herself.

Lightfoote cocked her head to one side, staring at the screen. "Sara's right."

"I am?"

"This *is* a board. Look—the edge, *here*. That golden alien symbol—it's cut off, only part of it shown. Thumb tacks, tape. It's like something out of *A Beautiful Mind*." She began to type furiously.

"A beautiful mind?" asked Lopez.

Yes! Houston remembered—vague images of Russell Crowe, Princeton, and equations. "The movie? With the crazy economist?"

"John Nash. It was about John *Nash*. Not an economist. A *mathematician* who did economic work. Got a Nobel Prize. The file, remember? The *Nash* Criterion? Look!" Several biographical pages opened in her browser with photos of a gaunt, gray-haired man.

Lopez had joined them, staring at the screen. "That one of your cork boards?"

He indicated an image of hundreds of pieces of paper taped to a board and adjacent wall. Riotous handwriting and equations covered the scraps. Houston knew immediately they were on to something.

"My God, he *was* crazy," she said.

Lightfoote nodded, furiously scanning text. "Schizophrenia. Says here he thought aliens were talking in code to him through the newspapers."

"That qualifies," said Lopez.

Lightfoote continued. "See this timeline of his life? He was a new star in the '50s, went nuts, disappeared for *forty years*, then resurfaces half-sane to claim a Nobel prize." She read in silence down the page. "Says he's still crazy but—get this—he can recognize *patterns* of thought, split them into *crazy* and *not crazy* from observing other's reactions. Statistical analysis of sanity."

Houston was stunned. "Is that possible?"

"Hard to believe," said Lightfoote. "But this handwriting—look familiar?"

"Definitely," said Houston.

Lopez laughed. "Well, it looks like the same decorator was involved, that's for sure." Houston's head was hurting. "I don't get it. What would some insane university professor have to do with Fawkes or Bilderberg?"

Lightfoote continued to type at a mad pace. "That's what we need to find out, right?"

The haunting mask of Guy Fawkes danced in Houston's mind, along with the bloodied head of the hacker Fawkes lying face down in Savas's office. "Maybe this really is just all for the *lolz*, Angel—Fawkes with a final, last laugh at us."

An image appeared on the screen of an open space within a building, a large display surrounded by onlookers in the middle of the frame. Houston squinted. *Was that—*

"Look at this," said Lightfoote. "Maybe Fawkes *was* trolling us. But this board is *real*."

Lightfoote zoomed into the image, centering on the display. A large cork board with numerous scraps of handwritten notes filled the screen. The extreme pixelation obscured the finer detail.

Houston felt a chill. "My God, it's the same. Where is this?"

"Nash Museum, Princeton University." Lightfoote rested her forehead on the top of her hand. "It's an exhibit—elements from his life, artifacts from his crazy time, too."

"Why would Fawkes send us a picture from a museum dedicated to the ramblings of a nutcase?" asked Lopez, his arms raised in frustration.

"A Nobel Prize-winning nutcase," said Lightfoote. "Prize in *economics*."

Houston nodded. "Fawkes was all about the world financial system, taking it down. His Bilderberg paranoia was tied up in that. Cohen's words, remember? Right before the soldiers descended. Maybe Nash knew something, wrote it down in his crazy period. No one understood."

"But only Fawkes did? Really?" said Lopez.

"He was a crazy genius too, Francisco. Maybe that's why he only gave us half the photo."

"Or maybe he wanted to make it difficult for just anyone to figure this out," said Lightfoote. "He's pushing us to go there. I can't get anything else online. Image searches only give the low res photo—can't do much with that. We need to see this thing. The whole poster board." She looked over her shoulder at Houston and Lopez. "We need to go to Princeton."

"I was afraid this was coming," said Lopez. "A dangerous journey. And, even if there is something in this, what if we can't figure it out? Maybe it's hidden in the crazy of this Nash? You're asking us to travel across a war zone—with military forces hunting us down—to try and decipher the ravings of a lunatic!" He stared at Lightfoote.

"Even Angel admits it's a strange mission," she said.

Houston reached over and touched Lopez on the cheek. "We're tired. We're fried from this and people trying to turn us into Swiss cheese. But it looks *real*. We have to figure it out." His face softened as she held his eyes.

"We might get some tutoring," said Lightfoote.

"From someone at Princeton?" asked Houston. "John Nash? He's still there?"

"Unfortunately, no. Says here he died in a car crash in 2015. Taxi."

"An eighty-six year old dies in a taxi crash?" said Houston.

Lightfoote nodded. "It's a strange one. But I meant this guy—Avi

Kaplan. He runs the museum. Some ex-Nash student who was close to him for decades. Worked on many of his important papers. Helped Nash's wife during his crazy years."

"I see this is destiny," said Lopez. "When do we leave?"

Lightfoote bit her lower lip. "Tonight. Angel needs one more hack. To send a message."

Houston raised an eyebrow. "To who?"

"President York. We need to talk to her."

18

TACTICAL STRIKE

"Y ou've made contact?" asked Savas.

They stood in the operations center beneath Manhattan, the labyrinth of tunnels snaking away from them in multiple directions. Military personnel and civilian staff continued to work close by, frantically orchestrating the coming journey westward. Savas could hear them debating the logistics, tactics, and threats. He tried to tune out the coming storm and focus on their communication effort.

"We think so," said York. She deferred to a boyish soldier in front of a terminal. "Specialist Turner?"

"Yes, ma'am! It's a Tor-scrambled secure chat—as secure as we can make it. Your friends, if these are your friends, have an extra serving of paranoid and all the software to work this with me."

"What do you mean, 'if' these are our friends?" asked Savas.

"That's just it, sir, how do we verify? We put out the codes and information you mentioned. They must have been monitoring a lot of information, and they took the bait. They reached out to us. But could be NSA or someone else."

York interrupted. "Hastings has control of the NSA servers. They have tremendous computational firepower and are spying on every internet and cellular network. Landlines too, of course."

Turner continued. "We need something specific, something that could distinguish friendlies from hostiles. Once that's done, we can risk more channels open."

Savas shook his head. "NSA a hostile. Half the US military a hostile. What the hell has happened?"

"Let me try," said Cohen.

The soldier nodded and stood up from the chair. "It's chat. Just type. They'll respond."

She sat down and typed.

"Gabriel's brother?"

Text appeared after a short pause.

"Archangel Michael."

"Who killed the wraith?"

"Gabriel."

"Cabin. What grows on the doors?"

"Rose creepers."

Cohen leaned back and sighed. "It's them."

Savas agreed. "Definitely."

Turner's eyebrows arched, and looked at York. She nodded and he resumed his position in the chair. "Okay, then let's initiate video."

A window opened on the screen. Pixelated blurs moved as if in a strobe light. The video improved, the resolution increased and movement smoothed. A bald woman with piercings across her face stared back intensely at them. Cohen leaned down to the screen.

"Angel! Are you okay? Where are Gabriel and Mary?"

Behind Lightfoote, two faces appeared.

"Right here, Rebecca," came Houston's voice. "We're fine."

"Where the hell are you?" asked Savas

She shook her head. "Can't tell you. Can't be sure who's listening or if you're okay. Not compromised. They're after us."

"We know," he said. "We were taken. Interrogated. They were very interested in finding you. You saved our asses, tracking us. We escaped and are in hiding with the President." He inhaled deeply. *Just say it, John.* "There's bad news. Frank's dead."

Lightfoote balled her hands into fists. "How?" She glared at Savas.

Cohen spoke. "We're not sure. They—" She couldn't finish.

"They tortured him to death," finished Lightfoote. "I get it. And from the look of his face, it looks like John was next. JP? He was dying when we left him."

"I don't know, Angel," said Savas. "My guess is they would see to him, give him medical attention."

"So they could torture him later," said Lightfoote. The silence answered her question. Her green eyes flared. "Who's doing all this?"

"Bilderberg," said York, pushing her way into the line of the camera.

"Then it's real?" came the deep voice of Lopez. "What is it?"

"Something impossible to believe. I've arranged to have some files sent to you. Look them over when you get a chance. But the bottom line: Bilderberg is a set of powerful puppet masters pulling strings across governments the world over. Anonymous nearly brought their system crashing down. I'm running for my life because I'm fighting it. There's been a military coup run by a high ranking soldier—Gerald Hastings. But he's only a front. The Bilderberg Group is behind everything."

"Who's in this group? Where are they?" asked Lightfoote.

"We don't know," said York. "We don't know one name or where they're located. For all we know they're distributed, all over the world. But their goal is to return the nation and the world to a pre-Anonymous status quo. In that world, they shape and guide the nations to their own ends."

Lopez spoke. "We're getting the files now. This is a little hard to believe. Tin-foil hat stuff."

"I know," said the President, "but I think the materials in those files and recent events will help things fall into place. If it helps any, I've *spoken* to them. After my election. They secretly contacted me, impressed upon me in ways I could not dismiss who was really in control of our world. For years I went along with it. Like other presidents. Like leaders across the world. I'm not proud of it, but there's no time to explain everything, what they threatened if I didn't. The consequences to me and others. But now—well, maybe we can stop them."

"Because of Fawkes," said Lightfoote. "And he's not done. He left us the file."

"Yes, John and Rebecca mentioned it."

"We've broken the encryption."

York leaned forward. "What does it say?"

"It doesn't say anything. It's an image file. One that doesn't tell us much right now. But it leads us in a clear direction."

"You won't say more?" asked Savas.

"Sorry, John. This is too important. Especially now after hearing the president."

"Angel's right," said Houston. "It's a long shot, but we need to follow up on it. We need to travel to unravel this. But we need to do it alone. We're a small group. We can hide."

"We can afford you the protection of a powerful contingent of the US military," said York. "We're going to NORAD. We'll fight our way there if we have to. Loyalists to this nation are waiting for us there. Come with us! Seek safety at Cheyenne Mountain to understand this puzzle."

Lightfoote shook her head. "Not putting the eggs in one basket. The file is leading us in another direction. We have someplace to go, and it's not the Rockies."

York frowned. "I can't spare anyone to help you, I'm sorry. And without knowing more about what you're doing, it doesn't seem wise even if I could. You won't reconsider? We can help you!"

Houston spoke firmly. "We think Fawkes gave us a key to Bilderberg, something we can use against them. But it's buried in an enigma we have to solve. We can't come with you. Not yet. Not until we know if it's useful. We have to commit to it."

Savas spoke to the screen. "Angel, you're sure about this? You really think Fawkes was on to something?"

"Definitely," she said. "Saying more might tip off our enemies. I'm sorry."

"My gut says you should be here," said York. "But there's no denying what you've done. I just wish you hadn't been so successful at stopping the worm. The one thing Bilderberg needs now is a return to normalcy. We have to prevent it at all costs."

"So now what?" asked Cohen.

"We turn these three loose," said the president. "And hope to hell they give us something to help fight this menace. Meanwhile, we muster out." She turned back to the screen. "You three stay alive and contact us when you can. The offer still stands. If you need us, if you can make it to us, we'll protect you."

"As best *you* can," said Lightfoote. "I assume Hastings isn't going to let you stroll over to NORAD without incident."

"No, he won't," said York. "But we'll be ready for him."

"Then maybe you're ready to hit him for us, too," said Lightfoote.

York arched an eyebrow. "Hastings?"

"His intel arm. The NSA. They're like ticks all over the internet, sucking info and tracking us. We were almost killed in Harlem because they tracked us. We need them off our backs, and away from the hackers that are working with us."

"You're working with hackers?" asked York.

"Parallel processing. That's how we cracked the encryption. We're counting on them. Right now, they're organizing. But it's all going to get bloody if the NSA spies keeping crashing the party."

"What do you want us to do?" asked York.

"Hit their data centers. Take them out. Fort Meade and Utah for sure."

"Isn't Utah on *our* side?" asked Savas.

York shook her head. "Not so clean cut, John. It's in our supposed range of control, but nobody has troops there and no one can commit them now. It's sided with Hastings. He's got the full power of the agency. Lots of cyberwarfare going on between NORAD and the NSA right now."

"Take them out," said Lightfoote. "Give us a chance to breathe. You don't even need to kill people. Those server farms live and die on cooling and electricity. Take out the water supply, local power stations."

"We've got the cruise missiles, but we're going to need them, too. I'll put together a team to analyze the most efficient attack, see what we can spare." York nodded, coming to a conclusion. "Actually, it will likely help our journey. Should of thought of this before. The NSA gets satellite information, monitors a lot of communications. Hastings can track us, get useful intel, just from whatever goes out from the areas our convoy passes. But not if their server farms are down. That'd jab a stick in his eye." She smiled. "Yes, Angel. I'm starting to take a real liking to your idea."

19

GANGRENE

"General Hastings, your first priority is to neutralize York."

The Director's rough voice spoke toward an enormous flat screen monitor, the deep bags under his eyes melding with his lined face to create the appearance of a melted landscape. The face of a heavyset man in a decorated uniform stared back, eyes darting left and right.

The general licked his lips. "We're looking at a full-fledged *war* if we continue. We risk fracturing the entire nation!"

"Let me explain the dynamics to you once again," said the Director, his voice cold. "We are at crisis point. If York solidifies her power base, and if the fugitives with the terrorist's documents survive, we risk the formation of a permanent front against our long-term interests. This would be unprecedented in recent history and could unravel decades-long efforts. We will not allow this. If you can't put an end to this rebellion, we'll find someone who can."

The general spoke through clenched teeth.

"I understand. We won't fail. But I warn you, there's going to be one hell of a mess to clean up."

"We will deal with it later. Find her, General. Kill her and her enablers."

The old man closed the connection and the general's face vanished. In its place, an array of faces appeared and tiled the screen. A woman with an Iranian accent spoke from the center of the screen.

"He is right. The simulations are in chaos. We are quickly oscillating outside our bands of prediction."

"I know!" shouted the old man, slamming his fist onto the table in front of him. "The hacker has disrupted everything. Hopefully, we can put this fire out soon and push things back into line."

"It may be difficult to do so within the models we have developed," came the clipped Germanic accent of a silver-haired man on the lower left tile. "Those models are statistically based. They rely on the *average* properties of large numbers of individuals, or, at worst, a few very well defined pressure points. The hacker was a completely random and extreme element. A *black swan*. His efforts are like a volcano erupting, scrambling all the weather forecasting. We might be basically starting over."

A man with Chinese features spoke from the wall of faces.

"We are at an inflection point. Those worst-case scenarios may not occur. Not if we end the social ripples of this *Anonymous* now. If we can bring the previous financial and political systems back online quickly, strongly suppress any deviations from it and any predictions of the past models, we may enter a quasi-stable tangent path. It will be different, but manageable. The simulations are still in flux. Nothing is fixed."

"All the more reason we must act forcefully," said the Director to the screens. "We must center our efforts on the anomaly in the United States. The other nations appear to be returning rapidly to previous trajectories in the forecasts. But not America. York is now in open rebellion against us. America is still the world's most powerful nation. Should she prevail, one hundred years of effort will be burned to the ground. She could undermine everything."

"If she prevails, we will also be hunted," said the woman.

The Director raised his voice. "I'm not worried about that! Eventually we can take her down and those who support her. Quench any investigations or covert efforts. They have nothing on us. No solid information, only the crumbs we gave her and the myths of the lunatic fringe. They will get nowhere. It is the damage to the *system* we have so carefully developed that will be devastating."

"Hastings may win," said the German. "York is vulnerable now.

Unless she can regroup with her supporters at NORAD. But there is a lot of land to cross in that nation."

"We will not rely only on him. Our assassins will infiltrate the military and every local population center along her path. We are flying in teams from across the world. Some will also be diverted to hunting down the FBI specialist, Lightfoote, and the fugitives aiding her."

"Still no progress with the file contents?" asked the woman.

"No. But there is little doubt as to its contents. The mention of Nash is clear."

The woman sighed. "The social engineering. It will be spelled out."

"Yes, and in the right hands, it will be understood for what it is. Our hidden plans laid bare. Countermeasures obvious. They will be able to undo nearly everything."

The German spoke. "They are as big a threat as York."

"Yes," said the Director.

The woman leaned back in her chair, long black hair cascading behind her head. "And if York or these fugitives elude us? Or do so long enough that they begin to capitalize on their threat? What then?"

The Director sighed. "It's one thing to be set back centuries. It is another to be made vulnerable to a death blow. If Hastings and our teams do not stop this soon, if the simulations show we are losing the ability to contain this catastrophe, then we will have only one choice left."

Silence descended, broken by the Chinese man at the upper corner of the screen.

"We have rarely used a failsafe. I had hoped we were beyond such measures."

The old man scowled. "Your weakness, Yigong, has always disturbed me."

Yigong continued. "Tens of millions will die. It's not 1945! With these kinds of numbers, the ends don't justify the means. The *ends* change as well."

"As a percentage of the human population, it is little different from the series of world wars we orchestrated in the 20th century."

A man with a Spanish accent interrupted. "Percentages tell one thing to statisticians. But absolute numbers—these are human beings, Director."

The Director held his hands up at his sides. "Are we forgetting our purpose, and what we have achieved? We've raised billions out of poverty, reduced death and suffering from infectious disease, raised the world life-span to unprecedented levels. Only because of *our* guiding hand has human civilization not torn itself to pieces, blown itself up, undoing all the progress in science and government, crashing back to another dark age!" He sighed and wiped his brow, sweat glistening on his face. "Some-times, to maintain this historical arc of progress, thousands, even millions had to die. Those deaths improved the lives of a thousand times as many!" He scanned the faces, his expression stern. "And now we have the science to do it with clarity, to know whether the lives lost will mean something down the road. Humanity *requires* guidance. *You know this!* But our ward requires harsh treatment when ill. And right now, the world is very ill."

"And so, if the criterion is reached, amputation?" said the Spaniard.

The Director took a deep breath. "Let's hope it does not come to that. But make no mistake, we will do what is required."

PART II

CIVIL WAR

"The biggest men in the United States, in the field of commerce and manufacture are afraid of somebody, are afraid of something. They know that there is a power somewhere so organized, so subtle, so watchful, so interlocked, so complete, so pervasive, that they better not speak above their breath when they speak in condemnation of it."

— Woodrow Wilson

20

BUGGING OUT

S avas stared across the ranks of soldiers and military vehicles. Part of his mind wouldn't believe it, couldn't accept the reality around him. Rows of drab transports, jeeps and trucks, lighter armored vehicles like Humvees—some mounted with rocket launchers—churned behind them as they rode up a steep tunnel incline.

They were inside a heavily armored vehicle, one supposedly resistant to major arms fire and explosive devices, disguised as a troop transport on the outside. Marines lined the interior beside Cohen and York, along with her advisers. It looked like something from a science fiction film with digital displays and operators monitoring troop movements and communications, speaking into headsets.

He turned to the President. "How has all this remained hidden?"

"It wasn't exactly hidden," said York. "New York City crews and administrations knew of it. They had to maintain the tunnels and concealed exits. Prevent anyone from breaking in and discovering it. What likely kept the secret was that it was on its way out. Something everyone knew about but didn't talk of because, well, it was over. A historical relic. Until we set up camp, it was mostly empty."

Ahead of them an enormous doorway opened in the rock. A stone wall split in the center along a vertical axis and continued to widen, orange light from outside pouring into the shaft. The doors themselves were made of steel more than three feet thick, the outer stone a facade textured to match the bedrock.

"This exit opens on the Jersey side of the Holland Tunnel, right in a wall of rock concealed with hazard signs and fake debris. Traffic, your odd onlooker, won't see it. Undercover soldiers have been guarding it for decades."

"Wait, we just went under the Hudson?" asked Cohen. "There's another tunnel?"

"Yes," said York. "There aren't too many ways off this island, you know. You didn't think Uncle Sam would build a secret underground shelter and not have an equally secret way to get the hell out of it?"

"Are there others?" Cohen's eyes widened.

"Two," said York. "By the Lincoln and Midtown tunnels. These emergency passages piggyback off the infrastructure of the others, lying alongside like leeches. We've got decoys exiting both of those right now. Hastings will be watching. If he has hard intel where we were holed up, he might be bringing fire to some or all of them. This way we'll spin their heads a little, hopefully give us time and space to get out. But we've hedged our bets in several ways."

"How many troops does he have? Equipment?"

"We don't know. The good thing is he doesn't know what we have. Anonymous took the satellite systems down completely. Including military and governmental. They're coming back online slowly, although we've lost a few probably forever due to orbit problems. But NORAD controls most of the birds up there. And we control NORAD. We've all been blind the last few weeks, but Hastings is going to stay that way except for a few inconsequential Navy sats, thanks to Angel's idea. While our vision slowly clears."

"The NSA attack? It's set?" asked Savas.

"Timed to our exit. Missiles are on their way now."

Ahead, the light intensified as the caravan approached. Savas could see the opening clearly now. Larger than he expected, the diameter surpassed all the tunnels he knew. Of course, the Abrams tanks and other large vehicles escorting them were wider and much heavier than even the biggest civilian transports.

"We're using their blindness to our advantage as much as we can," she said. "Have a look."

The convoy burst out of the tunnel and into a sea of military vehicles. The parade pouring out behind them was dwarfed by rows of tanks, highly mobile artillery, and massive numbers of troop transports. Soldiers lined the area. Vietnam-era helicopters thundered and he glimpsed their shadowed forms overhead. Cohen gasped.

"We've been positioning our forces nearby," said York, "They've been distributed for a few days, but tonight a large contingent moved to this exit. We've got a few birds for recon, but they're old and not suitable for combat. The ground vehicles and equipment are another matter."

They joined a group of heavily armored escorts and the convoy rushed onto the lined asphalt of an interstate. Savas could see the rest of the vehicles lining up to follow behind them.

"There were some minor skirmishes, but Hastings didn't have much in place. But soon he'll know we came through here and have some sense of our strength when his forces report back to him." She closed her eyes and exhaled. "Then we'll see what he does. For now, we need to get to the interstate and rendezvous with the main bulk of our forces."

"There's more?" Cohen asked.

"A lot more," said York. "We're fifteen thousand strong. Transports. Supplies—food, fuel, ammunition—enough for the journey and several major battles. It's nearly two thousand miles to the mountain. We can run most of these vehicles at thirty, maybe forty miles per hour. Three days minimum if we give ourselves six hours per camp. Lots of time and lots of land for Hastings to mount several offensives. Thankfully, all this Armageddon solves any traffic problems."

"Jesus," whispered Savas.

"Two thousand miles," said Cohen. "One long convoy. We'll be out in the open, exposed."

"Yes," said York. "Our asses hanging in the breeze. But with both sides' air power still reeling, it's feasible. And they aren't looking for a military victory. They just want slow us down. If they can stop us long enough to find me—well, that's the goal."

"Assassination," said Savas.

"NORAD can fight this war without me," she said. "But not the war for the people. If I'm not around to put a visible face—the democratically elected face of the people—against the forces of Hastings and Bilderberg, they win."

Bright light screamed overhead, a roar rattling the air around them.

"That was low," said Savas.

Thunder rumbled from the distance.

"Missile strikes. Clearing our way. Casualties are just going to climb from this point."

Cohen grimaced, her voice rough. "Sibling against sibling. The second Civil War."

21

THUNDER

Sara Houston stared out over New York Harbor, a cold December wind raking harshly across the bow of the boat. Darkness shrouded Lady Liberty, the post-Anonymous breakdown of order along the East Coast leaving the statue untended. Her upraised torch only a silhouette against the setting moon. The churning water along the hull of the craft began to lull Houston, ease her seasickness, and for a moment she wished she could simply let go of the madness around them, close her eyes, and lose herself to the sounds of the sea.

Instead, she looked toward the retreating lights of lower Manhattan and the enclosed cockpit of the vessel. The windows of the stolen pleasure yacht were tinted black, and she couldn't see Lopez and Lightfoote inside. She assumed the FBI woman still stood at the wheel, Lopez struggling to come up to speed with the navigational systems to help pilot them in the right direction.

Their plan was straightforward. They would continue south through the Upper Bay, passing alongside the Bayonne peninsula. Near its tip, they would change course with a sharp westerly turn into the Kill van Kull, the three mile stretch of tidal strait between Staten Island and Bayonne. It would get them out of New York by avoiding the major land bottlenecks of bridges and tunnels. The more open sea would make it far harder to monitor and control. If all went well, they should enter Newark

Bay within the hour, pass Shooters Island, and turn south toward the
Goethals Bridge. They hoped to find a place to dock somewhere near Port
Newark, steal a vehicle, and slip onto I-95 south towards Princeton. What
could go wrong?

"Helicopter!"

She heard Lopez before she saw him emerging from the cockpit. He
rushed alongside her.

"You were right about monitoring the police bands," he said, expression serious. "The NYPD and National Guard are working together.
Mostly just trying to restore order, it seems. I didn't hear anything about
us. But the curfew is still in force—still martial law. They'll bring us in if
we're spotted and we can't let that happen."

"Not sure we have the firepower to bring that down, Francisco," she
said. "Not sure I want to unless I have to. Probably some kid's dad trying
to do his job."

He sighed. "Agreed. Angel says we should go dark. It's a big pond out
here. Unlikely they'll spot us in the middle of it."

She nodded and followed him back inside. As they entered the cabin,
the boat shuddered as the motor cut off. Lightfoote moved quickly. One
by one, the lights on the boat went dark—green LEDs marking the starboard and port sides, a white stern light, and a bright lamp on the
masthead.

"Glad they modernized this one," she said. "Can you imagine trying
to pilot this boat without a manual? All hail the touch screen and auto
mode."

Houston gazed out the window. "Moon's nearly set."

Lightfoote followed her gaze outside. "Good thing. White fiberglass is
a bad color to hide in under moonlight. Okay—she's dead in the water
now. No need to drop anchor, should be a quick pass. Besides, if we're
made we'll need to move fast."

Lopez stood halfway in and out of the cabin. "I can hear it." He
motioned for them to follow.

The telltale rumble and thwack of the helicopter's motor and blades
were carried over the water by the wind. The winking red lights on the
craft were nearly lost in the blaze from a spotlight.

"Checking up on our girl," said Houston.

The helicopter approached Liberty Island and arced around it, the spotlight trained along its shores. They watched the bird do a complete revolution around the island, the light moving off the shores and onto the statue itself. Another full rotation had the craft's pulse coupled with a strobe effect from the spotlight, almost giving the towering figure the illusion of motion. Finally, the helicopter accelerated toward the Jersey shore. The light faded as it pulled away.

"Likely first of many flybys tonight," said Houston.

Lightfoote returned to the control panel and started the engine. "We need to get to the highway before sunrise. Great to hide out here at night, but we can't go dark in the day." The vessel shook to life, but she didn't turn the lights back on. "And I vote we stay dark tonight as well."

Lopez returned to the navigation system and switched the police scanner back on. "I don't know how many they have out patrolling, and there is no way to cover all the coastline. But some of this journey puts us in pretty narrow straits. We could get trapped there without many options."

Lightfoote nodded as the boat lurched forward. "Let's just hope their plate's full already."

"Going to go back out," said Houston.

"Still nauseous?" Lopez asked.

"Yeah. It's a hundred times worse in this cabin."

She opened the door and stepped back into the cold air. Immediately the wind and temperature drop began to relieve her symptoms. She walked back to the bow and leaned on the railing. Lady Liberty disappeared behind them in the blackness, lower Manhattan a foggy glow in the growing mist. Ahead, she began to see the outlines of the narrow opening to the Kill van Kull, traffic nonexistent. *Who would dare sail now, after all this?*

She hoped Lopez could get his head around the navigation. She didn't see much room to maneuver within the strait, and the sides were decorated with docks and moorings. They weren't even amateurs, and a collision could be ruinous. Ending their journey at the bottom of the New York harbor estuary was definitely not part of the plan. They had too much to do: A mystery to unravel. A shadowy organization and military coup in the United States to help thwart. And if a crazed terrorist's last words were right, in southern New Jersey an answer awaited them.

A glow flickered northeast of their position. The light revealed an approaching cloud front, dull orange reflecting off the low clouds rolling in from the northwest. The night rumbled and the light winked out.

And returned, the position slightly different, a trio of will-o-the-wisps in the far distance like someone had switched on and off several giant street lamps. An ensemble of rolling bass notes shook around them. Houston heard the cabin door open. Lopez and Lightfoote approached the bow and stood beside her, gazing north as the light and sound show continued.

"What is that?" asked Lightfoote. "Thunder?"

"It's not like any thunder I've ever heard," said Lopez.

Houston gritted her teeth. "Not thunder. Those aren't storm clouds."

"Then what?" asked Lopez.

A turbulent growl grew from the south and crackled, flashing through the air from port to starboard side. A flaming light screamed past them northwards, the rocket's burner searing streaks into their eyes. Its rumbling faded into the low throb of explosive detonations as it disappeared into the distance.

"Explosions," she answered. "From bombing runs."

Lopez placed his hand on her shoulder, squeezing firmly. "God help us."

22

GREETING PARTY

ouston squinted through the sunglasses as the morning sun glinted off the wet road in front of them. The mists had begun to clear but left a thin layer of water on the highway. It would evaporate quickly, but the surface blinded them for the moment.

"How's the glare, Francisco?"

Lopez grunted, his eyes behind shades heavy and dark from the sleepless night. He still favored his left shoulder, but it functioned better each day, the wound closed and shrinking. Houston knew the muscle damage would take longer to heal, and one hundred percent was months away. Dominantly right handed for most activities, it would have to do.

And they would need him. She had no doubts. Desperate men hunted them, assassins who stopped at nothing to prevent them from piecing together the mystery waiting in Princeton. The priest would have to become a killer again. His inner conflict would continue.

For now, she clung to the relative peace. The remainder of their voyage through the harbor and subsequent ride down the interstate had been uneventful—if one could call wrecking a cruise boat while trying to dock it, scampering to safety as it sunk beside a mooring, and hot-wiring an SUV *uneventful*. But by the standards of the last few weeks, it was almost relaxing.

Lightfoote slept soundly in the back of the black SUV, her body splayed out across the rear-most seat like an unruly teenager. She'd pushed herself more than anyone. Houston turned her head and stared at the strange woman—hacker, FBI agent, shaved and pierced cyberpunk, as much a mystery to her as whatever waited for them in Princeton. Houston sensed a darkness hidden within her.

Within each of us.

She returned her gaze to the road. "Two more lights and it's a right on Washington Road."

"I remember," he said gruffly. "We've gone over the route ten times."

Houston leaned across the seat and placed her head on his shoulder. "I'm tired too, Francisco. But we can't get down now. Everything is on the line."

"I know. Just on edge."

"Still, when we're together—it's a shield. Makes me feel we can do anything. I hold on to that."

He kissed her forehead, returning his eyes quickly to the road.

"God, and I thought working for my boss was a Hallmark card."

The rustling of fabric against the back seats was followed by a thud and vibration in the car. Behind them, Lightfoote leaned against the door, her feet flat on the floorboard.

Houston laughed. "Up already?"

She yawned. "So, where'd you two meet? Assassin school?"

"At a funeral," said Lopez.

"Touché," she said.

"He's serious," said Houston.

"Wouldn't surprise me. What funeral?"

Lopez sighed. "My brother's. Murdered by a madman who nearly brought down the CIA."

Houston cut in. "But that was before we were paraded across the front of the tabloids as some murderous, sex-crazed Bonnie and Clyde. Before we uncovered the CIA dirty laundry that got us smeared and on the most wanted list. Before your boss helped save our asses when we were caught hunting down the *real* killer of the former VP. The same man who killed his brother."

Lightfoote whistled. "Well *damn*, girl. John never said anything. He and Rebecca were unmovable. We all knew something was going on, but this? I've got to hear this story."

"Better story to hear than live through," Houston whispered.

"No time for stories," said Lopez, the car slowing. "Washington Road. Princeton University on the right."

Lopez swung the car off NJ 1 and onto Washington Road. The car sped through a short forested region, opening into extended fields of green as they approached a stony bridge. They passed over a body of water and into a tree-lined and well-manicured region.

Lightfoote mumbled. "Einstein. Woodrow Wilson. John Nash. Up ahead."

"On the left, actually. Faculty Road," said Houston.

Lopez turned at the junction and followed the road deeper into a forested patch. Just as they were getting used to the broken light and shadows, the environment shifted violently from pastoral to industrial and back again as they crossed railroad tracks. Lopez slowed at a sign reading Alexander Street.

"Right here, and then left on College, yes?"

"That's it," said Houston, staring at the campus buildings around them.

Ahead, a tower rose into the air. Stunted by Manhattan standards, in this rural enclave it rose majestically skyward, gothic spires and the gray stone facade giving the impression of medieval England more than southern New Jersey.

"Cleveland Tower," said Lightfoote, following Houston's gaze. "Built as a memorial for President Cleveland in 1913. Sixty-seven bells in a carillon at the top. Center of the Graduate College of Princeton University. Where John Nash got his Ph.D."

Lopez pulled the car into a circular drive in front of a row of stony buildings. He switched the engine off and got out of the car. The two women followed.

"It's completely deserted," he said. "We haven't seen a car or human being the whole way in. Where the hell is everyone?"

"A few weeks of Last Days events likely had everyone scrambling for home or the hills," said Houston. She turned to Lightfoote. "Looks like you've done your research. Where now?"

Lightfoote scanned the area. "Inside is the main quad. Tower's there on our right. The Nash Museum is directly behind it, built right beside a golf course."

Houston laughed, "So, after a hard day of schizophrenic econ, you can go tee off with the boys."

Lopez shook his head. "All right, let's go get the rest of that image."

"Don't move!" A man's voice shouted.

Footsteps sounded from behind them. They turned to see four men approaching, one with a raised handgun. Two of them seemed hardly out of high school, fear in their eyes. They dropped several bulging sacks to the ground.

A blond man walked slightly forward, the gun in his hand. A thin smile crept across his face.

"Well, what have we got here?"

23

ANGELS AND PANTHERS

"You boys from around here?" asked Houston with a smile. "We're a bit lost."

The two groups were separated by about ten yards, the car to the side. The men looked ragged, unkempt, and their thin leader stared with a wild glare. He kept moving the weapon from Lopez to Houston to Lightfoote, settling longest on the large form of the former priest.

"None of your business!" he yelled. "Who are you? Why are *you* here?"

"We're looking for someone," said Lopez. "We'll stay out of your way."

"Well, you found someone, asshole!" he barked, spittle coating the fuzz of blond hair on his chin. He inched forward, pointing the weapon at Lopez.

"Come on, Henry, we ain't got time!" cried another. "Those fucking soldiers are *here!* We got what we came for. Let's go."

Henry licked his lips. "Shut the fuck up, Nick! We're going. Yeah, we're going. We're just not going empty handed." He motioned with his gun. "Wallets. Purses. Any fucking gold or jewelry, you throw it over here."

Lopez looked at Houston. She nodded. Lightfoote said nothing.

"No problem. We don't want any trouble," said Lopez, carefully fishing his wallet out from his robes and tossing it to the feet of the man.

"You bitches, yours! Now!"

"I have to get my purse from the car," Houston said.

"No, no, no, no. Don't go near the fucking car! Got your little 22 in the glove compartment, am I right?"

"Henry, fuck it! Let's go. We got more than we can carry."

"Yeah, yeah," said Henry, a smile on his face. "We don't need no more money. But it's a long trip. Lonely trip." He waved the pistol. "You girls are coming with us."

The other three men looked at each other. Two of them smiled while Nick continued to protest.

"Dammit, no! We can't take more. We got too many already!"

Henry spoke coldly. "That's for sure."

He turned toward Nick and pulled the trigger. The weapon cracked crisply in the cold air. The teen grabbed at his throat as his legs gave way. His screams turned to gurgles as he convulsed on the ground.

"*Jesus*, man," said a man behind him, his eyes wide as he gaped at the twitching form of the dying man.

"Shut up or you're next!" Henry stepped toward Lopez. "World's gone to shit. Ain't no rules, not no more. We do what we want." He glared at Lopez. "You, wetback! You want to be next?"

With a final glance at Houston, Lopez shook his head.

"*No mas, señor*. I don't know these girls. After all the crazy, I was just carpooling with them. Not my problem."

"Down on your face!"

Lopez kneeled and fell prostrate on the manicured grass in front of the graduate college building. Houston began to cry as Lightfoote placed her hands over her eyes.

"Now, you two, this way. You run, I shoot you. You try anything, I shoot you. Look at that!" He pointed to the corpse beside him. "*See?* I will. I'll blow your fucking brains out!"

The women moved slowly forward, their bodies shaking in fear.

Henry turned to his remaining companions. "I did all the work here for you pussies. I get a go at each before either of you. You understand?"

One on his right nodded. "Yeah, man. Whatever you say. Jesus Christ. I can't believe you shot Nick."

"No rules but my rules. I make the rules." He turned to the other on this left. "You got that, Bill?"

"Yeah. You make the rules."

He looked Lightfoote up and down. "You, metal face." She stopped. "Put your hands down. Come here. I want to get a look at you."

Lightfoote walked up slowly, Houston following a pace behind.

He smiled. "Green eyes. Cool. You looked *fucked up* girl. I bet you can do some shit. Twisted, huh? Fuck me good?"

Lightfoote smiled and looked into his eyes. "Yeah. I'll fuck you up good."

Her hands shot forward and grasped the gun as she sidestepped. Using her body weight in a continuous motion, she twisted the wrist, bones snapping audibly. Henry screamed, staring down at his arm in shock, the hand wrenched at a grotesque angle to his forearm. Lightfoote crouched on one knee, his gun in her hand, the barrel pointed forward.

Stunned, the other two men barely reacted. Like a drunk, the one on the right began feeling around the middle of his lower back for the weapon tucked in his belt. His head snapped backward as a gunshot reverberated off the stone. At the same moment, Houston sprang like a panther toward the man on the left. He swung his arm in a haymaker from the side, only to find himself in her embrace as she redirected his unbalanced attack into a twist and flung him onto the grass. He landed heavily, the wind knocked out of him. He wheezed as he looked up into the massive barrel of a Browning 1911.

Henry fell to his knees. He cradled his wrecked hand.

"What the *fuck?* You broke my fucking arm!" Tears streaked his face from the pain.

Lightfoote dropped his weapon on the roof of the car with a clank. She nodded to Lopez as he stood up. "We can keep theirs as backup."

Lopez examined the gun. "Only when we're desperate. What a piece of crap. Guy's lucky this thing didn't blow up in his hand."

"He's got other hand problems," said Lightfoote.

"Who *are* you?" asked Henry.

Lopez checked the chamber and removed the magazine, continuing to examine the weapon. "We need to question them about the soldiers."

Henry's face reddened. "Always get girls to do your dirty work, Spic?"

Lopez smiled grimly and walked to the trunk with the weapon.

"Hey, I'm talking to you!"

Lightfoote struck the man in the chest with her foot. He crashed to the ground with a groan.

"You bitch, I'm going to—"

"Shut up," said Houston, kicking him lightly in the head. He shut up. Her weapon remained aimed at Bill.

Lightfoote stared down at Henry. "Your dead friend said *soldiers*. What soldiers?"

"You'll find out. Not telling you shit!"

Lightfoote sprang forward to land on his abdomen, her right hand like a claw smashing into his crotch. He screamed, began to struggle but froze, a high-pitched squeal tearing from his lips.

"Yeah, I can do all kinds of shit with your junk." Her hand pinched like a vice on his pants. He screamed. "Two little balls. So much pain." She squeezed tighter and the man's face reddened, the scream cut off, his body paralyzed. "I'm going to ask this one more time. And you're going to answer, or you're going to learn about a pain you never knew could exist."

24

DIGGING GRAVES

"There's a shed over by those trees," said Lopez, moving in its direction. "Likely for the grounds crew. I'll be right back."

"Where is he going?" moaned Henry.

Billy and Henry were tied with hands behind their backs and set against the car. The bodies of their companions lay in the grass directly in front of them.

"Ah, God! My arm! It hurts!"

Lightfoote scowled. "Maybe we should just shoot the ass and put him out of our misery?"

"No, I like to hear him whine," said Houston, a dark look in her eyes. "Reminds me of what he was planning to do with us." She walked up to the man and crouched down. "Karma's a bitch, ain't it, asshole? If your friend hadn't sung like a bird, things might be much worse for you."

"Bad song," said Lightfoote. "Sounds like it's a scouting party. They're sweeping through Princeton, but my bet is they're headed here. I think the NSA mainframes cracked the encryption before York got to them."

"You're sure she hit them?"

Lightfoote lit up. "Oh, yeah. It's like a thousand digital gnats suddenly disappeared. I'd love to see them scrambling to get back up and running. But right now, we have our own problems."

Houston stood back up and nodded. "Yeah. We don't have much time. More will come even if we can take these out."

A strained voice came from behind them. "Let's divide this up."

They turned to see Lopez laden with a pregnant tarp over his shoulders. He bent his neck and tossed it to the ground with a heavy thud and rattle.

"You two go to the museum. Take photos of the giant cork board. We can analyze them later when we've found a place to hide out."

"What about you?" asked Houston, looking toward the bulging tarp.

He bent down and unfurled the stained fabric, revealing shovels and gardening equipment. His head turned toward the two men.

"We're going to dig two graves. Better than leaving them out to rot."

"We?" asked Houston.

"Dumb and dumber there," he said. "They'll dig."

"I'm not digging nothing," said Henry.

Lopez stood up straight and his arm pointed toward them in a fluid motion. A dark barrel gleamed at the end of it. He screwed a long silencer to the end.

"You're going to dig those graves. Or I'm going to dig all your graves. Your choice."

"You broke my fucking hand! I can't dig!"

He kicked a spade forward from the open tarp. "You've still got one good arm. Use it. Your friend will use the shovels, and I'll be keeping both of you in my sights."

The ground in front of Henry exploded, dust and rocks coating his face, snow and mud stuck to his blond locks. He screamed and turned his head from Lopez's gun, coughing as tears ran from his spattered eyes.

"And you'll do it quickly. We don't have much time."

The men nodded.

"Wise move," said Houston. She reached down with a blade and cut their bonds. Both flinched from the knife. Lopez kept his weapon trained on them. She moved around the car and opened the trunk, ducking under the lid and back out holding a red canister.

Lopez squinted. "You're going to torch it?"

"Not going to leave any clues in that place once we leave. Let those bastards spin their wheels and wonder what we found out. Bring the bodies. Save the digging."

"The older Catholic rites die hard," he said cryptically. He nodded to the canister. "That's our reserve. Hope the fuel pumps are working around here."

"I'll use sparingly," she said. "Place is full of paper. Should go up like a straw man." She jerked her head toward the tower and looked at Light-foote. "Ready?"

The pair set off at a jog to the museum.

Lopez never took his eyes off the two men as they winced, bringing their hands around.

"Now, both of you—dig."

THE TWO MEN were dripping with sweat when the women returned. Henry whimpered against a nearby tree, clutching his hand to his chest. Two shallow and uneven holes had been dug and the bodies dragged into them, the dirt placed on top barely covering the corpses. A light snow had begun to fall, coating the ground in a patchwork of white.

"Got the photos, several angles to make sure," said Houston breathing heavily, bursts of fog coming out of her mouth. "It's the same board from the file photo, but we have the rest of it. Still more than half the gas in this thing," she said, shaking the canister.

"Good, give me five minutes here."

Lopez held a flat black box and removed a folded red item from within. He placed the box on the thickening layer of snow and as he stood back up, unfurled a crimson stole trimmed along the sides with golden embroidery. He placed it over his head, the two tracks of red and gold offset strongly by his black robes.

"Blessed is God, Who poureth out His grace upon His priests, like the oil of myrrh upon the head, which runneth down to the fringe of his raiment."

Lightfoote leaned over to Houston and whispered in her ear: "What is he doing?"

"Giving them a funeral."

"Why *these* guys?"

Houston shrugged. "Not running for our lives right now. Got a little time."

Lightfoote smirked. "The Priest and the Whore."

Houston didn't reply. Her eyes didn't leave Lopez. The snow had begun to fall heavily, the day darkening from the heavy clouds.

"Lord God, by the power of your Word you stilled the chaos of the primeval seas, you made the raging waters of the Flood subside, and calmed the storm on the Sea of Galilee. As we commit the body of our brothers to the deep, grant all peace and tranquility. You promised paradise to the repentant thief; here also bring us to the joys of heaven. Gracious Lord, forgive the sins of those who have perished."

The two men looked on in shock at the proceedings. Henry had even stopped his whimpering.

"Lord God, whose days are without end and whose mercies beyond counting, keep us mindful that life is short and the hour of death unknown. Let your Spirit guide our days on earth in the ways of holiness and justice, that we may serve you, sure in faith, strong in hope, perfected in love. And when our earthly journey is ended, lead us rejoicing into your kingdom, where you reign for ever and ever. Amen."

He made the Sign of the Cross over the graves.

"All a waste, you stupid priest. They wasn't even Catholic."

"That's all right. I'm not a priest." He folded the stole and replaced it in the black box. "And I'm not Catholic. Not anymore."

An orange light flickered off the low-lying clouds. The brightness intensified near the peak of the tower and cut through the heavy snowfall. Lopez approached the men.

"Now, you two are going to get the hell out of here. I don't think I need to explain that if you try anything, or if we catch wind you have given the soldiers or anyone else information about us, we will not pause to plant you in the ground along with your friends." He fit his hands one by one into a pair of black gloves. "I might not even give you last rites."

25

SCREAMS

Again he woke to the sound of his own screams.

Savas sat up violently in bed, arm raised to ward off a blow. Daylight had barely begun to remove the shadows of night, but a chorus of birds piped in the surrounding forests. Muffled shouts and heavy crashing swirled around him. His breath exhaled in ragged clouds from his chapped lips as a hand reached over from his left, and pressed gently down on his arm.

"It's okay, John," said Cohen, her voice pained. She leaned up against him, tugging on the army issue blanket, brown hair tangled and strewn haphazardly about her shoulders. "Just another dream."

Savas stared blankly forward. "Where are we?"

"Mmmm. Tent on I-76, just outside of Harrisburg."

He closed his eyes. "The convoy. Right. We started to see mountains." He shook his head. "Damn. Sorry, Rebecca."

"Want to talk about it?"

"And say what?" He coughed. "Variations on the usual. Thanos died. Right in my arms. You were almost—the towers were falling on us. Cinder blocks, metal and glass pounding you and him. I tried to shield you, but I couldn't. And they kept hitting and hitting until the stones turned to fists and I was in that damned boat and strapped to that table. And you were screaming on the monitor."

"John—"

His hand made a fist. "I can't protect the people I love. No matter what I do."

She took his head in her hands and turned it to her. "No, John. You can't. Look at me!" He grimaced, the muscles tensing across his chest. "You have to accept it. You aren't Superman. You aren't a hero out of a book or a movie. We fight monsters. Someday something bad might happen to me. You have to look it in the face and accept it. Like I have for you, for a long time." Her eyes glistened. "Someday, time is going to take away as much dignity, inflict as much damage and pain, as any of these monsters could. I need you to be there and be strong, now *and* then. Knowing what will happen. I will be for you."

"You're stronger than me," he whispered. "It's easier to get angry, strike out at a threat with adrenaline coursing through you. Fighting the incoming sea without end? I don't know how to do that."

"You don't fight it," she said. "You ride it out as best you can. That's all anyone can do."

"And hope for something transcendent afterward? That this isn't it, this screwed-up world and decaying flesh?"

"I don't know, John," she said, shaking her head. "My mother always said the b'rakhot. After she died, we didn't hear many prayers. My father wasn't much for ritual."

"Yeah, me either. I wish I had Father Timothy's confidence."

Cohen ran her fingers through his hair. "No time for crises of faith. Let's see what the soldiers have us eating this morning. We're going to be moving soon."

They dressed quickly in the frigid air and stepped out into the blinding light of the sun rising over the highway. Savas marveled as he stared down an endless line of military vehicles and troops, metal gleaming, engines coughing and spewing soot into the crisp air, chatter and the sounds of mundane activities giving lie to the absurdity before them.

"They've laid out some tables over there," said Cohen.

Savas followed her lead and they made their way over to a line of soldiers waiting beside a makeshift kitchen. The smell of burnt protein and fat mixed with the cold air and stirred deep feelings within him. He put his arm around Cohen and pressed her to his side.

"FBI!" came the bark of a well-known voice.

They turned, straining to see around the jockeying soldiers scrambling for a meal. A mop of disheveled gray hair sitting at a long table waved them over. The president and her advisors were shoveling food into their mouths as they spoke over a large map.

York glared in their direction. "You two aren't good enough for the regular mess. Over here with the civilians."

Savas saw Cohen smile. He was still too shaken for such a display. They picked their way around the bustling troops and up a short hill to the president's table. A paper map was spread out over the surface. Bowls and trays of food weighed it down in the cold wind, and various items from rocks to condiment containers were arrayed along the colored lines marking interstates and cities.

"I'm a dinosaur and prefer a hardcopy," said York, spooning a heap of eggs. "About to gouge my eyes out looking at those blinking digital displays in the command vehicle. Here, grab some *grub,* I think is the technical term. Plate of eggs and bacon and something I'm not sure what it is, but it's runny as snot."

They quickly raked the food onto a free plate and sat down across from York at the table, several aides looking askance at them. York ignored the looks and gestured over the chaos on the table.

"So, what do you think?"

Savas chewed on a burnt piece of toast and shook his head.

"I'm not sure I can make out what you're representing here."

Cohen pointed at several aggregates of items.

"Major cities on the map. These must be troop gatherings. Enemy troops, if I can say that about other Americans."

"You bet your sweet ass you can, daughter," said York. "And they have gone off and picked the wrong goddamned side of this war." The president bent over the map. "This line of rocks, that's us, this convoy. We're just outside of Harrisburg, Pennsylvania. We made pretty good time once we got rolling. Luckily, Hastings's damn hit-and-runs have been poorly executed. We're on schedule to make Mount Cheyenne in three more days. Considering the slow start out of the gate, it's not bad. So far, so good."

Cohen pointed to a dense collection of salt and pepper shakers.

"What's that ahead?"

"The bad," said York. "We've got partial satellite coverage and some imagery, also some scouting drones. That right there is Columbus, Ohio, capital of the state and fifteenth largest city in America. Right now, Hastings is fortifying it with some serious strength: infantry, heavy arms from the recon images. West of the city," she said, tapping an overturned coffee tin, "is Wright-Patterson Air Force Base. The base is his, and they are quickly turning it into a center of operations for this campaign."

"Why there?" asked Cohen. "I thought air force was useless."

"So did we," she answered. "But reports show increasing numbers of Hastings-controlled aircraft going into use."

"They've solved the worm problem," Cohen whispered.

"Yes," said the President grimly. "We believe they have. It will take them some time to get their planes online, but more and more, the longer we're out here, the worse it will be. We're likely to see some heavy assault coming from the land *and* air when we get into Ohio."

"Jesus," said Savas. "What can we counter with?"

York frowned. "Superior numbers on the ground, especially with the break-away troops from Fort Bragg that managed to rendezvous with us last night. Meanwhile, our side is working overtime to crack the digital problem with the advanced aircraft, but Hastings has the aerial advantage until we're closer to NORAD."

"So there's going to be a battle?" asked Cohen.

"Outside of Columbus it looks like."

"I hoped it wouldn't come to this."

Savas squinted down at the map. "And this tactical advantage in the air. What does that mean, practically?"

"It means," said York, glancing grimly upward, "that come this evening in Ohio, the skies are going to be raining fire."

BATTLE FRONT

The convoy commandeered the entire highway.

Before sequestering within the command vehicle, Savas had stared out at the troop transports, tanks, armored trucks with antiaircraft missiles, and an assortment of different medical and more mundane vehicles pouring down one of America's most traveled civilian roadways.

The giant convoy was divided into several staggered contingents. In the far lead were a set of soldiers tasked with keeping the roadway clear. This involved engaging what foolish civilian drivers would brave the coming military force and getting them off-road as well as clearing obstacles—construction or hazards often the product of sabotage from opposing forces. More than one bridge had come under fire from Hastings, and repairs or complete detours slowed everything. Instead of the consistent jog at thirty miles an hour modeled in the underground Manhattan base of operations, they found themselves oscillating between crawling and all out sprints. The strain began to show on equipment as increasing numbers of vehicles failed and were left on the side of the roadway.

Despite the challenges, their progress managed to be significant, if in spurts. Small raids by worm-resistant, Vietnam-era aircraft or troop ambushes were countered effectively, although the intensity of some of the

assaults stunned even a street-hardened, antiterrorist agent like Savas.
After a particularly close explosion rocked their truck, leaving a prolonged
ringing in his ears, he turned to Cohen in disbelief.

"This is what Frank dealt with for years in Afghanistan."

Cohen nodded, her face a mask of tension. "Probably worse. Fine way
he was repaid for his service."

"I think worse is coming," said Savas. "Gunshots, even the explosions
at the airfield in Mexico when we tracked Mjolnir—nothing like these
bombs and missiles. My brain is still rattling around, I think."

"That last one was very close," said Cohen, glancing nervously toward
York. "It's a dangerous shell game."

"There were what, five decoys? Five command vehicles spread around
out there?"

She nodded. "I think so. And I heard the communications guy up
front say one was hit earlier."

"Jesus."

"They're going to target those preferentially. And the drivers know,"
she continued in a stunned monotone. "Who does that? Who salutes and
gets behind a wheel of a decoy knowing they're just bait to hide someone
else?"

"While we sit safe in here," he said.

"Not completely. Everyone's in the line of fire. Shell game is an odds
game. But our odds are better than theirs."

Savas shook his head. "An amazing job—this truck looks like any
normal troop transport on the outside. But in here," he said, gesturing to
the banks of military communications, computer monitors, and other
high-tech yet hardened technology, "it's a different story. Thick armor
cloaked by the false vehicle wall on the outside. I didn't know the army
could be so clandestine."

"Thick or not, I don't think anything would stop a direct hit," said
Cohen.

"Well, let's hope we don't get one of those."

They were nestled in the back corner of the truck, strapped to wall-
mounted seats and staring down at the military dance of soldiers and
equipment. Stiff and sore from over twelve hours of travel, they were cold
even in their coats, the interior unheated to conserve fuel. York sat alongside several soldiers who manned the equipment, their fogged breath like

a cloud around them. Her face was grim. She rose and headed in their direction. He guessed what she might say.

A series of blasts outside explained the situation forcefully. The vehicle heaved and rocked violently, and sent the president crashing to the floor on her hands and knees before the FBI agents. A flurry of curses sounded as Savas and Cohen helped her to her feet. A soldier leapt to her side.

"Ms. President," he said, "are you okay?"

She sat down beside Cohen and regained her bearings.

"Yes," she said hoarsely. "Getting a little old for combat, I think." She blinked repeatedly. "Get the plan in motion and I'll brief our passengers."

The soldier nodded and turned toward the front of the truck.

"Plan?" asked Savas.

"We're three hundred and fifty miles past Harrisburg, around twenty outside of Columbus. We've been positioning our forces in anticipation of what's ahead."

A whistle overhead presaged an earthshaking explosion.

"That bastard Hastings has let the dogs out," she growled. "His troops are advancing. Heavy artillery is first in line. We've also detected incoming aircraft and a few missiles already, although a last-minute sabotage of his naval assets has grounded most of his cruise missiles for the time being. "

"Cruise missiles." Savas could hardly take it in.

"The modern military is something to behold," said York. "This is not going to be easy or pretty."

Sonic booms shook the air above them as the sound of jet engines ripped through the sky. More explosions followed as did the screaming of men outside.

"What's going on out there?" asked Cohen.

"War," said York. "Better you don't see. Better none of us sees unless we have to. We need to keep our heads and stick with the plan. We stay low. We remain covert. Meanwhile, many good men are going to engage that son-of-a-bitch and die today so we can continue this journey."

She stood up and dusted herself off.

"It's going to get ugly fast. Hold on and hope for the best. If you have a god to pray to, now is a good time."

27

WHISKEY

"Princeton's finest, and the best they had was Jack?"

Houston slurred her words, her grin asymmetric and comical. She leaned heavily against the bulk of Lopez, his dark hair spilling underneath his cap and brushing her pale cheek. The three sat huddled together in a crowded dorm basement, clouds of water vapor escaping their lips, ice surrounding a nearby water fountain from a burst pipe.

Lopez took the bottle from her and shook his head. "This was supposed to help us forget the cold, not blast us to nirvana." He smiled at Lightfoote. "There's nothing in the world this little lady can't do better than me, unless it's hold her liquor."

"Not fair," snorted Houston. "You're three times my weight."

"And you're heavier than Angel, but I wouldn't put money on me to out-drink her."

Lightfoote smiled. "Cyborg. Hyper-metabolism."

"See?" said Houston. "Explains everything." Her eyes lingered on the FBI agent. "You're some mystery girl."

Lightfoote removed a woolen watch cap and rubbed her fingers vigorously over her scalp. A red film of hair had begun to grow out. "So are you two. Tell me," she said, replacing the hat and nearly pulling it over her eyes, "what's the story on the Browning? You don't shoot anything else."

Houston sat up clumsily. "What makes you think there's a story?"

"That's not just a gun, girl. That's *your* gun. There's a story."

Houston laughed. "Fucking cyborgs. Well, my dad gave it to me. Trained me on it. Brought it back from the Korean War."

"Korean war? How old is he?"

"He would have been eighty. Died ten years ago."

Lightfoote nodded. "But he gave you his issued sidearm?"

"War changed him. Sucked a lot of the life out of him. He never talked about it. *Never.*" She grabbed the bottle and swept it away from a frowning Lopez. "They didn't have things like PTSD or therapy back in those days. He put away his uniform—*pluke*—and everything he took back from the war. Shut it all up in a trunk. *Click.* Never opened it again. I never saw it anyway, even all those years later."

"Except for the gun," said Lightfoote, staring intensely at her. "So he robbed the cradle? To have you, your mom must have been a lot younger."

"Mom. Ha. Now there are *problems.* She hunted him down, daddy figure or something she thought she needed. I don't know. Course it didn't last. She was gone like a wild butterfly." Houston watched the liquid swirl as she shook the bottle. "He was a good father. Don't get me wrong. You know, back then there weren't too many single dads. He never remarried. Never dated as far as I know. I think the only thing keeping him alive was me." She opened the bottle. "Until I left home." Her eyes flashed toward Lightfoote. "So! What's *your* story, fly girl? And don't even bother. I know there's one, too."

Lightfoote didn't smile. "Dad was a cop. Followed in his footsteps."

"No son to do it?" asked Houston, wiping her chin as whiskey dripped.

"It's more complicated."

"He teach you how to shoot, too?"

"No. Never got the chance." Lightfoote paused. "He was killed in the line of duty. Until then, I didn't want to be a cop. I had other interests. Dancing mostly. But everything changed when he died."

"Why'd that change things?" asked Houston.

"It's complicated."

Lightfoote reached for the bottle. Houston nodded and handed it over, watching her take a swig.

"Gotcha. We don't have to—"

"I saw him die," she said. "I was just a few feet away. I couldn't do anything." She took another gulp. "I knew then there were monsters in the world. I think I was a bit lost afterward." She laughed. "Make that a lot lost. But I couldn't just *dance* anymore." Lightfoote stared off into space, the whiskey bottle dangling over her raised knees, wobbling back and forth as she swung her wrist. Her eyes moved to Lopez. "So, big guy, you do the *follow dad* thing, too?"

A deep laughter rolled in the room. His deep brown eyes looked at his feet. "I wish I could have. Not remotely smart enough. My father was a NASA engineer, recruited from polytechnic school in Mexico City. Test scores off the charts. Helped build rockets in Alabama during the Cold War and Space Race."

"A literal rocket scientist!" barked Houston, nudging Lopez with her shoulder.

"I guess I did try. Ended up teaching intro calculus at a Catholic school. But that was as smart as I was going to get. No rocket science for me."

Lightfoote put the whiskey down and hugged her knees. "So why the priesthood? Visions? Voice of God?"

Lopez smiled. "I wish that as well. But, no. My motives were earthly. Rebelling against my neocon brother." He reached over and stroked Houston's cheek. "And denial of something similar inside me."

"So who taught *you* to shoot? You're the best I've seen."

"He had the best teacher," said Houston.

"You?" Lightfoote smiled. "Really? Blind date activities?"

Lopez put an arm around Houston. "When we first met, in the middle of all that crazy, it was the one thing she wouldn't shut up about. *Going to teach you how to shoot.* Drove me nuts. I'd rarely held a gun. Certainly not a man killer. I didn't want to! Violence, killing—I'd turned my back on it. I was a peacemaker, turning the other cheek." He laughed. "Before the priesthood, I'd used my fists a lot. I tried to turn it around, suppress it, have God's word my sword and shield and all the St. Paul Ephesians *Armor of God* stuff."

Houston kissed his cheek and shook her head. "Poor bastard. He had to learn the hard way to use some other armor and weapons. Bad guys out there."

"Monsters," said Lightfoote, her expression distant again.

Lopez squinted slightly at her but said nothing.

Lightfoote continued. "So, what's the plan for you two, assuming the world doesn't end soon?"

Lopez shrugged. Houston leaned back into his chest. "No idea. We're FBI most wanted, and Savas can't change that. Nobody can. Dead or alive kind of pariahs. We killed the former VP! Hundreds of government agents. Blew up a fucking police station. He's a pedophile. I don't think you come back from all that."

"So, John really put you in deep witness protection? He kept it all under wraps."

Houston nodded. "With help from CIA. Fred Simon." She looked away and closed her eyes, nuzzling into Lopez.

"I'm sorry about what happened," said Lightfoote. "We were overrun with Fawkes's mercenaries. I was lucky to get the code out. They almost won."

"Don't apologize. You stopped a madman," said Lopez. "We'll see when all this is done what kind of world is waiting. But I'm not hopeful. We've resigned ourselves to new lives, new identities. Always hiding. Always running."

"Priest and whore. Gabriel and Mary."

"Something like that, right Sara?" Houston didn't answer. Lopez looked down and sighed, brushing his hand over her head.

She was asleep.

28

BLOOD AND ASH

Savas gritted his teeth as he trudged through the new-fallen snow. No longer snow, but a black slush from fires and exhaust that tainted the purity. Flames continued to lick at the metallic skeletons of blasted vehicles, chemical fumes from rubber and burnt machinery choking him.

His shoulders burned from carrying the stretcher. The medic at the other end of it walked with his head bowed in silence. Savas had lost track of the number of bodies he'd carried like this. *Less than one hundred?* It felt like more, but he knew he couldn't have managed so many. Perhaps much less. All clarity had disappeared and his mind reeled.

Savas had killed men. Had watched them die in numerous ways. He'd seen small skirmishes with terrorist groups, suffered wounds on several occasions. Had watched the towers fall in New York, mosques obliterated around the world, and witnessed a nuclear detonation over the Gulf of Mexico.

But nothing had prepared him for true war.

Bodies still littered the roadway and sides of the road. To his right he caught a glimpse of the burning hulk of a fighter jet, the shape only barely discernible from the mangled wreckage. Far in the distance, he could make out the skyline of Columbus, a small handful of skyscrapers like desolate redwoods in a devastated forest veiled in smoke.

Columbus burned.

They reached a medical tent. He knew they were close before they entered from the smell and the screaming. Hundreds of wounded soldiers produced an environmental-level impact. The snow around them was crimson as well as black.

They placed the stretcher outside the tent alongside rows of corpses. The woman they carried had died along the way. Savas had seen her injuries and known that nothing in modern medicine could have changed the outcome.

"I'm going to take a minute," he told the medic, who just nodded and went about his duties.

Savas sat down on a set of wooden boxes outside the tent. For the first time in many years, he felt an old craving, a desperate thirst for a drink that would burn and numb. It frightened and fascinated him to watch this old specter rise so many years after exorcism. *I'm more shaken than I realize.*

He turned his mind to the ear-splitting and grating sounds of metal scraping on rock, watching the engineering corps clearing the road of debris and smashed vehicles. He hadn't counted on the obstacles war would put in their way. They needed to deal with the human toll of battle, but the logistical nightmare—opening the path for what remained of the convoy—demanded attention.

He scanned the road behind them. He could not comprehend the carnage. It distorted his reasoning. He would have sworn truthfully that the overnight battle had obliterated the president's force. But as he took appraisal of what remained in the morning light, he saw it was much the reverse. The bulk of the convoy remained intact. Perhaps one in ten vehicles had been successfully targeted by weapons fire. Craning his neck, he could see that the human toll, especially on the part of Hastings's men who had recklessly assaulted their position, increased as one approached Columbus. Bodies carpeted the stretch toward the damaged city. A nightmare might surround him, but the lower levels of the hellscape awaited them ahead.

In the initial hours of the assault, he had absorbed some of the military strategy unfolding. Not a ground commander, Hastings had led his soldiers into a slaughter. Yet that assault had taken the lives of many in the presidential convoy. The air and artillery attacks had been devastating, as missiles and explosives strafed them along the highway. But the air advantage proved too weak to turn the tide on the ground. York's advisors claimed their superior numbers and far superior battlefield strategy had won the day decisively.

Abstractions. On the ground around him, a decisive victory looked more like a meat-grinder. The cries and weeping of the wounded had become a haunted chant from the plains of Gehenna in his mind, tearing at his awareness even when he was alone. Images of bodies broken, shredded, inverted in manners hard to imagine, trespassed before his open eyes. Young faces turned to cold cadavers. Voices silenced. *And voices crying out.*

As the sun crept over the fog of smoke clinging to the ground, he saw a silhouetted form ambling slowly toward him. The rhythm, the stride, the body motions—*Rebecca.* The vapors slowly revealed her sooty face as she came to take a seat on the boxes beside him. She leaned back against a tent support and closed her eyes.

"The president?" Savas managed to ask after a few minutes.

"Safe. On overdrive. She can't be human. We're going to move soon, John. I came to tell you."

"We aren't done."

"Doesn't matter. We can't wait to take care of everything."

"These are men and women here. We can wait."

She sighed. "If we do, we'll have more deaths on our hands. Every minute we delay keeps us from Mount Cheyenne. Every minute means Hastings has more time to plan another assault."

"Another?" Savas couldn't process it.

"I've been in the command module. I've seen the new recon. He fucked up here, but he's already regrouping. York says he's not stupid and he'll learn. Next time will be worse, and there's no telling how much more tech he'll have online by then."

"Where next? I mean, where are we headed? Where's the next battle?"

"Kansas City for both, unless Hastings gets a lot more creative." She placed her hand on the back of his head. "We've got to move."

Savas nodded and stood up, Cohen behind him. He looked over the battlefield once more.

"Kansas City. Another battle. *Worse.*"

She stared out toward the smoldering skyline of Columbus.

"Looks to be. Yes."

"My God, Rebecca. This is America. What are we doing?"

29

MADMAN'S PRIMER

"There's a code here," came Lightfoote's weary tones.

The three remained in the basement of a Princeton University dorm room. A wave of soldiers had come by the building, loudly thundering through several of the upper floors, but abandoned the search as they moved toward the smoldering remains of the Nash Museum. They'd ignored the lower floors.

Houston moaned and drank from a cup of cold water. Her eyes were closed. "God I need an aspirin. I'm breaking up with Jack for real this time."

"There's a primer," continued Lightfoote. "I know it. I just can't figure it out. There's a measuring stick in this mess!"

Lopez sighed. "So you've been saying since dawn. But it's a quarter to five and there hasn't been anything more. Don't you get hangovers?"

"Cyborg."

"Right. I'd forgotten."

They'd been staring at the reconstructed image for hours, assembled on the computer from several photos Houston had taken, completing the half obtained from Fawkes's file.

"What do you make of it, Francisco?" Houston had asked after they stitched the images together.

"Nothing," he'd sighed. "Just more crazy."

But from early on Lightfoote had disagreed. As the night had limped by, she continued staring at the news clippings, scrap paper, words and diagrams, equations and images John Nash had taped and pinned together across the giant poster board.

"Look. This isn't coincidence. Numbers!" she gestured to the image. "These number strings always appear over words or math symbols. It's like they're labeling them."

"But what's the significance? What does it mean?" asked Houston.

Lopez shook his head and yawned. "Modern art from a madman."

"We don't have time to sleep, priest!" Lightfoote stood up from the computer and came within inches of his face. "You're a mathematician."

"Math *teacher*. Remember? *High school.*"

"Do any of these equations mean anything?"

He rubbed his eyes and stared again at the image. "It's a chaotic patchwork. These are mathematical symbols, no doubt. But no true equations. Pieces of them, computational instruments without substrates. Incomplete. Might as well be random."

"They're *not* random."

Lopez shook his head again. "I can't see the pattern."

She turned back to the image on the computer, tapping with her index finger on the screen.

"This then. In the center. It looks like some weird symbolism. It's huge, colored strangely."

"Everything here is strange," Lopez added.

Lightfoote ignored him. "We only had half the image from the file, split down the middle. But look, here we can see it's a gold circle with a long black line underneath, and underneath that, a short gold line. *That* has to mean something!"

"Yeah, to aliens on Stargate."

Her eyes flashed. "Try, dammit! There's something here, I just can't see the pattern. Find the primer to interpret it. This thing stands out the most. In the middle. Gold on black. It *means* something."

Lopez sighed and squinted at the screen. "I've been staring at the image for hours, Angel. Yes, it stands out. A golden circle over a golden line. I don't—"

His words stopped abruptly.

"You don't what?" asked Houston, opening her eyes. They were bloodshot.

Lopez leaned in closely. "A golden circle over a golden line. A golden ratio." He laughed. "Holy shit."

"Well, coming from a priest," said Lightfoote, "that sounds promising."

"Former priest. But, yeah, maybe. Look, the gold line underneath is the perfect length to be the diameter of the circle above."

Lightfoote shook her head. "Okay?"

"The length around a circle, the circumference, divided by the diameter! It's the most famous number of all!"

"Pi," Lightfoote said.

"Yes, Pi."

Houston frowned. "Okay, so what? How does that help, even if that's what it's about? Who cares about Pi?"

Lopez continued to scan the image, tapping his fingers in several places. "Look, *here*—a large golden three over this word in a newspaper article: *External*. And, here, another golden number, 14, over this scribbled word, what is it—*Equilibration*."

"And here," said Lightfoote, "a golden 159 over the word *in*."

"You two have lost me," said Houston.

"Three point one-four-one-five-nine-two-six-five-three-five-eight...well, that's all I have memorized," said Lightfoote.

"Memorized?" Houston asked.

"Pi!" said Lopez. "The decimal expansion of the number Pi. My God, it's so simple."

Houston put her hand over the image. "Okay, geeks. Explain."

Lightfoote moved her hand and grinned broadly. "The numbers. Over the words. It's a code! The primer was the image of the circle and line. Telling us the code is centered on Pi. The decimal expansion of Pi is a series of numbers. Infinite. Doesn't repeat. Nash put pieces of the numbers over words."

"Not just single numbers," added Lopez, "those will show up again, over and over in an infinite expansion. He's used the *groupings*. The first few colored in gold to make it obvious. See, a golden three here over *External*. Three is the first digit of Pi, in the one's place. Then the next two digits, 14, again gold, here over the word *Equilibration*. We get two more gold numbers: 26535 and 89793238."

Lightfoote held up her smartphone, a list of digits running across a calculator app.

"The decimal expansion of Pi out to nineteen places. Divided into five groups of numbers. Colored gold."

"What does it say?"

"If we're right, the first four words of something: External Equilibration in Non-cooperative," said Lopez.

"So, nonsense?" Houston asked.

"Maybe not," said Lopez. "Sounds almost mathematical."

Lightfoote spoke rapidly. "Nash specialized in an area called Non-cooperative Game Theory. It's math meets economics. This sounds right!"

"So where is the rest of the code?"

Lightfoote frowned. "A few more golden numbers, then just...numbers. Lots of numbers. Different sized number strings."

"How to we know which clusters of numbers are next?" asked Lopez.

"Pi, of course."

He shook his head. "Yes, but which pieces of Pi. This could take forever. Unless..." He shook his head. "Golden ratio. I said it in the beginning but didn't make the connection. Nash was brutally literal in his symbolism."

"*The* Golden ratio?" asked Lightfoote. "Artistic ratio the Greeks loved?"

"Yes," he said. "But not only. It shows up in many early cultures, in nature, in snail shells, flowers. Weird Catholic and Jewish numerology. And it shows up in a series called the Fibonacci numbers."

Lightfoote nodded. "I remember. Take the last number and add it to the number before last to get the next number."

"Exactly! One, two, three, five, eight..."

"Thirteen and twenty-one!" said Houston. "Look! Here and here. Two more golden numbers, thirteen and twenty-one digits long."

"You're catching on," said Lopez. He turned to Lightfoote. "They match the next sequences in Pi?"

"Yes!" She showed them the numbers on the calculator.

"Then it all repeats, I would bet, starting the Fibonacci numbers from the beginning again. Seven golden numbers, the first seven Fibonacci numbers giving the length of the string of digits from Pi," said Lopez. "The sequence lengths would get too big, otherwise, but this way we know quickly how to order the search and compare to Pi."

"Good grief," said Houston. "I thought you said this was simple!"

Lightfoote nodded. "It *is* simple for a code. A little messy for humans but not for any cryptographic analysis by computer. But we're going to need a lot of digits from Pi."

"But the first seven, all golden numbers. What does it say, Angel?" said Lopez.

She wrote down words and read aloud. "External Equilibration in Non-cooperative Games. John Nash." She looked between her companions.

"Oh, my God. This is it."

30

OUTSOURCING

A fine dust circled the room. Part chalk from the nearby blackboard, part disintegration of the rows of cardboard boxes lining the walls and filled with decaying books, the floating remains testified that the Princeton study room was evaporating like so much of an older world.

Lightfoote and Houston sat together beside a laptop plugged into a nearby outlet. Both were disheveled, their clothes matted and filthy, Houston's dyed-brown hair showing her natural blond at the roots. Several of Lightfoote's many piercings showed inflammation around the holes.

"Let me get this straight," said Lightfoote, her green eyes intense. "You two chased down this lunatic to the VP's house, where he'd basically taken on a legion of secret service agents, blown a hole in a fortified bunker, rappelled down and taken on more agents, killing them all, and then killed the VP? This guy superman?"

"I got this all second hand. I was basically bleeding to death outside from the shrapnel from said lunatic's bombing of the CIA safe house. And he didn't directly kill the VP. Heart attack." Houston took a sip from a bottle of Jack Daniels.

"Thought you'd dumped Jack."

"I always forgive him." She laughed and drank from the bottle again.

"But can you believe it? Ten years of revenge planned out and executed like James Bond and he's about to kill the VP, but the fuck drops over from a heart attack. Irony's a bitch."

"You realize that story is not remotely believable."

"I suppose not," said Houston nodding. "But if you'd told me back in 2000 that a bunch of Arabs trained in caves in Afghanistan by a diabetic Saudi prince would sneak unnoticed into America, train on small engine aircraft, hijack planes with fucking box-cutters and steer two goddamned jumbo jets precisely enough to hit each of the World Trade Towers and bring them both down—I'd have said you were full of shit, too."

"Point taken."

Houston offered the bottle to Lightfoote, but the FBI agent shook her head.

"I know my limits. Besides, tastes awful."

"Really? Old Jack ain't half bad, though I'm not a bourbon woman myself. Texas whiskey, now *that's* another story."

"So the priest kills the wraith."

"Sort of." Houston pulled up from her slouch and placed the bottle on the table. "More like suicide by fugitive. Guy was fucked up good. All his targets were dead. Mission accomplished, but the demons were still inside or whatever. Basically begged Francisco to shoot him. I'm glad it was so easy. The wraith would have killed him under different circumstances."

"Your man seems a hell of a fighter."

"He is. But he's been trained up good. Five years ago, he was just a priest with a lot of untapped potential." Houston grabbed the bottle and took another swig. "We were toxic waste by then. Fingered for the veep attack and ten other things. If Savas and Simon—poor bastard—hadn't pulled us out of that war zone in Virginia, we'd be on death row or worse. Instead, we got a pretty little cabin in the mountains. Far from everything. I trained him there."

"Yeah, bet it would be fun *training* him," said Lightfoote. "You must have hated every minute of it."

"Girl's gotta do what a girl's gotta do." Houston closed her eyes. "Little stir crazy. Fucking cold as hell in the winter. And we kept switching cabins on different peaks. But better than this shit we're swimming in now."

"How'd you end up in the CIA?"

"Oh, that's a random one. I was looking at law enforcement. Never thought to be a spook, but the Agency's got eyes in a lot of places. Learned all this later. They identify possible recruits early, track them over a few months, few years. You've got to do well enough in school, show the right kinds of interest, have a clean security history—your family, too. A man came up to me at an ROTC session in college. Said he had a job proposition. Handed me a card. Happened pretty fast."

"How'd your dad handle it?"

"Same as with everything. Quiet. Supportive. Mom was something else. Hippy-firebrand-alcoholic on her fifth husband by then. She was in and out of rehab and other men's trailers." She swished the whiskey around in the bottle and looked between it and Lightfoote. "I like to live on the edge."

"She disapproved?"

"Said I was going to work for the empire and all that. Baby killers and hegemony. 'Bout sealed the deal for me. Everything that bitch said I did the opposite. And flipped her the bird." Houston sighed and stared at Lightfoote. "I'm tired of me. Your turn. Who were these monsters that killed your dad?"

Lightfoote held her gaze for a moment and turned away. "Not worth telling."

"Come on, that's not how this works, girl. My cards are on the table. Let's see your hand."

Heavy footsteps tromped outside the cramped room. Houston placed a finger over her lips, grabbed her Browning, and moved quickly to the side of the door. Lightfoote drew her gun from a hip holster and crouched behind an overturned study cubical. The footsteps grew louder.

"It's Francisco," came a deep baritone from outside the door.

Houston twisted a knob on the bolt lock and opened the door. Lopez shuffled inside and placed a gun on the top of a filing cabinet. Sighing, he dropped a large plastic garbage bag to the floor.

"No sign of the soldiers or our burglar friends. No sign of anyone." He motioned to the bag. "I raided several pantries and a few functioning refrigerators. Anything that could spoil has. What's left is mummified bread and a lot of cans."

He glanced across the study room, his eyes lingering on a blackboard full of incomprehensible physics equations.

"I wish the graduate students were still here. Maybe one of them could figure this out." He bent toward the computer screen. "Anything?"

Houston sat down in front of the laptop.

"This is it," she said, scrolling through pages of text and figures on Lightfoote's computer. "This is the entire paper, but we're no closer to understanding what the hell Fawkes was trying to tell us."

"Fawkes? We're not even sure what Nash is trying to tell us," said Lightfoote. "Five hours of decoding and transcription and we have a Nobel Laureate economics paper we can't understand."

Lopez stared at the pages. "I recognize some of the math, but I don't know the theory, why it's being used. And a lot of the math I've never seen before. Way beyond my pay grade."

"We do have this note," said Lightfoote. She zoomed in on an image with scrawled text.

"What's this?" Lopez asked.

"We found it while you were out," said Houston. "I'm still not sure it's part of the encoded message."

Lightfoote shook her head. "Has to be, Sara. It's the last sequence of Pi on the board. The econ paper ends, one more piece of Pi sitting over this little note. Read it for Francisco."

Houston sighed. "*This is why we are not free. The puppet masters pull the strings.* There's this smudged part. Unreadable. Next, *their fingerprints are in the global numbers. Once the criterion is reached, they pull the trigger.*"

"Very different than the rational content of the paper," said Lopez. "It sounds like mad ramblings. Angel said he oscillated between lucid and insane states over the years."

"He did," said Lightfoote, "although everything claims that in his later years he was more stable than not. Got better and better at *classifying* and ignoring his crazy thoughts."

"But we don't know when this was written?" he asked.

"Well," said Lightfoote, "some of the clippings are over fifty years old. It's really old."

"He never published this? You're sure?"

"Yes, Francisco," said Houston. "Angel's gone through all the online databases. Enough are up again. We can be pretty sure this paper never saw the light of day."

He turned his palms upward. "But why? Okay, so it's old, from a time before he went nuts, right?"

"Right."

"But why not publish it later, when he recovered?"

Houston shrugged. "Maybe he'd forgotten about it. The illness and treatments erased it from his mind."

"Is that likely?" Lopez asked.

"No," Lightfoote responded. "He didn't lose the knowledge of his field in the later years. Continued to publish. I don't know why he shelved this one."

Lopez exhaled slowly. "How about this—he didn't just file it away. He *buried* it in this encoded crazy. Here is a work discussing something about the global economy, with analysis of multiple nations we can't understand. Written at the height of his productivity, the height of his powers. He never publishes it. Instead, right around the time he goes insane, he builds this Crazy Wall where he embeds the entire paper in a geometrical and numerical code. Why would he do that?"

Houston shook her head. "Like you said, Francisco, he was crazy."

"I'm starting to doubt my conclusions. I think Angel may be right—there's something important here. He was trying to tell the world something, but he couldn't do it openly. He was *afraid.*"

"Afraid of what?" asked Houston.

"And what was he afraid to say?" said Lightfoote.

Lopez stood up. "Back in New York, you said his student set up this museum. Maybe he knows something."

"Maybe it's no accident this poster board ended up where it did," said Houston.

Lopez paced, gesturing. "We decoded it and hoped we'd be able to get to the root of this message. But we can't. We need to outsource—speak to this guy if he's still here. Still alive. If he'll even help us."

Lightfoote closed the laptop and stuffed it into a backpack. "*Agreed.* Sara, you still have the last address?"

Houston nodded. "It's about ten minutes from here."

Lightfoote walked to the door. "Let's move the stuff to the car. If this doesn't give us an answer, we might as well ride out and meet John and Rebecca and the fucking Presidential Caravan. Nash's student is our last hope."

31

LION'S CLAW

No one spoke during the drive through the deserted township in New Jersey. Lightfoote piloted the car through tree-lined streets with the lights off. The night weighed heavily on them, each quiet and introspective, exhausted from the unending tension. Lost in thought, the address seemed to appear before them instantaneously, the time traveled like a vanishing dream. They exited the vehicle and walked up the short steps to a porch.

Lopez knocked on the creaking wood of an old door. No one answered. Houston and Lightfoote faced away from the house, weapons at the ready, scanning the dark street. He knocked again, each series of strikes against the wood harder. Frustration mounting, he struck vigorously, the knob vibrating and dancing back and forth past the frame.

"Any harder Conan and you might as well just knock the thing down," whispered Lightfoote.

"I know I saw some movement in the curtains," said Houston. "Someone's there. With everything that's happened, I can't blame them for laying low."

Lopez grasped the handle and set his shoulder against the panel. "There isn't time for norms. Angel's right—this old thing is ready to fall over."

"Got you," said Houston, pivoting and pointing her pistol at the door. "Angel, eyes on the road."

One try was enough. With a lunge his thick frame crashed into the door near the lock. The wood splintered and burst into shards, a cloud of dust following it inward.

Houston and Lopez moved in, followed quickly by Lightfoote. Creaking under their weight, a wooden floor extended down a dark corridor.

"We know you're in here!" shouted Houston. "There are three of us. We're armed. Don't do anything stupid. We're not here to hurt you. We need information."

They could hear their own breathing in the silence.

Lightfoote called out. "We're here to talk to Avi Kaplan. It's a matter of national security! Don't make us dig you out."

A muffled thump shook a doorway near the end of the hall. The three trained their weapons on the sound. The door creaked open and a trembling voice called out.

"Please, don't shoot. I'm unarmed."

As the door opened further a gaunt man in worn pajamas shuffled out with his hands in the air. He looked like an old image of Albert Einstein, complete with a shock of unruly hair and a mustache.

"Who else is here?" Lopez asked.

"No one. I live alone."

Houston walked toward the man cautiously. "I'll check him. Sweep the house."

"It's the truth," he said.

"Yeah, maybe."

Houston turned him against the wall and padded him down, glancing inside the closet and closing the door.

"Where is Avi Kaplan?"

"I'm Avi Kaplan."

"Nash's former student? The one who set up the museum and worked with him?"

"Yes, I cared for him for many years, off and on, since his, well, health problems."

"Health problems?" asked Houston.

He smiled wanly, his voice hoarse. "Who are you?"

"We'll get to that in a minute," said Houston, looking down the hallway. "That's a living room?"

"Yes."

"Okay, in there." She motioned with her Browning.

Kaplan's face tightened. "Yes, of course."

He walked in front of her, trembling. They entered a crowded room of chairs, a sofa, and boxes of papers. Houston had Kaplan take a seat on the couch, a cloud of dust rising as he sank into it. Lopez and Lightfoote returned.

"No sign of anyone," said Lopez.

"I closed the door and tied it shut with some wire," Lightfoote said. "It's busted all to hell. Won't slow anyone, but at least it's unlikely to attract the attention of an open door."

Houston turned to the old man. "Nash used to live here with you. Under nursing care."

"Yes." The old man hesitated. "That's what everyone was supposed to believe."

"Supposed to believe?" asked Lopez, holstering his weapon.

Kaplan nodded. "You said you were here for a national security concern. Regarding John Nash?"

"Yes," answered Lightfoote.

"Then surely you won't be surprised to learn that there have been forces interested in keeping John Nash under firm control."

Lopez loomed over the skeletal form on the couch. "What do you mean? The truth, and quickly."

He smiled and stared up at Lopez. "You don't scare me. I'm sure you could torture the information out of me, but this old heart would pop before you got enough pain going to open my mouth. I'm ancient, my friends. Had a long life. Seen a lot of things. Always John was with me. My last act in this world won't be to betray him. You'll have to find another way to persuade me to divulge his secrets."

"And what would that be?"

"You could start with your names. Tell me what important matter concerns my old friend. Convince me there's some reason I should trust you."

Lightfoote opened her backpack. "What if I told you we have a sixty-year-old, unpublished paper by John Nash?" She removed the laptop and opened it. "One that was encoded on the poster board in the Nash Museum."

"The fire in the news? That was *you?*"

Lightfoote marched across the room and sat down beside the old man.

"What if we told you we were pointed in this direction by a terrorist who nearly brought down the world financial system last month?"

She held the screen up to him. He squinted and read aloud.

"*This is why we are not free. The puppet masters pull the strings.*"

The three stared intensely at him as he met their gazes, one by one.

"This is supposed to impress me? He saw conspiracies everywhere. Left delusional messages in code everywhere. He was a schizophrenic, you know."

"This isn't the paper. It's only a last comment he made at the end of it." She scrolled on the trackpad. "*This* is the paper."

"External Equilibration in Non-cooperative Games?" he read slowly.

Lopez rumbled. "Look carefully. The world outside is going to hell. Somehow, the terrorist who triggered this disaster knew about this paper, this coded message from six decades ago. It's never been published. Isn't available anywhere."

"Can you increase the font size? An old man's eyes," said Kaplan. Lightfoote obliged. He scanned the text and spoke in a distracted tone. "So, you're chasing after the work of one madman on the words of another?"

"Both geniuses," said Houston. "Something's going on. This may be a key to understanding it."

The old man slowly scrolled on the trackpad, furrowing his brow. He didn't speak for several minutes.

"Yes," he nodded his head at last. "Dear God, yes."

"Yes, what?" asked Lightfoote.

Kaplan leaned back against the back of the sofa and closed his eyes. "*Tanquam ex ungue leonem.*"

Lightfoote cocked her head. "Sorry?"

"The lion is known by his claw," said Lopez.

"Indeed," said Kaplan. "You have found something remarkable. It can be no one else. The wording, the logic. This is John Nash."

"Can you explain it to us?" asked Lopez.

"Probably. But not right away. I would need days to digest this. He was the genius, not me."

Houston exhaled. "We don't have days. We have a nation falling down around us."

"And the note?" asked Lightfoote. "*Their fingerprints are in the global numbers; once the criterion is reached, they pull the trigger.* What does this mean?"

"I don't know. It sounds like too much that came from his paranoia over the years."

Lightfoote put a hand on his shoulder. "What if it's not? What if he was on to something and this paper reveals something we just can't understand?"

"Then you'd need to speak with John."

Lopez growled. "No longer an option. As you know."

The old man nodded. "Inconvenient, isn't it? As soon as I set up that museum, which contained this encoded paper, poor John met with a strange death."

"What are you implying?" asked Houston, her eyes narrowed.

"I was planning the museum for a number of years. John had become quite the celebrity. Recovery from madness, like it was some sort of twelve step program. Nobel Prize. Hollywood film and Oscar. The money flowed in from it all. We hardly had to break a sweat fundraising." He coughed, the sound ragged and ominous. "Sorry. Bad lungs. We all used to smoke in those days. Now, John begged me to include this poster in the exhibit, you know? So strange. Not the most flattering of displays. But of course I said yes. Who was I to deny him something so small at this stage?" He shook his head. "Governmental delegation swept the museum several times. Removed several items citing national security. Always passed by the poster board."

"Governmental delegation?" said Houston.

He smiled. "It wasn't the first time they had micromanaged our lives. Always so interested in John, since his consulting years. Took him away to special retreats many times. A pact with the devil. Money and support during his illness. Some kind of favors I was never privy to."

Lopez sat on the coffee table in front of Kaplan. "You sound paranoid."

"Do I? What if I told you I could help you after all?"

Lopez growled. "Then help us!"

"First—who are you? Don't lie to me. Tell me who you are."

Lopez leaned forward and looked the old man in eyes. "Here is the truth. No lies. We're fugitives: Falsely accused and judged because we uncovered something dirty in the heart of Washington. We helped stop the digital worm that has brought so much destruction. We captured the man behind it. Before he was murdered, he claimed his actions were to stop something even worse. He pointed us here, to Nash, to this encoded paper. We're trying to discover what he was talking about, and we've been targeted for death for doing so. We need your help."

Kaplan held Lopez's gaze for several seconds. He nodded and closed his eyes again.

"Truth is always in the eyes. Let me change. We'll need my car."

Houston blinked. "Why? Where are we going?"

Kaplan laughed softly. "The car accident? *A lie.* Staged. Someone felt John Nash needed to disappear. But they still needed his mind."

"Wait," said Lightfoote, her eyes widening, "you mean—"

"John Nash is very much alive."

"Where?" she whispered, her voice hoarse.

"A care facility, nearly an hour away. But you won't find it on any maps or in any directories."

"John Nash, alive," repeated Houston, her eyes locking with Lopez.

Kaplan nodded, appraising each of them in turn. His eyes lingered on their weapons.

"And you may want to bring those guns along."

32

JOHN NASH

"How many guards?"

Houston stared from behind the wheel at the old man beside her. Lopez and Lightfoote were fully suited up with body armor, checking their weapons in the backseat. They'd been on back roads in New Jersey running northwest of Princeton for forty-five minutes. The ride had been mostly quiet, the directions given by Nash's former student punctuating the stillness as they drove across the rural landscape. As they approached, Kaplan had begun to describe the location.

"Not sure. More in the beginning after his death was announced. But less of late. John's weak. He actually needs a lot of the care of a nursing facility. There are many patients in case someone stumbled across the location. To keep up appearances." Kaplan pointed through the window. "Here. Left here."

"Why did they let you visit? Why let you know?" asked Lopez. "You could have blown the entire thing wide open."

"Their threats were all too clear. John's their prisoner. I'd be killing him if I spoke publicly."

"That he's in a special nursing facility is one thing," said Houston. "But why on earth is it under armed guards?"

"For reasons that only the US government knows. Likely the same reason they faked his death."

"It is starting to sound like the man's paranoia wasn't so delusional," muttered Lopez.

Kaplan sighed heavily. "It's been a world of shadows and mazes. I've only wanted to make sure John's cared for. I had to make certain compromises." He gazed out the window. "The age of the paper you brought to me tonight, it's part of this. That's when John began to lose touch with reality. It was the same time the government took such a fascination with his work. Everyone speculated as to why. That film even assumed it was part of his delusions. But no."

"No?" asked Lightfoote. She leaned forward over the seat.

"It was real. They came. John left with them on many occasions. He was never the same after that. I never knew why. But this? Maybe there's an answer now. Maybe it has something to do with this paper. Something he was trying to tell us through it. I brought you here to seek my own answers as much as for what you hope to accomplish. Answers to a lifetime of struggle with pain and uncertainty." Again he motioned toward the window. "Okay, slow down now. It's around that bend in the road."

Houston pulled the car to the side of the two-lane country road, trees of a forested patch surrounding them.

"If you don't want them to know you're coming, I recommend approaching through the forest, on foot."

Houston nodded. "We can't bring you with us, Dr. Kaplan."

"I suffer no delusions. I'm long past my clandestine spy years." He smiled.

"We'll let you know what he said."

"Thank you. I'll try to visit him tomorrow if they allow it on such short notice. I want to talk to him in person."

They exited the car quickly, leaving the economist in the front seat. Lopez opened the trunk and removed a duffel. He unzipped it and retrieved a rifle fitted with a telescopic sight, along with several handguns. Popping open an aluminum case, he handed a large dart with a clear middle section to Houston. Liquid sloshed inside.

"Do you think the tranqs are still good?" she asked.

"I don't know. Not a biochemist. So, a test." Lopez walked to the passenger side and opened the door, brandishing a dart before Kaplan.

"I'm sorry, professor, but we need to test these tranquilizers. And while your trust in us is refreshing, I'm too jaded."

"You're going to knock me out?"

Lopez nodded. "That way you don't cause us any unexpected trouble, and we find out if these things still work."

"You're going to drug the guards?" asked Lightfoote.

"Not going to kill them unless we have to," Lopez answered. "And there are a lot of variables in hand to hand. We'll see how many we spot outside, try to take them down quietly, and make our way inside."

Lightfoote shook her head. "Best laid plans."

"Yeah, I know."

The tranq worked.

Lopez lay the seat back as the old man dozed. He closed the trunk as quietly as he could. Then the three of them made their way through the forest in the direction of the nursing home, keeping the curve of the road in sight. They crested a hill that opened to a compound. A driveway off the main road ended in a circular path before a one-story building. It was surrounded by barbed-wire, several security cameras visible around the fencing even from that distance.

Houston gazed through a pair of binoculars. "Guards inside are going to spot us. Likely there's some kind of motion detection system as well. No prep on this one, Francisco. Going to be messy." She continued her reconnaissance. "Two guards at the gate, none along the perimeter. It's not much on the outside."

"Why don't you take those two down and blow the power lines?" said Lightfoote. "It will blind anyone inside."

"And signal reinforcements when the alarm system fails. Also, some of those inside might be on machines they need. Maybe Nash."

She nodded. "You're right. Not worth the risk."

"You two make a run around this hill," said Houston, "come along the right side wall by the main entrance. Try to stay clear of sensors if you can spot them. Send me an alert and I'll drop the two at the gate. You keep an eye on the main door while I get down to the gate and check them for access cards. Drop anyone who comes out. If we're lucky, one of them has a keyed access to the place and we're in without triggering any alarms."

"Good a plan as any," said Lopez.

"Okay, go!"

Lightfoote and Lopez left her side and sprinted through the trees. Houston dropped to the ground and rested the rifle on a bipod, angling herself to the scope. She rotated the butt plate and loaded the first dart, closing the housing. She peered down the barrel and adjusted the focus. An alert buzzed her cell phone and she raised the binoculars, training them on the building. Lopez and Lightfoote were positioned along the wall by the entrance.

"No alarms. No movement inside," she said, scanning the building. "Nice footwork."

Houston texted back and pocketed the phone, lowering herself again along the rifle. She checked the gas cartridge a final time and switched on the laser.

The guards were in heavy coats, pacing along the front fence on opposite sides of the driveway. Houston didn't envy them that duty in winter without a gatehouse, but the clothing complicated her mission. The dart might not penetrate the coat, depending on its composition and thickness. She would have to hit below the coat, in the leg or buttocks.

She angled the rifle slowly, bringing up the green circle of light along the leg of the nearest guard. She estimated the distance to be about 50 yards. He paused a moment, lighting a cigarette, providing her with the perfect shot. She exhaled, paused a second with the light on his thigh, and pulled the trigger.

The projectile launched with only a swift expulsion of air into the night. She switched off the laser and blinked, peering into the scope. The figure jerked backward and grabbed his leg. The dart dangled from his upper thigh.

Reload. She ignored the form of the other guard moving toward her first target and flipped the end of the rifle butt ninety degrees. Grabbing a second dart from the case, she inserted it in the mechanism and closed the butt. When she peered in the scope again, the second guard stood over the kneeling form of the guard she'd hit, trying to help him to his feet. She fired again.

This dart struck the second guard in the ass. He dropped the first guard, who tumbled limply to the ground. Houston watched him stagger as he grabbed his right butt cheek. He fell beside the first guard. She left the dart gun on the hill and sprinted down toward the prone men.

Five minutes, a guard's keycard, and several hallways later, they stood in front of room 117. No other guards were present in the building. A handful of elderly patients slept in rooms scattered haphazardly throughout the building. A frightened nurse had been locked in a closet. A front desk search revealed a chart of patients and locations. John Nash was near the back of the building.

"All right, here goes," said Lopez, pushing the door open.

A small desk lamp beside a window spilled frail light into the room. An empty bed rested against a wall on their left, a table and sofa on the right. The lamp cast a ghostly hue on a wizened form in a bathrobe, an angular face with sunken cheeks staring with empty eyes at the wall.

The three approached the figure, geometric doodles covering the surface of the desk beside him like some mad child's scribblings. Light-foote passed her hand in front of his eyes. No reaction. She crouched down to match her eye-line to his.

"John Nash?" she said.

The face didn't move.

"Dr. Nash? We need your help. We need to ask you some questions about one of your papers. The one you never published. *External Equilibration in Non-cooperative Games*. Please! Dr. Nash?"

The old man blinked and focused on her face. He studied the two beside her, nodding solemnly.

"Yes. Yes, I've been expecting you for a long time."

33

ASIMOV'S MULE

L opez and Houston pulled up chairs as Lightfoote held her crouch in front of the Nobel Laureate.

"You've been expecting us?" she asked.

His lips moved in a silent mutter, his voice rising as from some dark depth.

"They said you would come. Well, of course they didn't. I know they don't exist. These creatures. So much knowledge they have! But it is suspect. Always suspect! It must always be examined, filtered. *Tested.* But they said you would come. I had to analyze. I had to distinguish the real and the misfirings of the mind. It wastes so much time, this madness. So much time. I could have done so much more."

Lightfoote looked desperately at Houston and Lopez. She continued to prod him.

"Dr. Nash, the paper?"

"Where's Alicia?"

Lopez mouthed toward Lightfoote. "Alicia?"

Nash continued without an answer. "They said she died in a car crash. I don't have enough data. Not enough to classify these voices. Lies? Truth? Is this place real? It is new. New walls. New voices. Too soon to know. Where is Alicia?"

Lightfoote continued. "Dr. Nash. The paper. *External Equilibration in Non-cooperative Games*. Do you remember it?"

A sharp bark burst from the old man's lips. "Remember it? It's the only damned thing I did of any importance in my life." He reached out a trembling arm to Lightfoote and grasped her hand. "Murdered. Killed in the womb. They would never let it see the light of day. Did they kill her, too? Can you tell me?"

Lopez leaned forward. "Who's they?"

Nash leaned back in his chair, still holding Lightfoote's hand.

"They they they they. It is the delusional pronoun. Always a *they* somewhere to do something and whisper nonsense and be the conspiratorial cause of this and that and the prime mover." He closed his eyes. "They keep me alive only for the hope of more material. I refused at first. Such a mistake." He leaned forward and stared wild-eyed. "Pain rules all things. Pain erases personality. Pain they brought and branded and cut and I could not hold. They needed predictions. I developed the theory. Never enough. They kept coming. It broke me. Into pieces. Each piece a voice. A thousand voices. From the stars and the pits of hell."

Lightfoote placed her other hand on his and looked into his eyes. "Predictions?"

Tears dripped down his face as he stared into her eyes.

"Yes, yes. I see it in your eyes. I see it in your soul. Burnt soul. You have been to hell, too. Yes, poor child. The demons have branded you. And now I know it." He closed his eyes. "She is dead."

He sat shaking for several moments weeping silently. Coughing, he pushed Lightfoote away and wiped his eyes. "Social. Economic. Population. The numbers were available to us finally. Data had been collected for decades by that point, for the first time in human history. They saw my work. Saw the embryonic theories. They knew what I could give them and the devils made me do it."

"Dr. Nash, what did you do?"

"I gave them the key to total control! Centuries and centuries, they had lumbered clumsily. But now, in an age of god-like computation, they too would become gods. Thanks to John Nash." He growled like some frightened dog. "But I had a last ace up my sleeve. My *paper*. I knew I couldn't publish it openly. They would stop me. One way or the other. But it turned hard. The thousand voices were tearing at my soul. I was going quite mad from it. But I persevered. I put it down in a way they could not see. And the voices told me, 'One day, they will come. They will understand. They will come and end it.' And here they are." His mouth opened into a macabre grin.

"We don't understand it, Dr. Nash. What does the paper say?"

He startled upright, his expression incredulous. "But it's so obvious! Any mathematical analysis of the markets with anything remotely like my models would reveal it. How can it be no one has seen it? Perhaps, yes, perhaps they were taken. They could not allow it. Yes."

"Just tell us what it means," said Lopez.

"The models are predictive. Even I was amazed how well it all worked. Socio-economic movements of populations. Market cycles. Political movements. Predictive, except that they are not!" He laughed maniacally. "How could they predict accurately when unseen hands steered all from the darkness? Maxwell's demon moonlighting in socio-dynamics!" He bent forward, his index finger extending rigidly toward them. "But put in variables to model external modulation of the models—bang! There it was! The demon hand behind history. Controlling everything. Steering humanity to their purposes. Like a closed thermodynamic system, entropy, distribution of resources. To ensure control, predictability, they needed to preserve *low* entropy. Funnel resources upwards. Vast income inequality, power imbalances."

Lightfoote furrowed her brow. "So, you are saying that—"

"Sorry! Yes. I must select the vocabulary carefully. I have to speak with the subsets of ideas that are rational. *Silence* the voices." His gaze turned distant. "I proved *mathematically* that the markets were being manipulated by a powerful influence. One outside of any of the known economic variables. Is *that* simple enough for you? But more than this. Yes, so much more. More than they understood fully. There are cycles between nations and groups, statistical mechanics, the billions making it predictable. There is a turning point that recurs with temporal predictability, a phase transition of instability. An hour of revolution when a maximum in instability is reached."

Lightfoote gasped. "The Nash Criterion."

Nash laughed. "Yes. They should name it after me. That is as good a name as any. But no one will ever know."

"We know," she said. "And your paper, it shows how to calculate it? How to determine when these instability points will come?"

"Yes. That's the whole point."

She nodded, her words spilling out rapidly. "And they want this desperately. It will allow them to know when the revolutions will come and ride them out."

He shook his head. "Too naive. Much more than ride them out. To destroy them. Kill, and kill millions to maintain their course, their control. They only guessed I had this answer. They only had metrics for when the criterion neared. But not a predictive model. They never got it from me."

Lopez shook his head. "I don't understand. Why would you give in to their demands on all but this?"

"Because it is the key to their long-term survival, Francisco," said Lightfoote.

"A great weakness," finished Nash. "Social cycles they cannot avoid, but can control if they are predictable." He pointed with his finger. "But which their enemies could use against them if they held the predictive power."

"Are we in a cycle now?" asked Lightfoote. "The world is falling apart. They act threatened."

"No," said Nash, shaking his head. "What has happened—an anomaly. It's Asimov's Mule. *Unpredictable.*"

"What?"

"The predictions rely on statistical patterns, patterns that only exist, that are only predictable when there are very large numbers of people to smooth out the random noise. Like the thermodynamics of gasses. A few molecules and quantum chaos rules. But Avogadro's number? The gas laws are obeyed! Of course, there is always noise—individuals, small groups, doing unpredictable, random things. Random for the models. But if five billion do the predictable things, the world is predictable, the noise averaged out. Unless you have a Mule."

Lopez grumbled. "What the hell is a Mule?"

"No one reads anymore," Nash sighed. "An individual that introduces a systemic randomness. It rarely happens. So few have the ability, and they hunt them down ruthlessly now. But this Anonymous—it had to be a Mule. No other explanation. Now the system is off model. The curves of prediction diverge from events. They have to steer it back. But until they do, they are vulnerable. Discovery. Intervention. Assassination. This Mule has deliberately exposed and weakened them. Now is the time to act."

Houston shook her head. "But Fawkes didn't reveal where they are."

Nash exhaled, his posture slouched. "It's in the numbers. You can't hide the source of the external stimulus. Follow the numbers back to them. It can be computed. You will find them."

Lopez threw his hands up. "Dammit, who are *they?*"

Nash turned to him and grasped the priestly robes.

"Bilderberg."

With that word the room was plunged into darkness, the central air silenced, the power cut. Everything fell still.

Nash sighed.

"Too late. Too late. They're here."

34

GRENADES

"Down on the floor!" cried Houston.

They dove to the ground just as the windows exploded. Glass sprayed inward as bullets whizzed over their heads. Paneling splintered, fabric burst open, and dust filled the air as shards tinkled to the ground. They rolled away from the exposed wall, gunfire trailing them and pocking the floor with holes. Lightfoote and Houston dove behind a couch, Lopez rising behind a ventilation pipe jutting out from the wall. He reached into his robes and removed two grenades clipped to his body armor. And pulled the pins.

"Frag out!"

He hurled the grenades through the battered window and turned his head. Light flashed and two thunderous claps shook the building one after the other. Dust and debris spilled into the room through the shattered window. Then silence as the gunfire stopped.

Houston cried out from behind the couch. "They'll be in the building. We've got seconds until they can pin us at the door!"

"Nash!" cried Lightfoote. Her head popped over the couch. The professor lay dead on the ground, his head a gruesome impact zone of multiple rounds.

"Tell me you have more grenades, Francisco!" yelled Houston.

"One."

He didn't need instructions. Together he and Houston darted toward the door, both unleashing a hailstorm of bullets through the window into the night. No one returned fire. Lightfoote took up the suppressing fire as the pair reached the door.

Lopez pulled the pin and tucked the grenade to this chest. He motioned downward to Houston. They both crouched.

"Now," he whispered. She turned the knob, flinging the door wide.

Lopez rolled the grenade outward and Houston slammed the door shut. The pair dove face first to the ground. An eruption of gunfire punctured holes in the door above them, the discharge terminating with an explosion.

The door blasted inward in pieces, fragments of wood and metal embedding themselves in the walls. Houston screamed out and clutched her leg. Lightfoote leapt over her body, firing into the hallway. Short return fire followed, and a guttural cry.

In the sudden silence, Lopez pulled Houston away from the window and behind the couch. He tore open the black fabric of her pants to reveal a black gash in her thigh.

"It's a nick, Sara. Shrapnel sliced you open, but nothing inside." He sliced and ripped segments of his robes.

"How deep?" she gasped as he stuffed fabric in the wound and tied a band around her leg.

"Deep enough. But the bleeding is manageable. We need to get you out. Stitched. Up!"

She placed her arm around his shoulders and neck, hopping alongside him toward the door.

"We're sitting ducks," she muttered.

"Inside is clear," called Lightfoote as she darted into the room. She glanced at Houston's leg and at Lopez. "Can you carry her? Fireman's style? We need the speed." Lopez nodded.

"Shit," gasped Houston as Lightfoote helped hoist her onto the broad shoulders of the former priest.

"All right, let's move!" said Lightfoote, dashing quickly down the hallway. Lopez followed behind, awkwardly navigating the shattered doorway. The bodies of three soldiers in gear lay strewn around the entrance. Inexperienced, or underestimating their quarry, they had foolishly made a fatal close approach. They were a horror show.

Two more bodies lay prone on the ground as he sped down the hallway, his thick frame bowed under Houston's weight, footsteps sounding thunderous to his ears. He felt his breath coming in gasps, the muscles of his back beginning to burn.

Lightfoote held up a hand as he approached the entrance to the building. Stopping on a dime proved more strenuous than the run, and he nearly lost balance.

"Dammit, Francisco!" said Houston as he slammed her into the doorway. "I don't need more damage!"

Lightfoote scanned the area outside with night vision goggles. Satisfied, she nodded to the pair.

"Can't see any movement. There might be an ambush waiting, but I'm hoping they overcommitted in there. Anyway, we don't have much of a choice. We have to go before more arrive."

"Agreed," gasped Lopez. "I've got one shot up that hill and need to take it soon."

"Let's go. You first and if you draw fire at least I'll have a chance to counter."

They ran. Lopez lumbered up the grassy hill toward the forest with Lightfoote waiting several seconds before following. No one waited in ambush. No shots were fired. She exited at a full sprint and quickly overtook them, scampering up the hill into the trees. As he crested the top of the hill, she passed him again, the goggles strapped on, and scouted the facility below. Lopez lowered himself to one knee.

Lightfoote returned. "Clear. Nothing moving down there."

"I'll need a minute," said Lopez.

"No time," said Lightfoote. "We'll make a basket."

They grasped each other's wrists in a square pattern. Houston stood on one leg and dropped into the seat. The pair hoisted her, shuffling quickly through the underbrush. Five minutes later, they had reached the car.

It was clear even from a distance that they wouldn't find Kaplan alive. The vehicle had been damaged, the tires ruptured by gunfire. Blood covered the inside, coating the windows in crimson.

"Motherfuckers," whispered Houston as she rested against a tree beside Lightfoote. She watched Lopez remove several bags from the trunk and place them on the ground. "At least they were too much in a hurry to search the thing."

"We need a vehicle," he said flatly. "We could ditch the gear, but we'll need to put some space between us and this place soon."

Lightfoote exhaled. "Those soldiers didn't teleport. There'll be a car or truck at the facility."

"Go *back* there?" asked Lopez.

"I'll run back. Either we finished them and the spoils are ours, or we didn't, in which case we're basically screwed anyway. I'll just find out before you do."

Lopez frowned. "Go. You better come back."

Lightfoote saluted and began a quick jog down the road.

"Meanwhile," groaned Houston, "get your ass over here and lower me to the ground. I'm not going to wait out our doom on one foot beside this damn oak tree."

35

KANSAS CITY

Miles of barren cornfields long-ago harvested surrounded them —mangled, yellowed stalks poking through a foot of snow. The convoy had halted fifty miles outside Kansas City, gleaming gray and camouflage spreading out for miles around them. In the cold December air, the president, her advisors, civilian and military, shivered around a long foldout table with a map. Beside it, a large flatscreen monitor had been erected, a lengthy power line running back to the command vehicle.

"What are the numbers this time, General Franks?" York asked.

"Double what we faced at Columbus," he said grimly, mouth drawn in a line. "Satellite data indicates they've cut off any reasonable routes this convoy could consider taking around their positions." He pointed to images on the flat screen. "You'll see they've learned from Ohio. It'll cost us to break through their lines. The only advantage I can see is that this time they've struggled to bring in the heavier artillery units. Half the number we saw before. Our guerrilla tactics and the weather have been very effective since we got some of the aircraft back online. But the increasing air power on their side might make up for it."

Savas spoke up for the first time. "So, we're looking at a longer battle, likely with far more casualties than Columbus?"

Several of the military men openly scowled in his direction. Savas knew many resented their presence at these strategy sessions, and he didn't know why York insisted they be there. But he would speak his mind while it lasted.

"Yes," said the General. "But nothing we can't take and remain fully capable of completing our journey. That's our hard assessment."

"With all the aircraft coming online," said Cohen, "is there a point in revisiting the option for the president's evacuation directly to NORAD?"

"No," cut in the General. Several of the aides and advisers nodded in agreement.

"Why not?" asked York, her sharp tone mollifying the hostile looks coming from her staff.

General Franks shifted to a more diplomatic tone. "Ms. President, while it's true the odds are better than they've been for such a mission, it is our opinion they are still far too risky, and the damage to our cause if you are lost, far too high."

"And what about the lives of the hundreds, probably thousands, of young men and women who will die at Kansas City? How high is the price on their lives?"

"It's not that we don't take into account the people serving—"

"Spare me, General. Taking their lives for granted has been a national pastime for decades." She gestured to the screen. "At this level, it's all abstract—marks on a map and numbers. And most of us here remain cocooned in our command bubble, even in this convoy placing us so close to those we're asking to die for us. To die for *me*."

The stout form of the General tightened. "We don't have the aircraft to give you a proper escort. If they were to get wind of the mission, we couldn't stop a determined sortie. Hell, some airborne or ground launched SAM could blow you out of the sky. And I don't even know what types of drone assets they have."

George Tooze, the Secretary of Homeland Security, leaned across the table, his gaunt frame trembling in the rising wind.

"Elaine, this is a hard choice. No doubt about it. But you'd be a fool to rely on a mad dash, vulnerable, exposed in an aircraft. The General and his staff say we can fight our way to NORAD. Many will die, yes, but it'll be much worse for the nation to lose you – for you to fall into Hastings's hands, and leave us without the force of your personality fighting his block. We're almost there! One more battle is all he has left in him."

York frowned and stared out over the vehicles. Savas didn't envy her. Every choice she made, even the right ones, would cost lives. Bad choices would cost more lives. He had never experienced such a burden of command.

"You're sure they can't mount another offensive?"

The General shook his head. "Not near enough time. They were stretched thin as it is here. Without compensating for the lost ground artillery with aerial power, even with their stronger positions, we're going to run roughshod over them. There's no way they manage to outflank us from here to Colorado. Not after two defeats. They can still snipe at us, but their stopping power's gone."

York nodded. She looked at Savas and Cohen. "God knows I want to spare our troops another battle. And I certainly don't want to be the reason for a single death. But we're in a war of hearts and minds as much as territory right now. I and what remains of the Constitutional government have to reach NORAD." She turned to the military men. "There'll be no evac. We face them. And goddammit, you better be sure we win this and win it big."

The meeting ended. The maps rolled up and the electronics rolled back into the vehicles. York turned to Savas and Cohen a final time, but said nothing. Then walked stiffly back to the truck.

"Looks like the weight of the world is on her shoulders," said Cohen.

"It is," said Savas. He shivered. "Let's get inside before we freeze."

36

CONVERGENCE AT OOSTERBEEK

A dark SUV sped through the New Jersey back roads. The license plate was damaged, impossible to read. A black antenna rose from the back, thick and unmoving even as the air rushed over the roof. Opaque windows reflected the night.

Inside, Lopez gripped the wheel tightly and tuned a scanner on the dash. Harsh voices barked out coded signals in military slang. He grunted and turned briefly to the back of the vehicle.

Behind him, in the place of standard passenger seats, flat screens lined the sides of the truck, stools bolted to the floor in front of them. Racks of weapons gleamed in the back, a makeshift cot beside them. Houston lay on it with her leg propped up and her upper thigh heavily bandaged.

"How's the leg, girl?" he asked.

"Hurts like hell. Thank God for the medkit. Best we can manage now."

Lightfoote spoke as she glared at a monitor. "Pretty damn lucky find, if you asked me. Mobile command vehicle, had their positions mapped out. We'd have been caught in a dragnet if our little commando team hadn't left us this baby."

"*Had* their positions mapped out?" asked Lopez.

"Yeah," sighed Lightfoote. "We just lost the readout. Matter of time before they figured it out. Took them longer than I thought. Guess they were spread pretty thin."

Houston leaned up in the cot. "You're sure you killed our GPS?"

"Yes, or we'd already be dead," she said. "But I'm not complaining. Positions, thread the needle to get out of the net. Medkit. And now a small arms locker back there. My favorite's the grenade launcher."

"Rack of M249s looks good," said Houston. "Boxes of ammo underneath."

"We can't keep this rig," said Lopez. "They may not be able to track us, but they'll be looking for it at the major junctions. We'll have to take those soon."

"I agree," said Lightfoote. "I think we have a long trip ahead."

"Oh?"

"Results of the calculations coming in fast now. Nash knew what he was doing. I think we've found them."

"You're sure?" Houston asked. "You said it could take weeks."

"There are levels of precision." Lightfoote glanced at the laptop on her left. "Once you understand what the equations refer to, it's just a matter of number crunching. Nash couldn't do this in the day, but we have computers now in our pockets people like Nash could never have imagined. Code was easy to write. And this little baby," she said, patting the side of the SUV, "is one linked mother. Saved a lot of time. Grabbed numbers online for nation-state GDPs, population, trade—all the variables in his paper. For controls I did repeated analysis at various time points in history. Major world events—everything fit the curves of his models."

"So it means he could predict it. Like the weather?"

"Yes, but the key thing is the constraints on the system to match the curves."

"What does that mean?" asked Houston. "Constraints?"

"In this paper, Nash includes a set of equations that aren't about markets and populations and trade and all that. These equations are like some external force pushing on all these variables."

"This is Bilderberg, whatever it is?"

"Yes. That's the key. These predictions assume there's something *outside* of our societies and economies, something actively shaping the course of history. To any rational person, it would seem like madness—

some divine hand. Any sensible person would just set those weird variables to zero—concentrate on those that relate to real world aspects of trade and population—then crank out the numbers."

"Except the real world doesn't agree," said Houston. "It agrees with having the outside force?"

"Right! The numbers coming out for nations, economies, populations: they agree with the equations that *have* the modifying external force. You need to tweak it, tweak the strength of those variables, but it's clear. *Something* is out there, something pulling the strings and levers, pushing the pieces across the board."

"So, back to Bilderberg. It was the last thing Fawkes said before he died."

Lightfoote nodded. "And coincidentally the last thing Nash whispered before *he* died. *Bilderberg.*"

Houston sighed and lay back, repositioning her leg. "We need to find out what it is, then. Is it related to Cohen's Bilderberg group? Is that a front? Is it something else?"

Lopez spoke up from the front of the truck. "Whatever it is, whoever they are, Anonymous has them shaken. Fawkes nearly blew up the entire system they were using for—well, for whatever they are using it for. It's clear they have friends in the US government. They've taken out Fawkes, imprisoned our friends, hunted us down. This has pushed them into the open. Nash was right about that. This is our chance."

"And then there's the back-trace," said Lightfoote.

Lopez stiffened. "Did it finish? Did it work?"

"It's still computing, but it's converging on a single answer." Lightfoote shook her head. "It's amazing really. He said it could be done, and it can. Some of the variables in the external force equations are geographic. Money and power flow like a river that can be traced to its source."

"And where is it converging?" he asked.

"We need to wait a few days more to be sure, but looking at these confidence levels—I don't think the answer's going to change. It's centering on Europe. Maybe it's too obvious. Too simple. But it could end up focusing right on Bilderberg."

"But what *is* the Bilderberg Group?" asked Houston.

"Not the name. The fucking place itself."

She turned her laptop to Houston, revealing a world map decorated with thousands of colored lines. They crisscrossed the globe from city to city, nation to nation. A million small tributaries, the lines flowed from a central point, converging into a dense web in northern Europe.

"Oosterbeek, the Netherlands," she said, tapping her finger on the focal point. "Home of the Bilderberg hotel. Location of the conspiracy theorists' meetings of doom. Travel stop of dignitaries, CEOs, Rockefellers, politicians. It's the goddamned nexus of it all."

Houston squinted at the FBI agent. "You mean it's real? The survivalist basement dwellers actually got this one right? There's really a shadowy organization running the world out of a hotel in Holland?"

"Bilderberg's looking like it might be the solution to the equations," said Lightfoote.

"Maybe so," grumbled Lopez, "but equations don't kill. Bilderberg does. We need a solution of our own."

"And a place to lay low," said Houston. "I've got a few weeks of recovery before I can be of any use. And it looks like we've got a long trip to make."

Lightfoote tapped frenetically on the laptop. "I've got something for that, too. There's a hacker underground, as you know. Well, I've been working with some of them to create something less abstract. Now there are a bunch of hackers *underground*. Outside of Newark. Abandoned fallout shelter. They've been setting up for a few weeks."

"What do you mean?" asked Lopez.

"Some who helped us with the decryption, some who believe in Fawkes's crazy quest," said Lightfoote. "Some are just anarchists who want to take down the system. They're expecting us." Lightfoote stood up and walked toward the back of the van, steadying herself on the side walls. "There's shelter and what's more some serious computer firepower. We can tap into their system and increase our attack on this problem one hundred fold. Should be able to confirm what I've done and go beyond it, narrow down the location for certain."

"You trust these people?" asked Houston.

"No," said Lightfoote, eyeing the weapons racks coldly. "But we have a tactical advantage."

HACKER UNDERGROUND

T hey stood in front of the ruins of an abandoned factory, rusted fencing and untended wild grass waist high and swaying in the cold wind. Several inches of snowfall from the night before conferred on the grounds a peace alien to the turmoil around them. In the distance, the taller buildings of Newark could be glimpsed in the morning sunrise.

Lightfoote struck the butt of a rifle repeatedly against a convex metallic plate embedded in the ground. Clouds of vapor escaped her lips. Nearby, Houston leaned heavily Lopez's shoulder, her wounded leg suspended slightly above the ground, her face a mask of pain.

"You're sure this is it?" asked Lopez.

Again Lightfoote struck the disk. "Yes," she grunted.

"You sure they're *here?*"

Before she could strike the plate again, a muffled impact rang several times from the object.

"Yes." Lightfoote smiled and lowered her weapon. A metal-on-metal screeching howled from the disk. "They're here."

The disk flipped sideways, revealing it to be a lid over a wide hole. They sprang back just in time as the barrels of multiple weapons pointed up through the opening, and one jerked back as it fired. A cloud of smoke induced a fit of coughing from inside the tunnel.

"Damn it, Morgoth!" someone choked. "Give me that gun!"

A head poked up quickly from the hole. It belonged to a heavily bearded, unkempt man in his twenties. He peered out from the hole, squinting in the morning light. He spun nearly a full circle before he saw them, eyes lingering on Lightfoote.

The beard smiled. "You Angel?"

Lopez exhaled. "Save us."

"Yeah, that's me," Lightfoote answered, stepping forward.

The man strapped a rifle over his shoulder and scampered up a ladder that extended from deep below. Behind him two men and a woman followed clumsily.

"I'm De-frag," he began, swallowing overgrown chunks of hair as he spoke. "Two dudes here are SixtyFour and Morgoth."

SixtyFour, baby-faced and gaunt, sported blond hair to his shoulders. He stooped and shuffled his feet incessantly, hiding a face pocked with acne, patches of unshaven hair scattered across his chin. Morgoth was older, graying hair trimmed to a millimeter in length contrasting with his deep black skin, a pair of smart glasses glinting in the rising sun.

"The little lady is Medea."

A heavyset woman squinted at them, hair dyed red. She wore a pair of taped glasses, a faded Wonder Woman shirt, and a suspicious expression.

De-frag continued. "We all use our handles here. We're the First Anarchists. Kinda the leaders but not really, 'cause you know there ain't supposed to be leaders in anarchy, right? But nothing was gettin' done, so we hadda come up with some kinda compromise, you see. Didn't go down great with everyone." He paused. "Sorry about the shot, yeah? No one's hurt, right?" He smiled awkwardly.

Lopez chanted under his breath. "Hail Mary, full of grace. Our Lord is with thee...."

"So," began Lightfoote loudly. "I'm Angel. It's good to meet you in the real world, De-frag. The big guy here is Gabriel," she said, nodding to Lopez.

Morgoth interrupted in a thick Kenyan accent. "And what's he supposed to be? Some priest? We don't need any priests here."

Lopez held the man's gaze. "Former priest," he growled. "Defrocked for sexually assaulting young boys and as an enemy of the state. Wanted by the FBI for multiple murders and acts of terrorism. But I am open to giving last rites over anyone I kill here. I also do weddings." The four hackers gaped. "Leaning on me and bleeding into her wound dressings is Mary. Now, are we going to stand out here, freezing and misfiring our weapons into the air, or can we get the hell inside and find her a place to rest?"

De-frag nodded spastically. "Oh, yeah, sure. Right, man! No problem."

Morgoth hissed, pointing at Lightfoote. "And that one, I don't care what you—"

"Morgoth, shut the fuck up and get SixtyFour down in the bunker." He glared at the black hacker who continued to eye Lightfoote. "Medea— how about you help Gabriel bring Mary over here and down the chute. *Now*, guys! Come on!"

Faces still in shock, the hackers obeyed. The two men entered the large entrance and bolted down the stairs. Medea walked slowly over and continued to eye the new arrivals with suspicion. She allowed Houston to place an arm over her shoulders, however, and showed surprising strength in helping Lopez carry her to the entrance.

"Holy God-damned Angel!" piped De-frag, his face exploding into a boyish grin as he stepped alongside her, watching Lopez and Medea orchestrate lowering Houston down the three-foot wide metal tube. "You and Gabriel and Mary. It's like some backwoods revival!"

"Uh-huh."

"Everyone's psyched you were coming. I mean, holy shit, it's Angel! You fucking beat *Fawkes* and let loose the most goddamned crazy code into the wild—from the fucking FBI servers! You an agent? What's your real name? You don't have to say."

"Angel," she said, her face strained as she watched Houston disappear from sight.

"Oh," he said with evident disappointment. "Anyway, like I said, you coming was *sweet!* But you fucking brought presents! The priest, ah man. Murder, terrorism, FBI most wanted! *Really?* Shit!"

"And child molestation."

His face clouded. "Uh, yeah. Um, okay that ain't so cool."

"Don't worry, that part's a lie. Big Brother. Framed."

"Really? That's even better! He must really be a bad ass!"

Lightfoote turned sharply to face him. "Look, De-frag, we're here for a reason. We need those servers you promised me. Tell me you have them."

He nodded vigorously. "Yeah, yeah. For *sure*. I mean *stability* is still an issue in this old shit hole, but mostly, *yeah*."

She held his gaze. "*Mostly?* You better not be jerking me around or that killer priest will be the least of your concerns."

He shook his head. "No way, man! But, ah, look, it's just, well—"

She grabbed his beard and yanked him toward her.

"It's just *what?*"

De-frag's voice raised slightly in pitch. "It's just that not everyone gets *why*, you know? We got all these people together—man, it wasn't easy, let me tell you—we promised them to fight for Fawkes. Help bring down the system. Dot gov, FBI, CIA, whatever, they get that. But what the heck's this Buildingburg?"

"Bilderberg."

"Yeah, that. You know, not everyone's on board. So, you know, maybe like you could smooth things over down there? Make it clear why we're all doing this? You got all kinda fans, Angel. And maybe some who'd like to take you down, too, you know? Hackers always gotta one up."

Lightfoote let go of his hair and scowled.

"Yeah, I'll make it clear all right. One way or another."

She marched off to the hole.

38

ROCKSTAR

L ightfoote released the ladder rungs and landed loudly on the metal floor at the bottom of the tube. De-frag swung the heavy lid shut with a grunt, cutting off the morning light above. Balancing on the wall-embedded ladder, he turned the wheel handle to lock the hatch shut, and the poorly oiled threads cried out and reverberated through the steel walls of the shelter. She tasted a staleness in the air as dust rained from above.

Lightfoote let her eyes adjust as De-frag climbed down slowly. Weak LEDs glowed along walls. Away from the chamber, a tunnel jutted into foggy light. Indistinct mumbling and chatter echoed down its length.

"It's down that way," said De-frag, wiping dirt from his hands on his checkered shirt. "Pretty damn big inside, actually, but this tunnel's a squeeze."

"Where's the electricity from?"

"Well, we got some big-ass batteries and a diesel generator. But we don't start it 'cause we all fucking suffocate. Morgoth wanted to put some solar panels topside, but I was all like, 'Dude, it's like an advertising sign saying we're here.'"

"You're not running this off batteries."

"Right, no. So, this thing's built close to an old transformer. Sewage line too, which helps some, you know. Some paranoid old boys back in the '50s. Russian nukes, bam! You know?" Lightfoote eyed him impatiently. "Yeah, so we got some electricians who rigged a connection. Course they're not really trained in grid-leeching, so we've had surge problems and whatnot. Lost some servers. Now we've got the boxes on layers of protectors. It's a bit ridiculous, but so far so good! Ready for the hacker-pocalypse!"

"Okay. Let's see what you've done here," said Lightfoote, and she crawled quickly down the tunnel. De-frag sighed and hefted his bulk into the tube and slowly wormed his way forward.

Lightfoote reached the end of the metal cylinder and rose to a crouch, her shaved head scraping the lip of the exit, her eyes parsing the expansive space in front of her. The entrance opened three feet above the floor of an extended corridor that ran forward for perhaps fifty yards. The height of the ellipsoidal shelter reached ten feet at its apex, but forced stooping near the sides as the ceiling tapered off. Along the length of the main hall, doorways opened to side rooms.

People milled about the space, congregating at makeshift computer tables hosting monitors and keyboards, or at a long, central table where meals were taken. The walls and floor were a hazard of cables and wires running in bundles or loose, duct-taped in place or left unsecured. Dark power cords slithered along the length of the shelter, daisy-chained with adapter cords.

De-frag thumped to a stop behind her, panting. "This is the common area. Business end's the rooms way in the back—hold our server farms, as much as we could stuff into this place. The rest are bedrooms and stuff. Have their own toilets. That's probably where they took your friend. Makeshift medical. We have a real doc, too!"

By now, the din inside had begun to taper off, all eyes turning to Lightfoote. People had stopped eating and turned from their computers as heads cocked her way.

De-frag chatted on, oblivious. "It's a functional hacker terrorist cell! We got some of the area's best. Well, and not so best, too, if you want to the truth. But man! Fawkes started it all and then you two duked it out in cyberspace for control! Country's down for a long count. This is it! Just look at it!"

A strange wind of whispers replaced the rowdy conversations, and Lightfoote could catch repeating instances of "Angel" and "Fawkes." A heavily pierced woman at the end of the table stood up and faced her. She raised her hands and began an exaggerated and slow clapping. Other's joined in, some standing, some remaining seated, and the sound swelled and accelerated. Yells and whoops topped the ovation as stomping feet climaxed to the calls of "Angel, Angel, Angel!"

She turned her head back to De-frag. "Seriously?"

He beamed. "I told you you had fans!"

39

NO FEDS ALLOWED

"Well, let's get this over with."

Lightfoote coiled even tighter at the tube opening and sprang outward, the impact of her boots reverberating through the metal shelter like thunder. Hackers swarmed her as she moved toward the table in the center of the long room, back-slapping her, many with looks of awe. Behind her, De-frag lowered himself awkwardly from the tube and straightened his twisted shirt.

The crowd parted roughly. Annoyed cries were stifled, and people moved away to allow a group of men to march toward Lightfoote. At the head marched Morgoth, his expression fiery. Two brawny men stalked behind him. They held metal pipes.

Lightfoote watched them approach silently. People near her instinctively moved away, leaving her and the three men in a circle of onlookers.

Morgoth sneered. "She's a Fed. She's not one of us. *Come on,* people! She sabotaged Fawkes's code. If it wasn't for her, he would have taken the system down once and for all. She's the enemy and shouldn't be here."

The chamber echoed with a chorus of boos. But some nodded their heads in agreement. Lightfoote stared impassively at the three men.

"Aw, shit!" came the voice of De-frag, and he pushed himself through the crowds. "Morgoth, fuck this, man! That's enough! We agreed to—"

One of the large men beside Morgoth stepped forward and came at the bearded hacker with a pipe. De-frag cursed and warded off blows with his arms, but he had little fight in him. The men drove him out of the circle.

Morgoth stepped closer to Lightfoote. "This is an anarchist commune, De-frag. You can't tell me what to do. And I'm not going to let this Fed stay here." He raised a gun and pointed it at her, inches from her face. Gasps erupted like steam leaks. "You're going to leave, or I'm—."

Before he could finish the sentence, Lightfoote's torso swept left and her hands darted in a blurred motion. There were two slaps barely separated, a snap and the gun was airborne, landing with a clank on the floor. Morgoth screamed and cradled his right hand.

"You fucking bitch!" He moaned. "You broke my finger!"

Lightfoote resumed her stance in front of him. "You were saying?"

An electric buzz spilled across the crowd. Morgoth backed up, doubled over, his mouth frothing. He turned to the pipe-wielding men. "Fuck her up!" he spat.

The two men approached her warily, their steps staccato, feinting to make a strike, hopping back, repelled by some unseen force as they approached within a given distance. Lightfoote balanced on the balls of her feet, never flinching. She rolled her eyes.

"You boys just do foreplay or are we gonna get it on?"

The man on her left growled and leapt toward her, drawing the pipe behind his head. He swung, but Lightfoote sprung into him, one arm locked and outward, her shoulder impacting his arm at the elbow, dissipating the strike. Simultaneously, the other hand assumed the shape of a slab, the fingers curled tightly, presenting the knuckles. They plunged into his windpipe, paralyzing him. She slung him into the onrushing form of his partner. The second attacker stumbled backward as the first assailant dropped to the ground clutching his neck, wheezed gasps erupting like barks.

Lightfoote had obtained a set stance again, eyeing the panicked man before her. "Time to quit, asshole."

But she only riled him up. With a yell he charged forward holding the pipe over his head. Lightfoote sidestepped as he swung wildly downward, thrusting her hand to his bent form and augmenting his twisting motion.

Losing control, his upper torso overturned and he flipped onto the floor, the impact knocking the wind out of him. The pipe clattered and rolled across the floor. The other man gulped awkwardly beside him, still clutching his throat in pain.

Lightfoote scooped Morgoth's weapon off the floor. She stared at him as she held it up. "Not even competent street fighters. Let's see, no bullet chambered." She ejected the magazine and pocketed it. "I wonder if you even have another mag. Can you shoot lefty?" She tossed it at his feet, glaring at him. He turned away, his appetite for conflict vanished.

"Well, if that don't beat all the shit out of a horse." De-frag wandered back into the circle, nursing his bruised forearms.

Lightfoote turned her gaze around the gawking faces. She raised her voice.

"I could have killed this asshole! But my guess is he's not the only one to think like that—want me out. So I want him and any sympathizers to hear what I've got to say." All eyes were on her. "I don't give a damn if you don't agree with me. Between me and my friend," she cast a glance toward the back of the room, "we'll put anyone who tries to stop us six feet under." Heads turned. Lopez stood silently in his priestly robes, a shotgun held across his chest.

A low murmur spread. She stood on the table now, brandishing her own weapon. "You don't believe it? Try us. Right now." She cast a withering glance across the crowd.

Stunned silence greeted her.

"Now that that's clear, let me tell you why you're going to let me do what I came here to do. Morgoth said I'm a Fed. He's right."

More murmuring. Louder.

"I took down Fawkes's code because it was the wrong fucking way to fix a broken system! *I* have the right way."

"She betrayed him! Betrayed us!" came a voice from the crowd.

"I watched Fawkes die, but I didn't kill him! It wasn't the Feds, or the CIA, or the police or government."

"Then who?" came another cry.

"They're called *Bilderberg*. An organization you need to help me stop. Fawkes's last words—given to me—gave us the key. He sent me an encrypted file that *you* all helped me break. You've seen it. An image of a madman's poster board. I've seen the online discussion—none of you could figure what it's about. But we *did*. In that wall is the code to reveal the hiding place of a conspiracy that's been controlling our world for centuries."

"The Illuminati!" "Aliens!" "Fucking Jews!"

"*Bilderberg!*" shouted Lightfoote over the growing bedlam, turning in a circle. "I'll distribute to you the proof. Make up your own minds. But I'm telling you it's *real*, and it's everything the worst conspiracy theorists have feared and more. And we have a way to track them down. A mad Nobel prize-winning economist gave it to us: economic equations to trace their center of influence."

"What did De-frag promise you?" came a woman's voice.

"Your servers. I need your raw computing power. You've all been fighting a long time. You just didn't know the real target. Today, *here*, I can give you that target. We're close to finding them. You can help me. And you can do it willingly. *Or* ... we take control of this place until we're finished."

Several shouted protests.

"No, it's not fucking democratic of me! It's dictatorial. Right now we don't have time to form a parliament or play teenaged anarchist. In case you haven't noticed, the nation is tearing itself apart outside. Maybe that's what some of you want. But if so, you're gonna have Mad Max and worse. Or you can help us reboot this world, help kill a very real Big Brother, and stop people who've been secretly controlling all our destinies!" She shone with sweat, towering above the crowd. "There's no more time for debate. I've got to get to work. Who's with me?"

No one moved or spoke. Lightfoote scanned the room, jaw set, as Lopez stood silently in the back. And then, a slow chant.

"Angel."

A few softly repeated her name. Others joined a growing chorus.

"Angel. Angel. Angel."

The chant swelled and people stomped their feet or banged the table or walls. The chamber rattled and shook. Lightfoote glanced back at Lopez. He simply nodded.

Slowly, the applause died down. As the chanting stopped, Morgoth looked furiously at Lightfoote and cried out:

"She's not one of us. She's antithetical to the movement. You're making a terrible mistake!"

"Your objections are noted," said Lightfoote. "Gabriel, let's put him and his little gang into lockup."

HAIL MARY

S avas and Cohen sat atop an armored Humvee, its surface-to-air missiles spent, the soldiers inside asleep even as the thundering roll of explosions continued around them. He shook his head. The human mind adapted quickly, even to the insane—the foundation, Savas knew, of PTSD. After a day of intense assault, counterstrikes, endless violence and death, the men were exhausted. Far behind the main battle, they could now rest as the front of the conflict moved toward the urban center of Kansas City itself.

Savas couldn't sleep. Cohen breathed slowly, her head on his shoulder, her eyes closed. He tried not to disturb her as he stared into the interrupted blackness, waiting for morning. The stars were constantly dimmed by blinding explosions, weapons' flashes, and manmade clouds rising into the sky.

He could taste it in the air: a burnt, acrid cloud the wind could never fully dissipate. It sank into their clothing, formed a thin layer of dust in the vehicles, and induced bouts of asthma in the susceptible. As if on cue, one of the soldiers within startled from sleep into a coughing fit.

It has been over a week of fighting, ten days of push and retreat, artillery and blast, carnage, and a slow victory. Their opponents had learned from the last engagement. This one had been much costlier. But finally, they held the upper hand. The president's troops had pushed Hastings' force nearly inside the Kansas City limits. Soon, they'd been assured, it would be over.

The road ahead drew his attention. A man in fatigues sprinted toward them, the cap on his head marking him an aide to the command center. *This can't be good.* He shook Cohen gently.

"Morning already?" she rasped.

"Rebecca, we got company."

Her eyes flicked open, one hand rubbing the sleep out, and she focused on the approaching soldier. His pace didn't abate, and when he finally came to a stop in front of the vehicle, he doubled over for several seconds to catch his breath.

"Evening," began Savas. "All okay on the western fr—"

"Come with me now!" he gasped out. "No time to explain. The president wants you at her vehicle immediately."

"What's going on?" said Savas. Cohen sat upright.

"I'm not here to talk or take no for an answer. *Now,* sir!"

The FBI agents exchanged glances and hopped down to the asphalt. The soldier turned and motioned for them to follow. "Double time!" He began to run.

The pair followed at a fast clip, wordless, dashing past sleeping soldiers and quiet vehicles toward the command vehicle. As they arrived, the tension spiked: high-ranking officials and military personnel were congregated around the president's war table. Soldiers inside spoke rapidly into headsets as they scanned computer screens. Faces were grim. Savas and Cohen edged closer to hear the dialogue, suppressing their gulps for air.

"If they're gonna launch," said a heavy-set general, "there's no way to clear the battlefield. It's a logistics nightmare. This many men, this much equipment, it's a day's bug out and you know it!"

"Then it has to be faster!" cried York.

"Impossible!"

Tooze leaned in. "Elaine, that's it. You've done what you could. It's time to leave. We can evac you and other VIPs on a few of the older choppers that still fly."

"It's a massacre! A slaughter!"

"If they follow through, it's already assured, Ms. President!" yelled the general.

York removed her glasses and squeezed the bridge of her nose. "Give me the assessment again."

An aide to the general suppressed a sigh. "NORAD detected SLBM activation. The boats are parked off the East Coast. For those missiles, we've got fifteen minutes after launch, less perhaps depending on trajectory."

The general spoke clinically. "They don't need precision accuracy, Ms. President. An air blast. We're not fortified. They'll umbrella the area. From the initial NORAD data, it's likely a Mark 4 type, fourteen warheads. Each is a hundred kilotons. They'll carpet bomb the convoy and surrounding area."

"We'd won, dammit!" she shouted, pounding the table, spilling small pieces marking positions across the map. "Nuke his own people? His own army?"

"It's *because* we've won," said the general, wiping sweat from his brow. "Like I told you, this was their last stand. They know they've lost it. This is a Hail Mary."

"More like a Hail Satan," she said. "NORAD can't shut it down?"

"They're still trying," came the voice of another high-ranking officer. "But there isn't much of a chance."

"Tens of thousands of our troops, this *entire* city, are going to die, gentleman. That's what you're telling me?"

"Yes, ma'am. And we can't stop it."

"Elaine," began Tooze softly, "We have—"

"Prep the aircraft," she interrupted, staring coldly at her military advisors. "Go with the Migrant protocol, worst case scenario. Get as many of the VIPs out as you can." She paused and sighed. "Don't say anything to the troops. Not yet. If Hastings steps back from the cliff, we need to hold this location. We can't afford to scatter—it could be a feint and Hastings trying to gain an edge here. But the second we have a confirmed launch— God forbid—I want everyone notified with details. Tell them the truth."

"It won't be enough to get them out."

"Maybe, maybe not. But they deserve a shot. God forgive us all for what we're doing." She looked them over. "All right. That's an order. Move!"

The military men saluted and raced off to enact her commands. Tooze remained beside her, and Savas and Cohen were slowly revealed to York as the crowd of soldiers dissipated.

"You catch all that?" she asked wearily, slumping into a foldout chair.

"I'm not sure I can believe it," said Cohen.

"I know I can't," said Savas.

"You'd damn well better believe it. What's more, you two are coming with me, part of my personal entourage when we fly like bats out of hell." They simply nodded. York closed her eyes. "Just like bats out of hell. Because hell's coming."

41

MULTIPLE MAXIMA

They sat together at the long table, the shelter's hackers giving them a respectful space, and dined on scavenged canned goods and a never ending soup of protein powders from a GNC store raid. Lightfoote scowled as beige goop dripped from her spoon.

"I don't know how many more artificially sweetened, vanilla-flavored amino acid blends I can slurp down." She turned to Houston. "How's the leg?"

"Wound's closed," she said. "I won't be running the one hundred anytime soon, but walking's good. Limited weight bearing drills: squats, lunges." The former CIA agent turned the bowl up and drank down the goo. "Thank God for these protein shakes. Good to rebuild the tissue."

Lightfoote frowned. "Tastes like liquid cardboard."

"Pretty much," laughed Houston. "Our prisoners won't stop whining about it."

"How secured are they?"

Houston chewed on stale crackers. "Physically, not very. We rigged some locks on the doors. But the best bars are psychological. I think you broke them. That and Francisco's silent shotgun-priest thing." She smiled. "Works every time."

Lopez cut in: "Nothing from Savas and Cohen?"

Lightfoote shook her head. "I've tried several times. I've left emails, texts, whatever I could. No response and I can't raise them on the emergency line."

"You sure you had a connection?" asked Houston.

"Not in here, but I went topside. Phone was ringing. No one home."

He exhaled. "Something's wrong. They've never gone dark so long. I'm worried."

Lightfoote nodded. "Me too. But it's getting pretty nasty out there if we're filtering the local Hastings propaganda accurately. The other hacker communities at least help with that."

"Let's see," began Houston, "after translating Pravda, what do we get? The president is leading an armed resistance. That's her trying to get to NORAD, of course. Hastings is unsurprisingly claiming she's trying to establish a dictatorship. The military is split between them. And fighting has begun. Huge battles reported Midwest, East Coast, West Cost, Philly. Our friends are likely caught up in all that insanity." She gestured around her. "Makes this shelter seem rather foresighted."

"Caught up, and how badly?" asked Lopez. "Battles like that—I don't care what your army, sometimes you don't walk away. Look at what happened in Princeton."

"Jesus," said Houston, closing her eyes. "They sterilized it. Couldn't find us, so why not burn the entire fucking place to the ground? I kind of liked the gothic look they had going on there."

"If something happened to York, we're toast," said Lightfoote. "The country will fall to this Hastings, or whoever is put in his place to pull the strings. No way out of that. And we *need* York. Especially now, right when the numbers are converging."

"Any updates?" asked Houston.

"Good news, sister!" popped in De-frag. He landed heavily at the table, a tin plate piled with ketchup-plastered beans rattling and partially spilling its contents. He shoveled several plastic spoonfuls, speaking through a full mouth. "Cause we got ourselves an answer!"

"WELL, WE KINDA GOT OURSELVES AN ANSWER," said De-frag, scrolling through lines of incomprehensible output. The group sat in one of the back rooms, centered around a group of monitors.

Lightfoote leaned in and examined the screen. "What do you mean? I see a clear peak, here, Northern Europe, right where—wait a second..."

"Exactly," finished De-frag.

"How can we have other maxima?"

"Don't ask me, sister. I'm just running your code. Them's Nobel Prize equations."

Lightfoote squinted. "The second maxima is far smaller, but the statistics are good. What the hell?"

"Lay-agent translation, please," barked Houston.

"Yeah," sighed Lightfoote. "Okay, first—we got the precision convergence in Europe. And what do you know, it's in the Netherlands. In a one hundred mile radius that includes the damned Bilderberg Hotel. That's the major convergence. Cross-checked and independently verified with control data removed. All the external manipulation of the economy and political trajectories center there."

"Well, yeah, except that they don't, really," added De-frag.

"Right, except that they don't," said Lightfoote. "There's a collection of nodes, weaker, but they look real. One stands out the most—some sort of major influence is tied into this one as well."

"Well, where is it?" asked Lopez.

Lightfoote reached over De-frag and keyed in several commands. A map of the world appeared, a wild crisscrossing of lines converging on Europe and the northern United States.

"Here," she said, pointing to North America. "New York City."

Lopez turned to her. "New York? Right under your noses?"

"It might not be anything like the Bilderberg center. It's a minor peak, and maybe tied to the fact that New York is a financial and world political center, an 'echo node' that reflects its influence, but isn't causal."

"Isn't causal?" repeated De-frag.

"It isn't a power center in and of itself."

"That makes sense," said Houston. "There are minor nodes at most of the main financial centers—London, Shanghai, Tokyo."

"Maybe New York is more important."

"How can we know?" asked Houston, grimacing as she repositioned her injured leg. "Do we have two fronts in this fight? More? Do we need to take out the others, too?"

Lightfoote shook her head. "There's no way to know, and everything we're doing here is experimental, anyway." She set her mouth. "I say we ignore the weaker nodes. Everything—history, the strong signal on the Bilderberg node—it all points to Europe."

"And we don't have the resources, or the time, to make ten pit-stops," said Lopez. "I agree. Let's take out the big dragon."

"Whoa," said De-frag, his eyes large. "Take out? What—ya'll are headed overseas to, you know, *kill* people?"

Houston shot him a hard look. "We'll do what we have to. They have to be stopped."

Lightfoote stepped back from the monitors. "We've got to reach out. We need help."

"York again?" asked Houston.

"She's the only one with the resources. It will take us ages to get there. I'm not even sure *how* right now. It's not like commercial airline traffic is back up."

"Go above ground to call out," said Lopez. "We'll come and provide cover, scout the area. Stay up there all day if you have to." He stood up. "This is the endgame. If we can catch them unprepared, we might have a shot at stopping them. Once and for all."

42

DE-FRAG

They exited the computer room and marched from the back of the shelter. Lightfoote toted a bag with her communications equipment. Houston limped behind at a slower pace, refusing any help from Lopez. De-frag trailed behind like a kid in a candy shop.

At the sight of their passing, conversation stalled and heads tracked them. SixtyFour sat in front of a makeshift security center, blond hair spilling around bulbous headphones that covered his ears. A grainy video image flickered jarringly on a monitor in front of him. It showed only static. He turned, sensing their presence, removing the earphones.

"Up?" he said softly.

Lightfoote nodded. "We're all going. Probably a long session."

SixtyFour shook his head. "Wait."

"We don't have time—" began Lightfoote.

"Hold on, hold on," De-frag cut in, his brows furrowed. "SixtyFour's quiet, so, you know, when he talks, you gotta listen. What's up, dude?"

The gaunt teen pointed at the screen. "Video's dead."

"Yeah, okay. Not the first time," said De-frag.

"Sounds," said SixtyFour, tapping the earphones. "Too much. Rustling. Impacts. Can't identify. Someone's up there. Sentry's silent."

"Sentry?" asked Houston.

De-frag looked pale. "Yeah. She's posted in the rubble, couple hundred yards out. Claustrophobic. Couldn't take this tank."

"She's actually a sentry?" asked Lopez.

"Right," said De-frag. "Chatty as hell, too. No way she went quiet. No way she wouldn't respond." He looked back at SixtyFour. "I think we got trouble."

A shout from the back of the shelter dropped all conversation to silence. Medea hustled toward them, waving her arms, a blur of dark clothing and a red streak from her dyed hair. She shouted again.

"We're blown!" Her heavy form came to a stop in front of them. "Damn they're good! Must be NSA or something. They've traced us, ID'd our location. I don't know how. We're getting penetration tests coming up our asses!"

"I thought York had bombed them!" said Houston.

"She did!" said Lightfoote. "Slowed them, just not enough."

"They know we're here?" Houston asked Medea.

She nodded. "No way they didn't geolocate us by now."

Lopez looked into the metal tube in front of them. He removed a handgun from his robes. "That means—"

A thundering clank turned heads in the room.

"That means those aren't friendlies upstairs," said Houston grimly.

"That means we're screwed!" cried De-frag, grabbing at his hair.

A deafening hammering began above them, the sound echoing through the tube.

"Ah, man, ah man, ah man," cried De-frag, spinning in circles. "The hatch won't last long. Then what?"

Lopez steadied him with a firm hand on his shoulder. "Then, if they don't drop a bunch of grenades down here, we fight them hand-to-hand."

"Hand-to-hand?"

"Do you have weapons? Firearms?" asked Houston.

De-frag nodded. "Yeah, sure. Some brought their guns and stuff. It ain't much. We pooled them all in a locker."

"Get them," said Lopez. "We're going to be facing trained special operatives. We're going to have to organize a front to prevent any significant penetration through the entrance—trap them in the tube. It's the only hope to fight them."

"Fight them," muttered De-frag. "We got guns, man, but, you know,

I don't know if we got many who can shoot straight. You know what I mean?"

"What else is there?" said Lopez.

Medea leaned in and hissed at De-frag. "Or, dumbshit, we could use the escape tunnel in the back? Remember that?"

De-frag's eyes widened. "Fuck, yeah! Why didn't I think of that?"

"Because you're too busy pissing your pants," said Medea. "We've got to get them out."

Lightfoote turned to Medea. "Take us there."

"Yeah, before half this place figures out what's going on. That's going to be a bottleneck, let me tell you."

Lopez stopped them with his arm. He glared at De-frag. "Get them armed."

De-frag looked at the blond kid. "That's SixtyFour. He's the only gun-nut here. You got this, buddy?"

SixtyFour nodded and raced off toward a row of storage lockers along the sidewall.

"Let's move!" said Lightfoote.

The group filed past. Frightened hackers staring toward the entrance tube, the hammering continuing. Medea ducked into a back room and single-handedly shoved aside a wall of servers, revealing a hatch in the wall.

"This is it," she said.

"You've tested it?" asked Houston.

"Ah, not exactly," said De-frag.

Lightfoote locked eyes with him. "Explain."

A loud explosion rocked the shelter. Screams came from the chamber outside.

De-frag shifted into a higher pitch. "Just schematics, man! It's a tunnel, leads out along the sewage line, then up and out, a couple football fields away."

"But you've never tried it?"

Medea shook her head. "Never even opened the damn hatch." Another explosion. More screams. She stepped up to the wheel and set her shoulder to it, her hands turning white as she pressed with all her strength. It didn't move.

"Damn," said De-frag. "She's stronger than all of us. What now?"

"Move," said Lopez. He grasped the wheel in his massive hands and angled his body sideways, his legs taking the brunt of the force. Nothing happened. His broad form tensed. A wrenching scream ripped through the room and the wheel inched counterclockwise.

"Help him!" yelled Lightfoote.

Medea grasped the other end of the wheel, and together they forced it across its shredded threads. Lopez yanked and the hatch spun inward.

"Ah, shit," said De-frag, his words muffled with his hand over his mouth.

"Near the sewage lines, huh?" said Houston. "Is this a thing with us now?"

The sounds of machine gun fire echoed through the shelter. Intermittent pops of smaller ordnance peppered back.

"Smells great to me," said Lightfoote, and she stepped through the hatch, her large bag of electronics clanging on the side of the opening.

Lopez guided Houston through the opening, turning back to the room. "Medea, come with us. De-frag, these are your people." He nodded to the chaos outside. "You can't save them all, but get as many as you can in here behind us."

De-frag looked crestfallen. "It'll lead them right to you. You won't have time. You got to stop this thing, right?"

"To hell with time!" cried Lopez. "You can't let them die." Houston called his name from within the passageway. "Go! Bring those you can here!" He ducked under the opening and disappeared. Medea followed immediately after.

De-frag stood frozen in the room, his head darting between the escape tunnel and the door to the main chamber of the shelter. Screams battered his ears. Gunfire. He looked down at the ground and exhaled slowly.

"Sorry, dudes."

He turned and grasped the hatch wheel and pushed the door until it slammed shut. The metal screamed once more as he turned the wheel several rotations. He heaved the tower of computers back against the doorway, the mainframes and metallic shelves obscuring the wall completely. Exhausted, he pulled up a chair and sat down, facing outward.

A soldier in battle armor pointed a weapon at him through the doorway.

"Where are the fugitives?" the man barked.

De-frag smiled like a terrified kid plunging over the edge of a roller-coaster for the first time. He extended the man his middle finger.

"Eat it, motherfucker."

Automatic discharge exploded in the room.

43

ELECTROMAGNETIC PULSE

T he passengers were bounced roughly. Savas, Cohen, the president's close adviser Tooze, high-ranking military officers, and other governmental officials were strapped into red seats lining the interior of the large troop transport—a hulking Boeing CH-47 Chinook from another era. Missing were any high-tech digital elements, the cockpit stripped and rebuilt only weeks before to render it invulnerable to any remnants of the Anonymous worm. The modern gear was replaced by a set of instruments and controls dating to the Cold War. Alongside an escort of Blackhawks shadowed their movements. York crouched beside the cockpit and spoke to a military man seated in the co-pilot's chair.

"How much more time?" Her voice barely penetrated the rumbling of the helicopter's engines.

"Unknown!" he shouted over the din. "Estimated launch window says ten minutes, but we don't know the trajectory. We can't accurately predict. It's a navy missile for sure, fired off the East Coast, so it's loaded and fast."

"Are we clear?"

"It depends on where they detonate! If they stick to the convoy and city, yes, we're out of the blast radius. Supposedly."

"Supposedly?"

He shook his head. "We don't have the number crunching here to check. NORAD's estimates. And too many unknowns."

"She's opened up as much as I can," said the pilot. "I've vectored us radially West from the coordinates you gave. Kansas City is behind us." Turbulence bounced them viciously, and York was thrown hard against the ceiling. "Sorry, Ms. President," he said as she regained her footing. "I don't know what they did to this bird. She's flying rough, but I'll get us there. I recommend you strap in."

Savas reached out and grasped Cohen's hand next to him. Their eyes met, but they exchanged no words.

York exhaled, rotating to the single empty red chair beside the cockpit. She shouted as she worked the restraints. "Okay, assuming we get through this, what's your plan?"

The pilot answered. "Follow yours, ma'am. Six hundred miles to Cheyenne Mountain. Running this fast, we'll need a refuel somewhere along that line."

"We're working on it," she said.

"If the duct tape can hold this old lady together, it's five or six hours. Maybe less if all goes well."

York nodded. "The other evacuees?"

"Behind but in communication. We got seven birds loaded, most a lot more packed than this one. Some with vehicles. It will slow them down."

"Can't be helped," said the military advisor. "The president's the priority. We leave anyone else behind and take the escort with us."

York turned to him. "We're looking into a contingency for—"

Her words stopped. A god's lamp was lit and the landscape around them brightened like an overexposed photo. Before anyone could process or react to the radiance, a shower of sparks burst like popcorn from the control panel.

The engines made a terrible screeching noise, and the helicopter lurched to the side. Passengers screamed. The craft dropped sharply and flailed side-to-side as the pilot wrestled with the controls.

"Putting her down!" he cried.

A shadow darkened the craft. Through the windows, the bulk of a Blackhawk could be seen dropping downward, nearly careening into their Chinook. Then it was gone, the Chinook itself quickly losing altitude as well.

"Brace! Brace! Brace!"

Passengers assumed a variety of positions, confusion and fear on their faces. Savas and Cohen brought their knees close to their chests. They continued to hold hands.

The machine slammed against the ground tail-first, the helicopter crumpling from the back like a tin can. Screams and rending sounds ripped through the air. A stomach-lurching leap propelled them back into the air before gravity jerked the vehicle down again and hammered the craft into the earth. Momentum drove it shuddering like an earthquake across the ground, the cockpit mangled, dirt and rocks breaking through the front windows and flooding madly throughout the belly of the dying beast.

And then it was still.

Savas opened his eyes, his body taut and constricted, a thick dust and smoke choking his vision and breath. Cohen opened her eyes beside him, unharmed. His eyes darted forward. Upturned earth covered the president. Savas released the five-point restraints and dashed beside her.

"Ms. President?" He shoveled away handfuls of dirt from her body.

She opened her eyes. "Holy hell," she whispered. "I hope to God you're not an angel." He stared back at her. "Heaven's gotta have better-looking ones."

He smiled wanly. "Sorry, no heaven. We survived." He continued to free her from the mud and rocks.

Cohen placed an arm on his shoulder. "We're maybe the only ones."

Savas looked around in shock. At the front of the helicopter, the pilot and advisor were crushed into the control panel. Behind them—grass and plowed earth. The tail end of the Chinook was gone, and along with it the other passengers—judges, senators, and Tooze.

"George!" cried York, and maniacally tore at the restraints, freeing herself and rushing out.

Savas grabbed her. "No Elaine! It's too late!"

Fifty yards behind them, an inferno engulfed the massive engine powering the craft, charred and mangled forms within. Black smoke vomited into the sky and spilled fuel ignited the tall grass around the amputated section.

The president stared at the raging fire in horror. Her hands shook.

Cohen whispered. "John, look—"

Savas followed her gaze. Around them like campfires were the wrecked hulks of the Blackhawk escort, the machines having struck the ground much harder than their craft. There could be no survivors in the wreckage he saw.

But Savas was no longer looking at the remains of the aircraft, but eastward, behind them, high into the sky. "Dear God." A line of monstrous apparitions sprouted into the air, dwarfing the smoking fires at their feet. Dark mushrooms tainted the blue thousands of feet above the plains, casting long shadows across miles of fields. The prevailing winds had begun to chip away at their structure, eroding the rising titans into trails of smoke billowing slowly east.

"EMP," Cohen whispered. Savas and York stared at her uncomprehending. She looked away from the nuclear blasts. "Why we all went down. Electromagnetic pulse. Fried the circuitry. Pilot lost control. We dropped."

York continued to stare at the flaming tail section of the helicopter.

Savas nodded. His jaw set. "The convoy is gone. Kansas City—gone." He looked around the carnage before them. "Our evac group—gone."

Cohen shook her head. "We got lucky."

"Not just luck," said York, finally turning her back on the flames and the remains of her advisor. "Our lift was the most outfitted to resist the worm. Engineers went back decades. Tore out the damn guts and built it back. There just wasn't as much to fry inside." With a final quick glance behind, she turned back to Savas and Cohen. "But enough to do the damn job."

"What now?" asked Cohen hoarsely.

York walked back into the shorn half of the helicopter. She grabbed several bags and weapons. "Salvage what you can. We've got six hundred miles in front of us." She glanced up to the towering smoke giants. "And a madman on our tail."

44

WORM-GIRL COMES CALLING

"Admiral Myers?"

The voice belonged to a young officer at the door of a chaotic office. A stout man with a gray shock of hair spun around in his chair, a landline to his ear, the cord wrapping taut around a desk lamp and bottle of scotch. Both crashed to the floor.

"Goddammit, son!" The young aide rushed over and began to mop up the spilled alcohol and glass. "Hendricks? Hold on, I'll call you back." He slammed the phone down. "That was a conference call to the Canadian air defense headquarters. I specified I was not to be bothered until we square out those damn false alarms on their infected computers! This better be good!"

The young man turned pale. Blood dripped from one hand as he cradled shards of glass. "Yes, sir!"

Admiral Myers sighed. "Benson, right?"

"Yes, sir! Jeremiah Benson. Deputy Commander Duval's aide, sir."

"They promote you Canadians quickly. Benson—spit it out."

"We've had contact with a flagged name from the York party. Part of the FBI team we were briefed on."

"Savas group?"

"Yes, sir. Lightfoote, Angel, Special Agent in Charge, Intel 1 Cybercrimes."

The admiral stood up. "The worm-girl?" Benson nodded. "Team Hastings knows about her. You verify her identity?"

"She claims to know the president. She knows details of the worm."

Myers shook his head. "Not enough. It could be a phishing attempt. How the hell did she reach us?" The admiral bent down and pulled out a handkerchief. "You're a bloody mess, Benson. Wrap it off and put the damn glass down. We'll have custodial take care of this." He looked toward the ceiling. "Maybe someone's trying to tell me something about the bottle."

"God? Sir."

Myers laughed. "Or worse—internal affairs." He frowned. "Lightfoote —how did she contact you?"

"Yes, sir. Sorry. That's just it. She's *inside* the system. She must have hacked in. We're getting contacts from internal email and instant messaging servers. It's a flood!"

"Hacked in? *Jesus.* Should've had that girl do our penetration tests. Well, that's probably better than a retinal scan. I don't think there are too many cyberwarriors at that level. It's got to be her with everything else."

"Yes, sir, that's what we figured."

"We'll make sure. York gave us some security questions. We'll use those. " Myers glanced down at the shattered bottle. "Damn I need a drink." He stood up, Benson mirroring him, the aide's hand wrapped in bloody fabric. "Let's get to the floor."

A SMALL CROWD gathered around a cubicle in the Command Center inside of Cheyenne Mountain. An array of monitors tiled the walls around them showing maps of the nation and world, newscasts, and streams of data comprehensible only to analysts. Heads craned from other cubicles lining the floor space, trying to catch a glimpse or overhear what was transpiring.

Myers stared into the green eyes glowing from one of four monitors on a wide desk. The girl's face was streaked in grime and blood, her head shaved, piercings decorating her ears and nose. Beside her sat another woman, brunette with short hair showing blond at the roots. On the other side loomed a dark face, Mexican, a broad skeletal and muscular structure mostly in shadow.

Myers nodded. "So, Angel Lightfoote, and the two ciphers: Gabriel and Mary. Normally I'd call this a con-job, but, miraculously, you fit the exact profiles we were given."

"You've spoken to Savas? To York?"

"One thing at a time," he said. "You need to answer a few questions. We need to be sure you're who you say you are."

"Understood." Her gaze didn't waver.

"Uh, Gabriel," he began, looking at a piece of paper, reading glasses now sitting on his nose. His eyes wandered to Benson. "Is this some kind of joke?"

The aide shook his head. "No, sir. That's what they gave us."

"Well, how the hell am I supposed to read this? It looks like Latin!"

"Boys school, Montreal," said a lanky officer in a foreign uniform. He put his hand out for the paper.

"You know Latin, Pierre?" asked the Admiral.

Deputy Commander Duval nodded and took the paper. "But it's been a while, Jim. Let's see—*Comple in Sacerdote tuo ministerii tui summam.* And there is a final phrase Gabriel is supposed to provide."

The dark figure in the monitor nodded. "*Et ornamentis totius glorificationis instructum coelestis unguenti rore santifica.*"

Duval nodded, his eyebrows raised. "That's it. What the hell is it? Some Catholic prayer?"

Lopez rumbled over the speakers. "A blessing during the ordination of a priest."

Myers shook his head. "This one's for Mary. Javed Ahmad, otherwise known as?"

Houston replied instantly. "The wraith."

"Two-for-two. Now, Lightfoote. Five years ago you figured out a pattern. You drew it on a computer screen. It was an object pointing to a target. What was the object?"

Lightfoote's face tensed. "A hammer. *Thor's* hammer. *Mjolnir* in Old Norse."

Myers nodded. "It's them."

"Now, can we stop wasting time and get to business?" asked Lightfoote. "Where is York? Savas and Cohen? We haven't been able to reach them. We're on the run, Hastings troops on our asses. If you know about us, you must know about Bilderberg."

"We do," said Myers. "And your mission. You've found something then?"

"Yes. We have proof this group is behind everything. They've been orchestrating world events for decades, breaking international law, under-mining national sovereignty. Most importantly—we now know where they are. We're going there."

"Going there?" asked Duval. "To do *what?*"

"Stop them," said Lopez.

Duval squinted at the screen. "Who are you?"

Myers cut in. "We're going on the president's word here, Pierre. York claims they're as good as a Seal commando team, and she's put them on point for this. Not that we have any real options. We can't get anyone out from here with Hastings on our asses 24/7." He gestured to the monitor. "This crew is our shadow force."

"This is insane," said the Canadian.

Lightfoote nodded. "Every bit of it. Now, where the hell is York? We need her to authorize transportation for us."

Myers exhaled. "We don't know where she is."

Houston leaned in. "What do you mean? What happened? She should be there by now!"

"They were outside Kansas City, six hundred miles out from here. Hastings put up a last stand to stop her. He lost, or was losing. Then, the unthinkable. He launched a ballistic missile and dropped a bunch of warheads on the convoy and the city. It's been radio silence since."

Houston angled back in her chair. "Oh, my God."

"We had advanced warning from satellites, and York and the FBI agents were being bugged out on an emergency flight. But before they got far the bombs hit."

"They didn't make it?" asked Lightfoote.

"We don't know. But with the EMP, there's no telling what happened. They could be alive with fried communications equipment, charred in the blasts, or pulverized when their aircraft lost power."

"EMP?" said Lopez.

"Electromagnetic pulse," muttered Lightfoote. "Nukes cause them. Supposedly fries anything except the most hardened electronics."

"Does that explain the power outages?" Houston asked.

Myers cocked his head to one side. "There were outages?"

Lightfoote nodded. "Middle of the afternoon two days ago. It's still down here. We're running off a stolen generator."

Duval leaned toward the camera. "Timing is perfect. Our reports from the East Coast are minimal—Hastings controls your territory. But that's the best explanation. We're heavily shielded here, but the pulse must have damaged more civilian equipment than we anticipated."

Lightfoote slammed her hand down on a table in front of her. "We need her help! We need a transport to get us out of the country."

"Slow down," said Myers. "We've ID'd you to our satisfaction. She's left instructions, said if you called—and I guess hacked-in counts—you'd need help. And we're here to give what we can. You say a transport? To where?"

"Europe. The Netherlands. ASAP. Bilderberg is holed up there. We know exactly where. If we can get there, stop them, we can cut the head off this beast and Hastings will be a clean-up job."

"One hell of a clean-up, by the way things are going."

"Yes!" cried Lightfoote. "But he's a puppet. Take him down and Bilderberg will replace him. Take down Bilderberg—"

"Yes, yes. We ax the puppet masters," said Myers. "I have to say, this is one of the craziest conspiracy theories I've ever heard. But I serve the president, and she says to give you what you need."

"Can you?" asked Lopez.

Myers stroked his chin. "Honestly, I don't know. You need a plane. Hastings owns the seas. But air is still risky. Ridiculously risky. Commercial traffic is grounded. Since the worm and through this civil war. We'll have to get you a military transport. But how we do that without Hastings finding out ... I don't have a goddamned idea." Duval leaned over and whispered in Myer's ear for several seconds, and the admiral nodded. "Where are you?"

"Outside of Newark. Big ass airport right next door," said Lightfoote.

"Hold your position. Monitor this feed. We'll get back to you."

Lightfoote pressed. "Can you help us?"

Duval nodded. "We might just have an idea."

45

BOSWORTH HOMESTEAD

Barric Bosworth stared at the flaming sunset, one hand on a rusted fence post, the other fingering the butt of his twelve-gauge pressed into the ground like a walking stick. The dust particles and debris from the atomic explosions scattered the low rays of the sun into the most spectacular color show he'd ever seen in his seventy-three years. It didn't even look real but reminded him of the artificial palettes modern filmmakers were so taken by.

He scowled. Something for poets and painters maybe, but not a farmer. Nothing could erase his fury over what had happened—the anger and shock of nuclear war in his own backyard. Not even when nature turned the monstrous into something miraculous.

His scowl deepened as his eyes were distracted from the sky to the grassy fields below his farmhouse. He squinted and turned his good eye toward three shapes moving toward him up the hill. *Three people.* Trespassing on his property, coming from the direction of the blasts. As they neared, he could see they were struggling. An older woman, a younger woman, and a man. Their clothes were filthy, sooted like they'd come out of a crop-burning, their faces sunburned even in the winter chill. They were ready to collapse.

Still he didn't move. Didn't raise his weapon. He let the trio approach within twenty feet of his fence.

"All right you three, that's far enough."

The older woman stumbled. Propped up by the other two, her head hung as breaths wheezing in clouds from her mouth. The man supporting her spoke.

"My name is John Savas. These are my friends. We need shelter. Food and water. A place to rest." He spoke hoarsely through cracked and bleeding lips.

Bosworth nodded. "You come from the blasts?"

Savas nodded. "Outside the city. We've walked for two days."

"Two days?" the farmer rubbed his chin. "At the rate you were walkin', that'd put you 'bout halfway from here to the city. But you ain't from 'round here."

"Our flight was knocked out of the air by the blast," said Savas, his voice weary. "We're the only survivors."

"Ain't no flights since the troubles started."

"It wasn't a normal flight."

Bosworth shifted his weight off the shotgun, his hand gripping the butt more tightly. "Well, that's what I was gettin' to. You're some VIPs, or I don't know nothin'. But what I'm wonderin' is *whose* VIPs." Savas simply stared at him. "Some are sayin' we got ourselves a civil war. Some sayin' the president's trying to take over, like Hitler. Others the military. Other's the goddamned Iranians. Even *aliens*." He shook his head. "The three of you, *flyin'*. Nuclear bomb in my home state. Just *whose* VIPs are you?"

"You gone plumb senile, Barric?" cried a nasal voice. A thin woman with wild gray hair scampered down the hillside from the house, kicking up a dust cloud, a heavily patched dress billowing around her.

"Irene! Get back in the house right now!"

She pushed past him with a grunt and bent nearly in two, squinting her eyes toward the three strangers, a clawed index finger indicating York. "I swear I'm gonna make you get that laser procedure. You're gonna give a sermon 'bout the president when she's a-standin' right there?"

Bosworth furrowed his brow and turned to York. The president looked him straight in the face. His eyes widened. "I'll be goddamned."

His hand grasped the weapon at his side firmly and he lifted it into the air, loudly racking the chamber and loading a shell. The barrel pointed above Savas's head.

His wife put her hands on her hips. "Put that damn gun down, Barric! You ain't shot it in twenty years!"

He ignored her, staring fixedly at the president. "They shot you down?" York nodded affirmatively. "Where were you headed?"

York sighed, beyond the point of disguise or deception. "To NORAD. The bunker in the mountains."

"Cheyenne Mountain?" he said, the weapon not moving.

"Yes," said York. "Government and military loyal to me are waiting. Holed up. We're trying to ride this out there. But I had to get there from Washington." She looked behind her. "It's not going so well."

"Barric—" his wife began.

"Hush, woman!" He licked his lips. "Who are these two?"

"FBI agents. Real heroes if you want to know. John Savas and Rebecca Cohen. Killed the terrorist who nearly caused a war a few years back."

Bosworth looked between the two agents. "I remember."

Savas spoke. "So, Mr. Bosworth, I think it's our turn to ask whose side *you* are on? Because if it's with our nation's rebels, you might as well shoot us now. If you're loyal to this president, to our elected government, then we need your help. President York needs your help. We can't go on much farther."

Bosworth scanned around them again, weapon at the ready. "Sons-a-bitches dropped the bomb on their own country. In *my* state." He glanced them up and down again. "You go much farther like that, they'll get you for sure." He looked at his wife. "Irene, put something on the stove. You all come on in. We ain't got much, but we got food, beds, some medicines. Maybe buy you a little time." He patted his shotgun. "And don't you worry, anyone coming after you is gonna have to get past me first."

46

BLACKBIRD

N ight fell, and nothing moved at Newark airport. Planes slept along the shuttered terminals, the tower looming above as a shadow in the starlight, the runways invisible and dark. The blackness was punctuated haphazardly with the faint glow of exit signs and flickering emergency lights, the electric gasps of a region still reeling from the both the worm and the EMP.

Lopez, Houston, and Lightfoote huddled on the tarmac, three small shapes beside a broad runway racing alongside the central terminal. A blue glow blossomed as Lightfoote opened a laptop, the glare forcing the three to squint as their eyes adjusted from the darkness.

"This is the longest runway," she said, indicating a black line on a schematic of the airport. "They said it would put down here."

"They're late!" whispered Lopez through clenched teeth. "It's just a matter of time before they hem us in. We're sitting ducks."

Houston scanned the skies. "I don't know what we're looking for. They'll be flying low, trying to screw with any radar scans of the area. The airport is down, thank goodness. I don't know what else the military could have looking."

"I assume the lights will be off," Lopez said. "No runway lights. How are they going to put it down?"

"I have no idea," said Lightfoote, shaking her head and closing the computer.

The three sat in silence as the minutes dragged by. The sounds of a truck caused them to catch their breath and draw weapons, but the noise faded quickly, leaving them in the quiet of the open space.

"We ought to consider a defensive arrangement," said Houston. "If they search the airport, we—"

"Wait!" hushed Lopez, his eyes fixed on the sky. "Listen! Can you hear it?"

For a moment, the two women followed his gaze, silent, listening.

"An engine, air turbulence, something," said Lightfoote.

"There!" hissed Houston, pointing north-east and into the sky.

A hole in the band of the Milky Way yawned above them, a gap in the stars blurring its way across the sky. The sound grew more distinct, the churning of some machinery that was completely outside their experience.

"It's almost on us!" said Lopez, rising from his crouch. "It's about to land!"

The three stood back from the runway. At the far end, the shadow expanded dramatically, a shape with unfurled wings descending like a hawk on prey.

"Are the engines off?" asked Houston. "It hardly makes a sound."

Tires screeched with a quick burst of light as the plane touched down. They watched silently as the rending sound of brakes engaged and the aircraft rumbled past them, the plane slowly coming to a stop.

"It's the damn bat-plane," said Lightfoote.

The three jogged toward the craft as it circled around an end of the runway and aligned toward the other, preparing for takeoff. Drawing near, they could better make out the details of the thing. Pitch black, a coating drinking all light, sharp wings framing a blade, the plane slowed to a stop. The vertical cross section was small, the engines placed like two boxes over the wings. The sounds of a hatch opening rang in the night.

"It's a stealth bomber," said Houston, awe on her face.

"Not a bomber," came a man's voice from the vehicle. From around the nose stepped a pilot in dark gear, a broad helmet like a fighter pilot's in his hands. He marched quickly up to them.

"It's a stealth transport. A prototype from Northrop for cargo, strategic airlift capability. Bomber doesn't hold passengers." He looked at the bald head of Lightfoote. "You Angel?"

"Stealth cargo transport? What the hell is that for?"

The pilot shrugged. "They always think up uses. But never went into production. NORAD said you needed a bird and we had to get it in without being seen. And this prototype runs on some new military-grade OS. Worm-proof. There weren't too many options."

Lopez scanned the aircraft. "It will hold all of us? Doesn't look like much room."

"It's for cargo. More room than you'd imagine. It looks like a B2, but it ain't. Doesn't fly much like one either. Now, come on. Let's get you three the hell out of here."

They didn't need any persuasion. The pilot led them to the cargo entrance, and they jogged inside. Cramped and lacking much light, they stumbled to seats along the walls and strapped in.

The pilot reached the cockpit and sat next to a helmeted co-pilot. Their hands moved over the instrument panels and the cargo doors shut. The engines powered up, the interior going completely dark as the plane began to accelerate down the runway.

"Please fasten your seat belts and stow your tray tables," came the pilot's voice over speakers. "Next stop, Amsterdam."

A dark shadow leapt into the air.

47

SURGICAL INTERVENTION

"So, it's come to this at last."

The words were spoken by a harsh face over a computer screen, a middle-aged man in a business suit. The Director stared at the monitor from his seat underneath the Bilderberg Hotel, a panel of other monitors displaying an array of ashen faces.

"Yes, Alpha. We are in agreement," said the Director. "York has perturbed the models too much. The equations are diverging. America is lost. Europe now has a sixty percent chance of diverging from the planned curves as well. Asia will be next."

"But is York still alive?"

"We don't know. But it hardly matters now. Had we secured the nation, suppressed her message earlier, exhibited her alive or dead with the proper propaganda, it might have been contained. But through NORAD and their broadcasts, it went on for too long. The Nash Criterion has been reached."

"And you have confidence in the metrics of this madman?"

"This is what we do, Alpha. You have trusted us and been amply rewarded by our numerical simulations. The Nash Criterion was always a calculation for *in extremis*, more to calibrate the models with a high bound. We never believed the model fluctuations could reach this point.

The hacker has been a disaster. There is now no way to salvage the global trajectory without dealing with America."

"Amputation?"

"Surgical intervention. Enough to render its world influence minimal, to absorb its economy and government into that of nations to be appointed as guardians over what is left. Otherwise, the equations can't be balanced or normalized. We will lose control."

"And you estimate Europe and Asia will fall back on path even after this drastic event?"

"Yes." The Director wiped sweat from his brow. "The models show a strong attractor to the established trajectories. A high confidence for stabilization within the envelope of error. But only if America is neutralized. The parameters are tight. Too large a strike and we risk major secondary effects, climate the most significant. Such disturbances could also doom us. Too small, and the divergence will not be contained. We have a set of models for minimal, decapitation strikes of government and industry. Strong ripples are unavoidable, but we believe they can be managed while putting our past models back on track."

Alpha nodded on the screen. "Zero has decided. Do it."

The Director glanced at the screen in horror. "Of course."

"We remain in control over the required systems?" asked Alpha.

"We have verified several times over the last few days. Launch codes, missile command and control servers, and our personnel—everything is in place, as well as other nations' systems to avoid panicked responses."

"The university is on the target list."

Alpha frowned. "You don't need to explain the obvious. You aren't going to impact America without a strike here. We will dismantle everything in New York and evacuate. We need several days to manage the logistics."

The Director looked down to his desk and shook his head. "After so long. Such a perfect disguise. We won't find another like it for some time." He returned his gaze to the monitor. "What of the scientists?"

"Them? They are only a front. Mostly a pack of Nobel-chasing sheepdogs imagining themselves to be prima donnas. They are no longer needed."

"And Zero?"

"His plans will remain hidden, even to you, Director. When we've completed our transition, you may learn more. Now, prepare everything and wait for our final contact."

The screen turned black and Alpha disappeared. The Director placed his hand to his temples.

"God help us."

PART III

PROMETHEUS BOUND

"The real truth of the matter is, as you and I know, that a financial element in the larger centers has owned the Government ever since the days of Andrew Jackson."

— FRANKLIN D. ROOSEVELT

48

INFRARED

"I still can't get used to the quiet."

Lightfoote stood in the middle of the stealth transport cargo bay. A constant purr and muffled sound of wind filled the cramped space. A black SUV with tinted windows sat chained to the floor several yards behind them, the vehicle unusually long with a substantial bed. The glow of a laptop screen painted the dim interior in a ghostly sapphire. She stared up at the surrounding walls, her body still. Her computer rested on a makeshift table culled together from small boxes. Lopez and Houston sat on either side, watching her quietly. After several more seconds, she shook her head and sat down with them.

"Invisible to radar and hardly makes a sound. Pretty amazing." She looked at Houston who grimaced while repositioning her leg. "How's the thigh?"

"Better, but crouching in this black box isn't doing wonders for it." Lightfoote continued to stare. "I'll kick plenty of ass when we get there, little girl. Don't worry."

Lightfoote half-smiled. "You better. Looks like we're going to be hitting a fortress."

Lopez pointed to images on the monitor. "So, these are aerial images that see underground?"

Lightfoote nodded. "They're brand new. NORAD moved fast on our request, using some of the newer imagining satellites. Infrared. Archeologists love them—found new pyramids buried in the sands in Egypt. Pretty powerful and high resolution."

"Looks it," he said. "More than one floor underneath, I think. It's at least three times the size of the above-ground structure."

"And it's not a parking lot," said Lightfoote. "I couldn't find anything about underground structures associated with the Bilderberg Hotel. As far as the internet is concerned, it's just a simple four-story structure in Oosterbeek."

"Can we get a sense of the security?" asked Houston.

"The resolution is good, but not miraculous," said Lightfoote. She switched to regular aerial photographs. "Nothing topside to raise any suspicions. But there has to be something serious given what we're dealing with. I assume it really starts near the entrance to the underground bunker."

"But we have no idea where that might be," said Houston. "We're going to be awfully exposed hunting around for that."

"Yes," said Lightfoote. She bent over, staring at the screen. "But maybe we can make some educated guesses."

"The power lines?" asked Houston.

Lightfoote nodded. "A hotel that size doesn't need so many cables. And look at the asymmetry here. A few lines to the main structure, and then what, *five* running where? To this wing only. What the hell is going on there? Stadium lighting?"

"You're right," said Lopez. "The entrance is there." He pointed to the satellite imagery. "The forest comes close to the extended wing *here*. If we can make our way to this point, we can recon the wing. Maybe remain unseen until we move on it. I bet there's a network of cameras sweeping the place."

"I wouldn't assume the forest is safe, Francisco," said Houston.

His face darkened. "Haven't forgotten, Sara. We've seen a few examples of paranoids wiring nature to hell and back. Still, I think it's the best approach. Remember, it didn't save the occupants we came across."

Houston nodded, her eyes distant, remembering. She snapped back. "I agree. We conduct sweeps through this sector. If we identify surveillance, we avoid or deactivate."

"We might alert them," said Lightfoote.

"We might," replied Houston. "But we don't have too many options coming in this fast. Unprepared."

"I also had NORAD compile the satellite imagery over the last few weeks," said Lightfoote. "I've strung the frames together, run it several frames per second. Watch."

She double-clicked on a file and a video player opened, displaying a still frame of the top of a building surrounded by land and roads. She pressed play. Cars and trucks came and went at blinding speed, shadows running across the frames right to left, repeating over and over. "Their birds get several photos a day. Notice anything?"

"Deliveries?" asked Houston. "Guests arriving? What?"

"The number of trucks is pretty low. About enough to handle a hotel that size and not much more. Unless they have an underground railroad bringing in supplies, what you see is what they get."

"They're minimally staffed," said Lopez. "We're not going to hit an army."

Houston smiled. "You're right. It's the best news we've had yet."

"I'm not sure why it's so minimally guarded," said Lightfoote. "I sure as hell hope we aren't wrong."

"The Nash equations? A huge and secret underground bunker with a massive supply of electricity?" Lopez shook his head. "*Something* highly unusual is being hidden there. We aren't wrong."

"Maybe they never feared discovery," said Houston. "Maybe automatic security systems with a few guards seemed enough. If they've been around as long as they have and never discovered, they might have gotten cocky."

"Maybe," said Lightfoote. "But let's keep our eyes open. I don't want any surprises."

Houston smiled. "I don't either, except the one we're going to drop on them."

49

SHOTGUNS

Bosworth opened the front door, using his foot to kick the scuffed wood at the bottom to force it through a sticking point. He lost control of the handle and the door swung wildly on its hinges, slamming into the wall behind it.

"For cryin' out loud, Barric! You 'bout gave me a heart attack." His wife stood in an apron over a gas stove. "I've told you to fix that damn door!"

"Have a seat," he said, ignoring her. He placed his shotgun beside the door, drawing the shades to the windows.

As Savas helped York through the entrance, he noticed the wall behind the doorknob had numerous indentations. Mr. Bosworth's kicks over the years had made their impression. The house was built of knotted planks of wood, stained a rich honey, the polish long worn away. A small fire crackled on the right side and helped to dispel the cold air invading from outside.

"We need to use your phone," said York. "I've got to contact NORAD and let them know where I am."

"Honey, the phones have been out since that interweb virus thingy shut everything down," said Mrs. Bosworth. "And look at this, my computer." An older model desktop PC sat with a dark monitor on a table by the wall. It appeared to be covered in dried foam. "Soon as the bomb went off, every damn thing with wires 'bout caught on fire. My computer did, sparks flying everywhere."

"Irene had to pull out that old extinguisher," laughed Bosworth. "Miracle it still worked."

"Laugh all you want, Barric, but it had all our records."

"I don't think Uncle Sam'll be feeling up to any audit right now," he replied

York looked between them. "So, no computers. No landlines. Cell phones?"

Mr. Bosworth shook his head. "We ain't got one, but I heard they're all down, too. Stuff takes longer to fix out here. That's why all the kids leave."

"So we're completely cut off," said Cohen.

"Welcome to the prairie," said Mrs. Bosworth. She looked at Cohen. "Your name again, honey? I can't remember my own, somedays."

"Rebecca."

"Rebecca. Nice church name."

"I'm Jewish."

"So was our Savior, honey. So was he. Can you hand me some of those candles on the shelf there? Night's gonna fall soon and there ain't been electricity for weeks."

Cohen reached behind her and grabbed a sack of candles, walking them to the old woman. "How do you keep warm?"

Mr. Bosworth grunted. "Battery back-up for the furnace helped, but course it wouldn't last. Couple of days we lost heat. That weren't no fun, let me tell you. I switched off the A.C. to the furnace and wired up a nine volt in place of the normal one. Fooled the damn thing. Gas valve opened and furnace started fine. To get things flowing, I popped the inspection cover. No fan running, but we got a good bit of heat. With the fireplace over there, everything was fine. Well, the blower safety switch kicks out and shuts things down every now and then and we got to let everything cool down. But it works. Until the gas supply quits."

Irene snorted. "That makes as much sense as government cheese. Just don't get him started."

"I was only answerin' her question."

Irene huffed and placed several candles on a long wooden table in the middle of the room. The light had begun to fail outside, and already the warm radiance of the fireplace and candlelight tinted the room orange. She placed a fat kettle of soup on the table.

"Haven't had guests for years." She looked at York. "Last gov'ment man we had was Jim Wilson from the local IRS in KC." Her face darkened. "I guess he's dead too now, 'long with that pretty family of his. I never was much for hostin', and we ain't got nothin' proper for a president. Anyways, come eat up. You look starved."

Eagerly, the three descended on the table, the first nourishment in days drawing them greedily. Conversation halted for several minutes as the famished visitors devoured the broth.

"Sorry to say, ma'am, I didn't vote for you," said Mr. Bosworth, opening conversation.

York laughed. "Well, that's quite all right, sir. I don't take opposition personally. Unless they're shooting at me."

"It weren't that I *opposed* nothin'," he said.

Mrs. Bosworth shook her head. "He just don't want to say he thinks a man ought to be in the big chair."

"Now, Irene, I never said—"

"Never said! You don't have a thought in your head I don't know beforehand, Barric."

York helped herself to a second bowl. "You have no idea how nice it is to think about someone voting against me rather than trying to kill me. It's what all this is about, you know." She wiped her mouth with a napkin. "Some people want to take your say out of what the country does. They want to rewrite the rules, remove the people opposing them. As you see, they'll stop at nothing."

"I knew you were tough as any man for the job," said Mrs. Bosworth. "I kept telling Barric during the election. 'She's army! What else you want?' Pair of dangling ovaries I guess."

Mr. Bosworth didn't answer but shook his head, slurping loudly with a spoon to his mouth. Cohen turned to the president.

"How did you end up in Iraq? Can't have been too many women serving in combat areas back in the nineties."

"There weren't," said York. "It's a long story, starting with enlisting. And it never would have happened if my father hadn't been so damn pushy for me to enter politics." She laughed. "Try to imagine a young girl flipping her big name politician dad the finger and signing up for the

army. Boy, was he pissed. Had the roadmap already laid out for me, probably when my mom was in labor. I was determined to blow it all to hell.
Of course, he did spin it for the press and gained some points for his
patriotic children."

"And yet," said Savas, "after it all ended, here you are. President of the
United States. Dad would have been proud."

"Life's never short on irony. But right now my title is on the ropes."
She placed her spoon down in the empty bowl. "And what about you,
Agent Savas. Your father an officer of the law, like you?"

"He did clash with the mob," said Cohen, smiling.

"Sounds promising," said York.

Savas shook his head. "The last thing my father wanted was to be part
of the law or crime. Now, my paternal *grandfather* is another issue entirely.
I really don't want to know what he had to do to become one of the
biggest shipping magnates in Asia Minor."

"So, you're from money?" asked York.

"Could have been. But there was too much chaos in the Balkans those
decades. My grandfather lost everything, every boat he owned during the
Greek genocide a hundred years ago."

"Greek genocide?" asked Mr. Bosworth. "Ain't never heard of it."

"Yeah, not as well advertised. And like the Armenian genocide, the
Turkish government would like to keep it that way." He stared off into the
distance. "But more than a million perished, the entire Hellenic population in Asia Minor either killed or driven West into Greece. An entire
culture perished. So did my grandfather's boats and our family's wealth."

"That's a horrible story," said Ms. Bosworth.

"Just one of thousands in Europe of the last century. Genocide after
genocide. Ethnic cleansing—love that word. Like they gave all the Greeks
a bath or something. Not as civilized as we like to pretend we are."

York exhaled. "No need to remind me."

"Afterward, my family settled in northern Greece. A piece of land
belonging to three different countries off and on before my father was
twelve. For the next Balkan wars, he was conveniently drafted into three
different armies. My grandparents put him on an Italian boat to the New
World."

"At twelve?" clucked Ms. Bosworth.

"He did pretty well. My father was a charmer and entrepreneur. By the time he reached New York, he was fluent in Italian and had a Sicilian girlfriend. Ran a restaurant under the Brookline Bridge for more than thirty years."

"And the mob connection?" asked York.

"Getting to it. He refused to pay the protection money."

"The money you pay the mob to protect yourself from them," said Cohen.

Savas continued. "They set fire to his restaurant three times. Three times he borrowed, built it back, and had better digs than before. I guess they finally just gave up."

"Amazing," said York. "But now I see why you joined the police. You were police before FBI, right?"

"Does it show?"

York smiled. "I've been around a lot of law enforcement. Got a good eye."

Mr. Bosworth nodded. "So how'd you get from the police to the FBI?"

Savas tensed but forced himself to relax. "My son followed in my footsteps. Joined the NYPD a little before the World Trade Center attacks. He died as a first responder." All eyes were fixed on him. "I joined FBI counterterrorism afterward."

Cohen reached over and put her hand on his shoulder. Savas drank down a glass of water quickly as she spoke.

"My story's similar," she said. "I had a lot of relations killed in Israel. Bombings. I remember as a kid my mom coming to me. 'Aunt Yael won't be coming to visit this year.' 'Cousin Ziva got hurt.' I was precocious: I watched the news. Looked things up in the papers. I loved detective stories. I decided before I was out of braces that I would be a detective."

York stared intently at the pair. "Your division has a lot of people familiar with trauma."

Savas nodded. "No accident, as you might have guessed. Intel 1 was set up by a man who had a dark but effective vision. He recruited some characters, including one who's now with the pair who rescued you in Washington. He felt we'd be highly motivated."

"If he could keep you sane," said York. "This was Larry Kanter?"

"Yes," said Savas. "Killed by Mjolnir five years ago. Blew his house up."

Mr. Bosworth stared at Savas with his mouth agape. "Well, goddamn, son. Sounds like you've gotten the tour of hell."

"More like he's been stationed at the turn off to hell, Mr. Bosworth," said York. "He and the others have had to stand in the heat and steer the rest of us away from it."

Savas put his spoon down. He smiled at Ms. Bosworth and changed the subject. "This meal has been as close to heaven as I could imagine food to be. And as thankful as we are for all of it, we need to consider soon what we're going to do next. The president can't stay here. Seeing what's happened, you shouldn't want her to stay here for long, unless you like a big bullseye painted over your house. We've got to get her to NORAD."

"I've been thinkin' on that," said Mr. Bosworth. "You need something you can hide out in. Car or truck, you're open on the road. You've got to find a place to sleep. You can't count on motels or anything. Most are closed. But I've got an idea."

"You don't mean that old camper?" asked Mrs. Bosworth.

"I surely do," he said. "I've got me a nineties Coachmen Leprechaun. She still runs."

"And smells like a swamp inside."

"She'll keep you on the road, out of sight, no need for doing much but driving—straight shot to Colorado on I-70 should run you a day, and if you need more, motel goes with you. I ain't got no more real use for it. You want it, she's yours."

Savas stared at him. "It will get us six hundred miles to Colorado?"

"No promises," he said. "But I've kept her in shape. I ain't no mechanic, but I can tinker the hell out of things. Like the heater. I wouldn't push her too hard: Keep an eye on the temperature. Stay under sixty. She should get you there."

"Beggars can't be choosy," said York. "We'll have a look. But we might just take you up on your offer, Mr. Bosworth. The nation doesn't have much more time. We have to end this conflict soon."

He nodded. "Nothin' truer said. We can fill you up with a few days' supplies. You shouldn't need more than that to get there." He stood up and walked to a floor-to-ceiling cabinet, pulling a key from several on a chain. He unlocked it and swung the doors open. "And we can supply you with more."

The interior of the cabinet was lined with shotguns. Boxes of shells were stacked along the bottom.

"Barric's been a collector for years," said Mrs. Bosworth. "'Bout drove me nuts with guns all over the house. Different makes, special handles, all kinds of money thrown away. I always said: 'What are you buying all these for, a war?'"

Savas stood up and walked alongside the cabinet, examining the interior.

"Well, Mrs. Bosworth, it looks like he was."

50

HARD LANDING

"Okay folks, time to take your positions," said the pilot. "Here comes the crazy part."

Houston and Lightfoote walked to the large SUV and opened the doors, entering the dark behemoth. Houston sat shotgun. Lightfoote took the back seat, spinning to look on the forms of two compact motorcycles strapped in the back, then turned back and belted herself in. Outside, Lopez looked over the vehicle, examining the chains and their attachments to the floor. He called up to the cockpit.

"These will release automatically?"

"Yes," said the pilot over the speakers. "Once the ramp is lowered. You follow it down, accelerating out and clear the aircraft. Then we're gone."

Lopez nodded and stepped into the driver's seat, slamming the door behind him. He pressed a button on the dash. "You picking us up?"

"Roger that," said the pilot through some static. "We're on approach, monitoring all frequencies. The airport is still shut down for all commercial flight, but they've started bringing in cargo planes and military aircraft. We've got some heavies around. Air traffic control can't see us, and as yet we've only had one pilot call in a UFO. It's getting dark, so—hold on. Make it two UFOs. Word's getting out."

"Jesus," said Houston. "How are we going to land in this mess?"

"Hold on!" cried the pilot.

The plane banked sharply, throwing them sideways. Lopez slammed into the glass, and nearly pitched to the other side of the SUV when the stealth craft leveled off, only his grip on the entry assist handle keeping him in position. He quickly buckled himself in.

"Looks like we land dangerously," said the pilot. "An Airbus Beluga super transport at takeoff. A flying whale for sure. Just missed it. *Jesus!* Okay, hang on, coming behind another plane on approach. Prep for wake turbulence. This is it!"

Their stomachs dropped as the plane descended rapidly and the stealth aircraft was pummeled and shaken violently. Lopez grabbed the wheel instinctively as the SUV convulsed around them. He could hear the crates of weapons and ammunition rattling loudly from behind.

Then a kick in the gut as the plane slammed onto the ground. The landing gear miraculously held together as they were yanked mercilessly forward. The pilot decelerated the aircraft forcefully, and they felt him struggle to keep the plane from pitching. The brakes screamed, and the smell of burnt rubber filtered into the SUV.

"Prepare to detach!" cried the pilot.

"Roger!" called back Lopez.

He released the brake and put the vehicle in neutral. Despite slowing, the plane still moved quickly on the runway. The failing light of dusk streamed into the dark cargo hold, a slit in the floor growing in front of them. The ramp lowered, the tarmac below racing madly past.

"Go, go, go!"

There were several loud pops, followed by the rattling of heavy chains. The SUV pitched forward down the ramp.

"Brace!" Lopez cried out.

The vehicle slammed onto the asphalt as he gunned the engine and accelerated, sparks flying from the ramp behind them as it scraped the ground. He quickly angled away from the runway.

"Clear!" he yelled.

A strained voice came over the speaker in the SUV. "We see you. Accelerating for takeoff." They heard the black plane scream into full throttle. "We aren't coming back. Good luck! Always check your six."

"Thanks, and get the hell out of here."

He steered toward the main terminal as the stealth craft rose into the air. Lopez scanned the planes and crew around him, dodging obstacles and bewildered workers.

"Map's a bit blurry in my mind. We head for the main terminal, then west, and the highway?"

Houston nodded. "Right. No one seems to have picked us up yet. I'm sure they were a bit distracted by the unexpected landing and takeoff. But it won't last forever. There, Francisco! Ahead. Follow the green line."

Lopez flew past parked airplanes, approaching a gate surrounded by booths.

"Boom barrier ahead. Arm's down. We ram it?"

Lightfoote leaned up from the back, straining against her belt. "No choice. Look!"

Bright red and blue lights began to flash from outside the SUV. Sirens howled.

"Police," said Lopez. "Well, that didn't take long." He shifted and accelerated, grinding his teeth. "Okay, hold on!"

"Guards! Take cover!" cried Houston.

Lopez had a millisecond to process the scene in front of him before he aligned the car to the gate and ducked. Two dark figures stood at either side of the barrier. They opened fire.

Impacts struck the front window, the shatter-resistant glass forming circular craters around the bullets. Other projectiles banged across the hood and roof of the car. The passenger side mirror exploded.

They crashed through the barrier and the shots momentarily ceased. Lopez jerked up, desperately steering the SUV out of the oncoming lane and onto the right side of the road, narrowly missing several cars approaching the gate. Horns blared. Several shots chased them, two thumping against the rear doors. But they were through!

Lopez gunned the SUV down the road and approached a turnoff to the main highway. He glanced in the rearview mirror, flashing lights from police clearing the gate in the distance behind them.

"Anyone hurt?" he cried out. Sweated beaded on his forehead.

"I'm good," said Houston, exhaling slowly and leaning back into her seat.

"Ditto," said Lightfoote. She laughed. "Your man can drive, sister."

"That he can," said Houston. "We clocked a hundred before we kissed."

"Don't get too excited," said Lopez, the SUV screeching as it rounded the exit ramp. "We're going to have the entire Dutch SWAT brigade on our asses in ten minutes."

51

COACH FORCE ONE

"Maybe travelin' by night might be more secret," said Bosworth, eyes squinting. Wisps of breath escaped from his mouth.

Savas shook his head, pulling the hood down behind him. "It might call attention. Typical RV is going to drive by day, stop at night. We'll leave as soon as we're packed, be out of here by sunrise. Should be in Colorado by nightfall."

"Don't think any vehicle on the road these days will look normal. Everyone's shut up. Fuel's mostly gone. I'd vote for night. At least then it's hard to see you."

"We'll need lights. It will stick out for sure."

Bosworth nodded. "There's that."

The two men stood beside the dingy sides of the old camper, its once-white paint chipped and yellowed, dents spread haphazardly across the vehicle. The garage was spacious yet crammed with tools and a small hydraulic lift. A rusted pickup truck was on the other side of the RV. The faint first light of morning began to glow through small windows in the structure.

Cohen and York stepped out of the camper, discussing what they had found inside. Mrs. Bosworth shuffled across the oil-stained floor loaded down with heavy bags. She set them down in front of the RV.

"You two look twenty years younger," she said, her eyes twinkling.

"Miracles of food and a shower," said York.

The old woman nodded toward the interior of the vehicle. "So?"

"You weren't wrong about the smell," said Cohen.

York smiled. "It's not Air Force One, but it'll do."

"Might lose your appetite, but here," she said, indicating the bags. "Some food and supplies. You won't be needing much for this trip. Maybe Barric's gun collection might prove more useful. But it's nothin' we can't spare."

"Thank you," said Cohen, grabbing the bags and heading back into the RV.

York stepped up to the two men. She pointed under the truck to a large metal box. "The auxiliary tank?"

"Yes, ma'am," said Bosworth. "It's not Department of Transportation approved, mind you. Set it up myself. But served well for a lot of trips. You got fifty-five gallons in the main tank and forty more there in the reserve. That's a good seven, eight hundred miles. Unless you do something stupid, you won't have to even stop."

"We don't plan to," said Savas. "Stop or do anything stupid."

"What we plan and what's happened haven't always been in perfect alignment," said Cohen, returning.

"You got that right, girl," said York. "But we'll go with the plan. Dawn to dusk, straight shot. I-70 is likely mostly clear. Hope for the best."

"Not much else you can ask for in life," said Mrs. Bosworth.

"I still think you're gonna be the only ones out on the road," said Mr. Bosworth. "If they're looking for you, it's got to call their attention."

"Maybe," said York. "But we can't wait. And most of Hasting's troops were at Kansas City. Don't know what he has left out here."

"Hastings," echoed Mr. Bosworth. "The general you mentioned?"

"That's the one."

Bosworth shook his head. "Bombed his own *troops*. His own *country*. What kinda man does that?"

"One we need to stop," said York.

The five of them stood silently before the large vehicle for several moments before Mr. Bosworth cleared his throat.

"I wasn't for your politics, Ms. President, but I have to say you make a good impression. My money's on you for this fight. God speed to you and I hope you make those bastards see justice."

Mrs. Bosworth flicked her hands at them. "Okay, get, all of you. Come back some day and see us. You're good company, and we want to find out how it all ended."

"And you two stay safe," said Cohen. "We don't know how long it will be until things return to normal."

"We'll do fine," said Mr. Bosworth. "Got supplies laid up through this winter. If'n things ain't better by the next, country's lost anyway. We've seen a lot of good. Feel bad for the young ones."

Savas slapped the old man's shoulder and grabbed a shotgun on the back bumper. "Thanks for everything." He glanced at Mrs. Bosworth. "We won't forget. Don't worry."

The three said their goodbyes and boarded the RV. York slid into a booth in the middle of the vehicle, unfolding a large map in front of her. Savas placed his hand on Cohen's shoulder.

"You sure you want to drive?"

She nodded. "If anything happens, you two are the gunslingers." She looked at his weapon. "Sit. You're shotgun."

"All right. Let's pray I don't have to chamber a single shell." He eased into the passenger seat, pointing the weapon to the floorboard.

Cohen started the RV, the old engine coughing loudly and catching, the entire vehicle shuddering. They'd agreed to leave off all climate control, both to save gas and not to risk overtaxing the engine. They sat in poorly fitting coats, Cohen's fingers poking up through finger holes in a set of frayed gloves, the winter gear supplied from the attic trunks of their hosts. She checked the mirrors, adjusting the rearview, and looked out the window. The garage door was opening, the pale light before sunrise spilling in. A light snow had begun to fall, the air dancing with ice crystals.

The Bosworths walked alongside the camper and stepped outside the garage as the door retracted. Standing motionless by the left side, their expressions were inscrutable. Cohen waved and shifted, the RV rumbling forward and onto the driveway, bouncing clumsily on its poor suspension. They left the farmhouse behind, the front lawn passing on the right, two stony protrusions marking the entrance to the property. She turned right and onto a local road.

"All right," she whispered, clouds escaping her lips. "Here we go."

52

ALWAYS SEE THE BODY

L opez accelerated to over ninety miles per hour. They passed the early morning traffic on the highway out of the Amsterdam airport like the cars were tied to the road. With five lanes and little congestion, he easily picked his way around smaller vehicles.

"What the hell does this thing have under the hood?" asked Houston. "It's as big as a bus with two cycles in the back!"

Lightfoote hung her arms over the two front seats. "And what was the military doing with it? Urban warfare?"

"Later," snapped Lopez, dodging a blaring commuter bus. The speedometer hit ninety-five. "Status of those blue lights?"

Lightfoote spun back around. "No visual, but you can bet they're in pursuit. They've likely radioed ahead. They're going to set up road blocks soon."

Houston laughed and glanced at Lopez. "Sound familiar?"

"Too familiar. Angel, the turnoff should be close! You have the maps?"

Lightfoote stared at her laptop, open on the seat beside her. "Saved by the bat-plane satellite internet. Take the next one. Puts us in some small town—not going to try to pronounce it. They sure like lots of letters here. Narrow streets. It's perfect." She paused to glance through the back window. "Update: We got company. Good half mile, but I can see the flashy lights. A lot of them."

Lopez growled. "This is going to be close."

"We need to be clear enough so they don't see the bikes," said Houston, "or else it's just another chase."

"I know," said Lopez. The speedometer read one hundred.

"That's it, *there!*" cried Lightfoote, again leaning into the front space, her arm pointing to the right.

Several signs indicated an approaching exit ramp. The beginnings of a town could be seen along the roadside. Lopez swerved toward the rightmost lanes, accelerating even more to pass several vehicles lining up for the turn, horns protesting loudly behind them. Once he hit the exit lane, he floored the brake, pitching them forward in the cabin, cycles rattling loudly behind them.

They swerved into the turn far beyond the recommended off-ramp speed, Lopez fighting the wheel, G-forces slamming them toward the left side of the SUV as they whipped around the curve. Bags beside Lightfoote thudded into the left door as she clung to the headrests of the front seats. Exploding through the turn, Lopez raced through a stop sign, narrowly missing several cars crossing the intersection. Tires screeched in their wake.

"Awesome!" cried Lightfoote as they bounced through a narrow road, old buildings rising like walls on either side of the car.

Lopez continued to decelerate. Already the highway was lost to sight. As they approached a four-way, he turned left and brought the SUV to a stop on a deserted street.

"Move!" he yelled, opening the door and leaping out.

Houston followed, her limp nearly gone. Inside, Lightfoote bent over the back seat, reaching toward the flatbed. She worked frantically at the restraints on the cycles. The back doors opened, and Lopez slung several heavy bags to the ground.

"Sara, set the charges," he said as Houston caught up, then leaned into the SUV interior. "Angel, are they free?"

"Yes!"

"In three, two, one!"

Lightfoote grunted inside as Lopez pulled on one of the bikes. The motorcycle rolled backward and careened out of the truck. He steadied it as it hit, wheels bouncing on the cobblestone road inches from Houston's face as she crouched over a large, black bag, a detonator in her hand.

"Number two!" cried Lightfoote.

The second motorcycle bounced down onto the street, Lightfoote following it out. Both vehicles were pitch black, even the metallic elements covered in a dark matt material. Black helmets were snapped into holders near the back of the seats.

Lightfoote leapt on one cycle, quickly donning the helmet. "The bat-bike!" she called.

Lopez handed her a heavy backpack, and she strapped it on. He swung his leg over the other cycle, handing the second helmet to Houston as she exited the van.

"Ready?" he asked, motioning toward the SUV.

She nodded, strapping on a second backpack, and taking the helmet from him. "Where's yours?"

"They didn't plan for three. Don't worry—likely the safest thing we're doing this week."

Lightfoote laughed. "They're quiet too. Light. Stealth Harley's next."

Her engine was running, but the sound was minimal. Lopez pressed a button and started his cycle, hardly feeling the motor.

"Electric, remember? More than enough juice to get us to Ooster-beek." His head whipped to the side. "Listen!" The unmistakable sound of the Dutch sirens wailed from the distance.

"Let's go!" cried Lightfoote, gunning her cycle and ripping off down the street.

Houston wrapped an arm around Lopez, her other grasping a small metallic box. "Go, Francisco!"

Their bikes raced past the SUV and down the hill. As they approached an intersection, Lightfoote banked left and turned, soon lost from view. Houston held up her free hand, the other anchoring her to Lopez, a red light winking in her palm barely visible in the growing sunlight. As they turned the corner, she detonated the charge.

The SUV exploded. A fireball rose into the air, fragments of the vehicle raining around the ancient street along with smoke and ash. Blue flashing lights approached the raging fire from down the road, the police vehicles slowing to a stop. One officer opened his door some fifty meters away and gawked at the inferno in front of him.

Racing back onto the highway, the two motorcycles merged with the rest of the morning traffic. Houston turned her head and stared behind them. A cloud of smoke rose from the receding town and into the sky.

"Tracks covered," she said, flipping a black sun visor over her eyes.

They raced south.

53

PIT STOP

"We're barely halfway through Kansas and the engine's overheating?"

York stood near the front of the RV, gazing down on the gauges. The engine light flashed while the thermometer danced in the red.

"We shouldn't have pushed it after we saw the helicopter," said Cohen, the RV's speed now dropped to fifty-five.

"It was definitely checking us out," said Savas. "I'm glad there's a little more traffic out here than Barric predicted."

"At least he got *something* right," said York. "I think his opinion of his mechanical skill is a little inflated. This thing's held together with wire and string!" Her lips pursed. "We're going to have to pull over, check the engine coolant, radiator. We can't have the damn thing blow on us. We'll be stuck."

"Pull over?" said Cohen.

"I think so. Do we want to risk losing the RV?"

Cohen looked at Savas. "What was it I said about plans?"

He ignored her. "Last sign said there's a stop a few miles down the road. We do it like a pit stop. Off road to a garage, have someone look at it, assuming anyone's there. Otherwise we do our best. Anyone a grease monkey? No? Wonderful."

"We don't have a choice, I'm afraid," said York. "We'll risk exposure, but nothing like the exposure we'd get broken down on the side of the road."

Several miles later, the dilapidated RV exited on a curved ramp and spiraled to a red light, gas stations and restaurants surrounding them. Savas pointed to a large station with a visible garage, and Cohen steered the camper to the lot on the light change. To their great surprise, they saw a crowd of people there.

"I don't get it," said Savas as Cohen stopped the vehicle in front of the empty garage. "No cars. The pumps are out. Look—a sign says *No Gas*. What's going on?"

"Phone!" said York. "Inside, through the window. A woman is talking on the phone."

"The line is for the phone?" asked Savas.

Cohen nodded. "Of course. The Bosworths said everything was down. Cells, landlines. Looks like this place has one of the few working lines around. And everybody knows about it."

A rap on the window startled Cohen. She spun the handle and rolled down the glass to stare at an older man in a greased jumpsuit.

"Overheating?"

Cohen smile. "Yes, how'd—"

"These old campers are awful. Hundred dollars says it's a coolant hose."

"Can you fix it?"

"Well, I'll have to take a look. But likely, ma'am. We got a lot of rubber that will patch you for a while until you can get it looked at properly."

York leaned over and whispered to Cohen. "Get her fixed. I'm going to that phone."

Savas turned to her. "What?"

"A working phone, John. I can reach NORAD. If I can, I *have* to. Tell them I'm alive. Where we are. That we're coming. To send *help*."

"You'll be recognized."

"Possibly. I don't have my TV crew to doll me up, and I've lost some weight from this adventure. But maybe. I'll have to risk it."

"Jesus." He looked at Cohen. "We're way off plan. All right then, Ms. President. You're the Commander in Chief. But I'm going with you."

The pair left Cohen with the mechanic, the hood already up and his torso obscured within the engine. The line stretched outside the convenience store and around the station, stragglers converging from random directions to extend the line on a regular basis. Ignoring hostile looks, Savas pushed his way through the store doors and walked past the line to the register. York held up her hand and he let her approach the counter.

"Excuse me, sir," she said, her voice ringing with an authority and grasping the clerk's attention.

A young man with several days' worth of stubble walked over. "Sorry, ma'am," he began, "no service. We're out of everything."

"I need your phone. It's an emergency."

The clerk's face darkened. Grumblings came from the line. "Well, ma'am, lots of folk got need of that phone. It's the only one east of Colby that's workin'. We got a line."

"It's a matter of national security," said Savas.

The grumbling became much louder.

"Yeah, right!" laughed one.

"Back of the line, grandma!" someone shouted.

"My son's sick!" came a woman's voice.

"It's York! It's President York!"

The room fell silent. All eyes centered on her, the clerk squinting and leaning forward.

"I'll be damned," he said.

Whispers ran like a wind hitting a wall of trees. York turned to face them, the oversized coat from the Bosworth attic swallowing her like a steal from a thrift shop. Savas instinctively backed away, giving her the spotlight.

"I *am* President Elaine York."

Savas let out a soft whistle and turned away from the crowd. He angled his body to York and whispered. "Might as well throw up a sign that says 'Bomb here.'"

York ignored him. "I am your elected leader. I'm here right now because there's been a military coup, one you've likely heard something about. I fled Washington, chased by the same people who bombed Kansas City." People murmured. "I'm going to Cheyenne Mountain, to the NORAD bunker to lead a resistance. But I'm not there yet. I need your help. I need that phone to reach them. They need to know I'm alive, that

I'm on my way. I need them to send help." She walked up to the landline, a brunette holding the receiver staring at her open-mouthed. "The fate of the country might just depend on me making that phone call."

"I'm sorry, Chief Kruger, but I'll call you back." The woman hung up the phone and stepped back.

"Thank you," said York. She removed the receiver and dialed.

~

THE MECHANIC SLAMMED the hood down and wiped his hands on a towel.

"And that, pretty lady, is how you do it. It's a patch, jerry-rigged, but anything's better than the leaky hose you had. You'd lost most of your coolant oil. You were lucky you got this far."

"She's good to go?" asked Cohen, a growing wind tossing her brown hair across her face.

"Yep. I topped it off. You got more gas than you ought'a be carryin', so don't think you need anything else." The mechanic turned his head to look behind Cohen, distracted. "What the hell?"

York and Savas walked toward them, a giant crowd following behind. Cohen stared back and squinted into the wind.

"Oh, lovely."

The clerk raced up and grabbed the mechanic's thick arm.

"It's *York*," he said, giddy. "*President* York!"

The mechanic nodded as the crowd came to a stop in front of him. He extended his hand.

"Mighty honored to meet you, sir. Uh, ma'am."

"You get us straightened out?"

Momentarily star-struck, he tried to recover. "Um, yes ma'am. Busted hose like I thought. You're all set."

York turned to the crowd. "All of you, I'm going to repeat what I said. Don't follow us. Don't tell anyone you've seen us. I mean it. We have killers chasing us. The same killers who murdered half a million people in Kansas City. People some of you knew. If they find us, they will kill us. If you follow or speak about us, it will make it that much easier for them to track us down." The crowd remained silent, stunned. "Whether you like it or not, you've just been drafted into a war. In wars, loose lips sink ships.

Help me get to NORAD. Pretend you never saw me. Go back to the line, call your loved ones. Take care of your emergencies. I promise you, I will fight to get this country back, and to bring justice to those monsters who have violated every decency."

The crowd applauded. Savas turned away and sighed.

"Great. Let's just send up a flare to attract more attention."

York waved quickly and stepped into the RV. Savas and Cohen followed. The crowd inched forward, unconsciously attracted to the vehicle.

"Try not to run them over, okay Rebecca?" said York.

"You reached NORAD?"

"Yes," York replied as she buckled in behind the booth. Savas lingered at the rear window, gazing outside. "They know the key details—what happened, where we are, where we're headed and how. I didn't dare stay on longer than to get a promise they'd pull out all the stops to help us."

Cohen nodded and started the engine. "Readings look good. Let's try to meet them halfway." She pulled out and turned onto the road, heading for the on-ramp to I-70. "I have to say, that was something. *Uplifting*. To find so many people behind you, supporting you."

"Not everyone," said Savas, his brows furrowed as he returned to the front.

"Trouble?" asked York.

"Several characters left soon after you were revealed to the crowd. They slunk out the back. Didn't look like their roots were in Kansas. When you were in the middle of that nice speech, an SUV with tinted windows pulled up across the street."

Cohen checked the rearview. "It's behind us!"

Savas grasped the handle of the shotgun by his side. "We've got company."

54

ON THE SCENT

T he Director of the Bilderberg Group lay back in a plush chair, his head indenting the black leather, eyes closed. His heavy jowls hung slack, his mottled skin resembling some snake's hide in the dim light. Flashes of light splashed across his dark features as an alert tone sounded on the computer in front of him. Slowly, struggling to summon the energies of motion, his eyes opened, the gray eyebrows twitching, and for several seconds he simply stared at the blinking light. Then he leaned forward and pressed a key.

"Director," he rasped.

Static hissed over the speakers, and a snowy image of a man with a chiseled jaw appeared on the screen.

"Fox team beta, sir. We've found her."

The Director raised a pair of eyeglasses to the bridge of his nose with a shaking hand. "What? *York?* She *survived?* Are you sure?"

"We have two confirmed sightings by assets on the ground and we pulled the surveillance video from a gas station near Colby, Kansas. That's about an hour from the Colorado border. There's no doubt."

"My God."

"It's worse, sir." The snowy reception garbled the man's words and face. "There was a working landline, one of the first restored to service.

We intercepted transmissions over the local network from your monitoring stations. She's contacted NORAD. They know she's coming."

"Dammit!" The Director pounded his armrest, falling back into his
seat and closing his eyes.

"We have a vehicle in pursuit and several more en route. It's four
hours to Cheyenne Mountain. That's a lot of time to handle the problem,
sir."

His eyes remained closed. "Call in all available assets. Pull aircraft off
anything else. If we have a fighter plane left I want her blown off the
highway."

"Ahead of you, sir. The front is decimated. NORAD controls most of
the airspace and we can't launch anything without them knowing."

"There must be something. We need something in the air."

"We're working on it. We might can commandeer local craft. It's our
only option."

He sat up and rubbed his eyes. "Do whatever you have to do. Run her
off the road. Firebomb her car. *Anything*. She can't be allowed to reach the
mountain. Terminate with extreme prejudice."

"Understood, sir. Will keep you informed."

The image clicked off and the Director sighed. He initiated another
video call, and the Middle Eastern woman appeared on the screen.

"Director," she said, her hair full and uncombed behind her, a silk
evening gown on her shoulders.

"Maryam, the news is bad, it seems—"

"A moment." She stood up, carrying the camera with her, the figure of
a powerfully built man naked in the bed. A door closed behind her,
cutting off the bedroom. "Good morning."

"Morning for you. It hasn't quite arrived here. And there isn't much
good to be had." She remained expressionless. "They've found York. She's
alive and making a run for Colorado."

Her dark face turned to the side and she cursed in a language he
couldn't understand. "Is there no way to kill that bitch?"

"We have assets in pursuit. She's exposed."

"Yet nothing is certain."

He nodded. "The real danger is her reaching NORAD, sealing herself
in the bunker, and surviving what's coming. Unless we find a way to kill

her now, or cut off NORAD completely, she could wage a war of ideas against us."

"What good will it do? There will be nothing left of the nation. She can summon an army of rocks and the radiation-poisoned."

He shook his head. "That's not the danger. It's Europe and Asia. If she can reach them, she could disrupt the world with that megaphone."

"If the assets fail, can we accelerate the program? Initiate it before she reaches the bunker?"

"No," he said firmly. "Zero must be out. It takes time."

"Then we'd better hope your men finish the job on the ground today, Director. I will brief the others."

She smiled coldly as the connection closed. The old man exhaled and once again crashed backward into his chair.

Damn these women.

55

WARTHOG

"There's a second one!" shouted Savas from the back of the vehicle. The RV screamed as Cohen pushed it past seventy. She glanced down at the gauges.

"We're running hot again!"

"How bad?" shouted Savas, moving to the front of the camper.

"Just in the red. But she can't take much more of this."

York loaded shells in a pearl-handled, double-barreled shotgun from the Bosworth collection. "No choice, sister. Those two trucks aren't looking to parlay." She slammed the barrels shut with a snap.

"Absolutely not!" said Savas to York. "Put the gun away. If they make a move, you're going to stay out of sight. You're the target. Don't be crazy!"

"We're not going to let them make a move," she said. "We're going to move on them first."

"Elaine—"

York looked sideways down the window along the side of the RV. "Your husband always have this problem with authority?"

"Pretty much," said Cohen.

"You want to let me drive, Rebecca?"

"I'm the analyst. He's Rambo."

"Then it's settled," said York. "This rig won't auto-pilot. We need as many guns as we can. I'm shooting."

Savas sighed. "Perfect."

"Second one is closing. It's going to be soon. Since you're worried I'm too delicate for combat, you take the rear window and I'll cover our flank."

"Back window is jammed, remember?"

York cocked her head to one side. "What do you think the shotgun is for? Bosworth will understand."

Savas moved quickly to the back as York rolled down the window beside her. The roar of rushing air thundered into the RV. He kept to the side of the window to avoid being seen by the SUV tailing them. Crouched beside it, he signaled to York with his fingers, and mouthed, "Three, two, one..."

He sprang backward, aiming the gun, and turned his head. A deafening explosion roared through the vehicle, dust and debris clouding the air. Most of the blast carried outward, slamming into the onrushing SUV. The truck stuttered and swerved, the driver nearly losing control. Savas pumped the action.

"The other's overtaking us!" cried York.

He pulled the trigger again, aiming the twelve-gauge through the window as the pursuing vehicle closed the gap. The front windshield of the SUV shattered directly in front of the driver, a hole the size of a fist punctured in the glass. A cloud of red burst inside and coated the windows, the truck veering violently to the right. It flipped, rolling wildly, and was quickly lost to sight as it smashed to a stop.

Two blasts in short succession followed from the front of the RV. Savas heard a tire explode, followed by the careening form of the second SUV veering into the median and plowing into the concrete separator.

"Good shooting, agent Savas!" cried York triumphantly.

"Two more trucks!" cried Savas. He dove to the floor and yelled to York: "Down, down, down!"

York dropped underneath the booth table. Bullets exploded through the camper. Windows shattered, glass fragments raining on the ancient carpet and upholstery. Cohen cried out as the rearview mirror popped. An engine roared and as the blade beats of a helicopter boomed from the left

Cohen shouted again. Instinctively, she swerved to an approaching off ramp, trying to slow the RV and control the exit.

"Sorry!" she screamed. "I thought it would ram us!"

"Forcing us off the highway," cried Savas, rushing to the back of the camper. "Got a little distance, but the SUVs are following. Helicopter is banking for another pass."

"Can you get a shot at it?" cried York.

"Maybe," he said, "but they've got automatic weapons. I won't last long enough to aim."

York turned and looked ahead through the front window. "Where are they herding us?"

Cohen sounded defeated. "Local road. Two-lane. Nothing but farms and fields."

"Take the on-ramp?" called Savas. "Quickly!"

Cohen turned sharply right onto the two-lane road. "Can't! Black SUV at the bottom of it waiting!" She accelerated, the lumbering vehicle rocking back and forth.

"Our bird is back," said York, grimacing. "What the hell is it doing?"

The craft sped in front of them, passing overhead and down the road for some distance. It turned and banked sharply, half a circle until it had aligned itself with the road again.

"Oh, shit," said York. The helicopter dropped altitude and hovered just a few feet over the road. "John, those SUVs still behind?"

"Closing the gap. It's going be a shooting gallery in a few seconds!"

"What do I do?" cried Cohen, the bulk of the helicopter approaching quickly.

"Side road!" shouted York. "There!"

Cohen swerved. Dust clouded the air behind her as the RV skidded on the dirt and pebble road. She fought the wheel and centered the vehicle, catching her breath as the uneven surface flung them up and down.

"SUVs following!" cried Savas from behind. He hung on like some trapeze artist to the bunk beds as the vehicle lurched side to side.

"That house," said York, top of the hill. "If we can make it we can go to ground there. Fight them off."

"It's too far," whispered Cohen. "We're too slow on this road!"

"Hush, child! Don't think! Do!" York stepped up and strapped herself in beside Cohen. "Gun it! Make for the driveway. Ram the gate!"

The sounds of the helicopter had returned, higher but still in pursuit.

"They're almost on us," yelled Savas. A shotgun blast sounded from the back. It elicited return machine gun fire, strafing the top level of the camper.

York pointed forward. "Rebecca, look out—"

The camper pitched forward. Savas was thrown toward the front, his form flying through the corridor and slamming into the back of the passenger-side seat. The RV shuddered, the nose diving down, the windshield darkening and shattering like a spider web. They reeled sideways and the camper fell on its side, sliding to a rending stop in a fog of dust and raining pebbles.

"John!" cried Cohen as she fought with her seatbelt. She crawled along the left wall of the camper, coughing in the thick dust. He lay unmoving, blood covering his face. A strong reek of gasoline filled the air.

York called, "We've got to get out! The front glass—it's peeled half back. Help me out!"

Torn between the unconscious Savas and York, Cohen paused, paralyzed. She turned to the front. York was suspended sideways above her in the passenger seat, the belt the only thing keeping her from tumbling down. Cohen braced the president's form with her shoulder and wrapped her arms around her.

"Release the belt," she said.

The belt clicked and the full weight of York's body pushed Cohen downward. She cushioned the older woman's fall with a grunt. They turned and kicked violently the remaining sheet of shattered glass, peeling it further from the window.

Dirt continued to spill slowly into the camper, and they could see an abandoned, unplowed field in front of them. York grabbed her gun and turned to Cohen.

"Pull him out," she coughed, the fumes thick and pungent. "This thing could go up like a bomb any second. Those bastards are likely right outside by now. I'll do my best."

Cohen stared at her in disbelief but needed no prodding to turn back to Savas. The old woman groaned as she wedged herself out the empty window frame, the gun dragged behind her.

The air above brightened with a flash of orange, and a rending, ground-shaking explosion shook the RV. York squinted, adopting a bent crouch, the gun aimed as she pivoted to survey her surroundings. Off to her right, a fireball plunged from the sky and exploded a second time on impacting a neighboring field. A powerful engine rushed over her head, and the shadow of a muscular aircraft darkened the sun. The wreckage of the helicopter burned in front of her.

When the plane had passed, York turned to look behind the camper. The men were rushing back to the SUVs, planting themselves behind it for cover, aiming machine guns upward. They opened fire as the engine noise returned. York followed their aim. Swooping in over the field like some demonic crop duster, a plane rushed right toward them, heedless of their gunfire.

York gasped. The plane opened fire from the nose, a trail of light spewing from a hunting dragon. A deep grating sound battered her ears. The SUVs and men around it simply exploded.

Not from a bomb or missile, but from the impact of thousands of rounds of heavy ammunition. The bodies were blown apart in puffs of red, flesh and limbs spraying behind them. The vehicles similarly disintegrated, metal filleted off the chassis, the gas tanks igniting and torching the remainder.

The aircraft passed over the scene of destruction like a bird of prey, and banked once more, coming in low over the neighboring field with wheels visible. It was landing.

York lowered her shotgun and leaned against it, sweat and grime smearing her clothes. "About damn time."

56

HOTEL DE BILDERBERG

Three shadows crouched in the thick foliage at the forest's edge, a manicured expanse of green erupting before them and crashing into a white and gray chalet-style structure. Bright walls trimmed with dark balconies and rain gutters were offset by a purple-tinged shingled roof. Two prominent gables fought for attention along the front of the structure, one centered over the window-studded ground floor entrance, large words in cursive script decorating its center: *Hotel de Bilderberg*.

Lightfoote placed a hand on Houston's left shoulder. "And you're sure that's the last of the security?"

Houston nodded. "Key was taking out the central power line. We could have played peek-a-boo with those motion sensors and cameras all day and still been spotted. But they didn't wire it redundantly. So, *pop*, find the main power line and cut it before it can branch out. Forest goes blind."

"I really need to hang out more with you two," said Lightfoote.

"We've seen a little more of this than we'd like," said Houston.

On Houston's right, Lopez scanned the grassy field in front of them through binoculars. "Any minute now they're going to notice the system's down. The security on the building is still doing fine, I'm sure."

"So we wait for them to come to us," said Houston.

"Then what?" asked Lightfoote.

"We'll see," said Lopez. "We'll either get a leg up or have to make a mad dash, and then all hope for surprise is gone. It'll be a first-person shooter at that point."

Houston took the binoculars from Lopez and made her own appraisal of the grounds. "Let's hope a leg up. And look, just in time." She offered Lightfoote the lens.

Lightfoote focused below. "Two redshirts."

"Redshirts?" asked Lopez.

Lightfoote looked over the binoculars at him. "Star Trek? Security guys that always beam down but don't beam up?" Lopez shook his head and shrugged. "Never mind." She turned her attention back to the approaching figures. "Two men. One's muscle. Well trained, fit, and he's packing. The other's not. He's clumsy. A technician I'd bet."

Lopez spoke to Houston. "Charges prepped?"

She nodded. "It's modified. More flash than bang."

"Assuming you got it right." He looked at Lightfoote. "She's our resident *untrained* explosives operative."

Houston shoved him upright. "Not by choice. Now, let's get in position."

Each grabbed a bag from the ground. They moved quietly twenty yards to the right, hugging the forest edge and keeping the two guards in sight. As the men reached the woods, the three of them lowered to the ground behind a large bush and fallen log. The power line snaked into the forest in front of them.

The Bilderberg workers approached. A heavyset man kneeled before the main cable, shaking his head and gesturing to a frayed gap in the line. A short conversation followed, the features of the trim man clouding with concern. He nodded and reached into his pocket and retrieved a mobile phone.

"Now, Sara," whispered Lopez.

"Look away!" she hissed back.

They turned their faces and shut their eyes. A blinding flash and a sharp crack sent the two men falling to the ground, writhing and moaning.

The three figures in black pounced: leaping over the fallen tree, they fell on the prone figures like tigers. After a brief contest, the two Bilderberg agents lay incapacitated and unconscious, hog-tied and gagged with duct tape.

"Got his cell," said Houston, tossing a roll of tape onto a black bag beside her. "Any of you understand this?" She held the phone up.

Lightfoote shook her head. Lopez laughed. "This is our lucky day. Guess the unemployment rate is pushing people out of southern Europe." He took the phone from her. "It's Spanish."

Houston smiled. "I think what he was planning to write was *shut the outer security system down*. Power linkage, need to isolate systems. Sound believable?"

"Maybe," said Lopez. "Let's see how it works."

As Lopez texted, Lightfoote continued to search the men, pulling out IDs and weapons. She called up to Houston. "Cards are magnetized. Might get lucky with them inside." Houston nodded. Lightfoote held up a black gun. "Another pistol."

"Looks like a Walther," said Houston. "Standard issue police pistol in these parts. German made."

"Good," said Lightfoote removing a shoulder holster from the man and fitting it to herself. "Never know when you're going to need a good German pistol."

"And the ruse pays off," said Lopez, shaking his head. "They're dropping the system for five minutes. They're sending backup. Guess they're nervous."

Lightfoote stood up and smiled. "A leg up."

"Maybe two," said Lopez. "Let's go."

They zipped up the backpacks and strapped them over their shoulders, leaping out of the woods and down the steep grass incline. Houston trailed behind, her leg slowing her pace. Pistols gleamed in their hands, eyes flashing between the ground and the door to the extended wing of the hotel to keep balance.

Lightfoote and Lopez reached the side of the building first, and the former priest reached into his black robes to remove a metallic canister, spraying black the lens of a camera mounted on the wall. Houston caught up with them, her face dripping with sweat. She placed her back along the wall, gun held to the side of her head, aimed up.

Lightfoote backed away from the hinges, hugging the wall as well. "Opens outward," she whispered. "I hear movement. They're coming."

At her last word, the door to the hotel swung toward her, and two men in suits exited. Each had a wired earpiece and showed a firearms bulge in their tailored jackets. They never got the opportunity to reach for them.

Lightfoote and Lopez caught them utterly flatfooted, a fury of disabling strikes bringing the pair down. The man beside Lightfoote had taken a heel to the back of his head and lay sprawled in front of her. Lopez followed a split second later, a powerful punch to the abdomen loudly cracking a rib, his target doubling over. He grabbed the man's head with his other hand and drove it into his knee. The body fell heavily to the ground.

Houston had already darted inside. "Clear!" she said, waving them in. "Francisco, get those bodies in here before we attract attention. Angel—"

"The transformer. On it." Lightfoote removed a gray block and set of wires from a bag and sprinted along the side of the hotel.

As Houston kept watch, Lopez dragged the unconscious bodies inside. The door opened to a small vestibule, revealing a second doorway. He tied up the pair and sealed their mouths with tape. His eyes darted sharply as the inner door clicked. Houston stood beside it, an ID card in her hand from one of the employees, the door open.

The building shook violently and a blast ruptured the air around them. The lights inside cut, the door making a loud and final metallic clip. The hallway behind it turned red from emergency lighting.

Houston tossed the ID to the floor. "Glad I tried this before Angel blew the thing."

Lightfoote bounded through the doorway panting. "Main transformer's down. Unless they've got a backup generator, power's dead for a good bit."

"Power looks out here," said Lopez, checking the mag on his sidearm, "but you can bet what's below has a redundant source. Question is how stable, and how long until it kicks in."

Houston moved down the hallway. "It won't matter if we don't find a way to get down there. This was the wired wing. The entrance is here, somewhere."

A sound of scraping metal screamed from the corridor, and they instinctively crouched and aimed. Two men bounded into the hallway space, weapons drawn, seeming to materialize out of the wall itself.

A storm of gunfire greeted them. The three invaders held the advantage, the Bilderberg guards shaken from the blast and orienting to the hallway. They were hit with multiple gunshots before they could even pinpoint the location of their attackers. One managed a wild shot into the ceiling. Their bodies fell heavily to the ground, groans escaping from one of them.

Three panthers bounded forward. One of their targets was clearly dead, two shots having struck him in the heart. Lightfoote crouched beside the other who moaned, crawling forward, a crimson soup pouring from his stomach and neck.

"He's bleeding out." She rose. "We move."

Blood splattered the corridor walls but for an opening in one panel, revealing a passageway down. A set of spiraling metallic stairs raced away from them into a red light that dimmed to a fog below. Shouts and the sounds of running feet echoed upward from the stone walls.

A door beside them opened, and the terrified countenance of a black woman stared at them. Houston pointed the barrel of her gun down the hallway. "Go," she said. The woman tore down the plush carpeting, dodging the bodies in front of her.

Lopez removed a pair of grenades. "Clear."

The two women stepped backward and away from the opening as he pulled the pins. He dropped them immediately along the sides of the stairwell, a two-foot buffer between the railing and the wall allowing them to fall without impediment nearly the entire depth of the shaft. He jumped away from the opening, placing his back against the wall.

Loud clanks followed, a cry of surprise from below, and two nearly simultaneous explosions vibrating the walls. Smoke poured up through the shaft and into the corridor. Screams of pain came with it.

"Leg up," said Lightfoote, stepping through the opening. She descended rapidly.

57

ESCORT TO THE MOUNTAINS

"Bad time for a selfie?" mumbled Savas. Blood stained his face and clothes, gauze and tape in and around his swollen nose.

"You might say," said Cohen, her tone flat as she tossed aside several bloody tissues.

"Camper packs a hell of a right hook," he said.

He looked up to the crowd around him—Cohen, the president, and an Air Force pilot in heavy gear. An oak tree towered above him, the broad branches spreading over their heads like an umbrella. Behind them gleamed the hull of a powerful aircraft. Several hundred feet to his right, a foul smoke continued to poison the air from the flaming remains of the vehicles. A blue commercial helicopter thundered in from the west.

The Air Force pilot turned to face York. "We've got to get you out, ma'am."

"On that?" asked York.

"All we had," said the pilot. "Not much of a selection out there right now. They called us in from across the front. Mopping up any of Hastings forces that didn't surrender and survived the bombing. I was given your vehicle description and told to neutralize anything else."

"You sure as hell did that," said York.

He indicated the approaching helicopter. "That bird was the only thing near enough—my Hog's a single seater."

York nodded. "Too bad. Yours is the plane I want."

The pilot smiled. "Smart call. She's a fortress. But I'll be escorting you if that helps."

The noise from the helicopter became deafening as it touched down several hundred feet from their position.

"Can you get up?" Cohen asked Savas.

"Have to," he groaned, grasping the tree trunk and rising unsteadily to his feet. She helped steady him as he grabbed her shoulder. Savas nodded to the pilot. "Fire her up. I'm coming."

The pilot instead escorted York directly to the helicopter. Savas and Cohen passed the huge airplane, the rugged exterior impressing upon them a lethal practicality. The hull and cockpit were heavily armored with thick plates of metal. Two hulking engines were mounted just in front of the tail, disproportionate to the body. The wings themselves were unusually thick and extended, housing underneath five or six missiles. Several slots were empty, the pilot likely having launched some of his arsenal already. An enormous Gatling gun was embedded in the nose of the plane.

"What the hell is this thing?" said Savas.

York climbed into the helicopter. The pilot turned back toward Savas, following his gaze to the plane. "A-10 Warthog. Hell of a fighting machine."

"That's a big gun."

He smiled. "Yes, sir. Made confetti out of your friends over there."

Savas looked slowly toward the skeletal forms of the SUVs. "Damn," he said, grabbing his neck. "I'm all kinds of beat up."

"Let's get you in the air, sir." With the pilot's help, Cohen eased Savas into the helicopter and he took a seat beside York. They buckled in, the A-10 pilot slamming the door shut and waving. He turned to jog back to his plane.

York spoke to the FBI agents. "Some interesting news from the pilot while John was down. We have assets in the Netherlands."

"They reached you?" asked Cohen.

"Not me, NORAD. Same folks as called in our escort. Seems your hacker busted into their system and demanded to speak to the brass."

"Angel. Then they're okay?" asked Savas roughly.

"They were, but all bets are off now. They tracked Bilderberg down.

Called in my directive to back them. Military and some remaining CIA support got them on the ground in Europe, flew them past Hastings. Now NORAD's lost contact. But they were headed to the hotel."

"Things move fast," said Cohen. "I hope they're right, and they can do something."

"We could use some victories right now," agreed York.

"Zhanna Mouradian, your pilot." A woman's voice came from the cockpit, her helmeted face briefly looking back into the cabin. "US Geological Survey, actually." She turned back to the controls and began to lift the craft off the ground. "Nothing to do with the pterodactyl over there. Called me in for my National Guard service. Proud to be carrying you, Ms. President."

"Just get me to the mountain," said York. "This bird can make it?"

"Yes, ma'am. We got about two hundred miles to travel and we're fully fueled. No problem."

York smirked. "Don't be so sure. There's been nothing but problems on this ride. Combat, nuclear weapons for God's sake. And firing shotguns out of an RV like it was some damned Old West wagon chase. Take *nothing* for granted. Some nasty folks want us dead."

The ground receded behind them and the helicopter banked sharply west. The roar of the A-10 rumbled around them as the airplane managed a takeoff from the empty fields behind. They watched the armored bird of prey gain altitude and turn in their direction.

"Well, ma'am, we've got the flying Terminator behind us, if it counts for anything."

The helicopter continued to climb rapidly. As the ground receded, the trio squinted into the bright light of the setting sun ahead of them. In the distance, the horizon blurred, a smear rising from the ground. Peaks formed at the top of the blur, some dusted with a faint white cap.

The Rocky Mountains.

58

STORMING THE FORTRESS

Weapons at the ready, they rushed down the spiral staircase, the smoke thickening as they descended. Fires flickered from where the blasts had ignited materials below. As they neared the bottom, Lightfoote stopped and held a hand up to stop Lopez and Houston.

"Ladder's disengaged."

The stairs stopped abruptly, exposing a ten-foot drop to the floor below. A ladder lay among the still forms of several bodies, its latch to the stairwell damaged by the explosions. A flashing red light from an alarm system strobed the walls around them.

"Watch the hallway."

Lightfoote holstered her pistol and turned her back to the passage. Bending and placing her hands near her feet, she grasped the edge of the last stair and swung down. Her hands anchored her to the stairwell for one swing before she let go to land a foot beyond one of the bodies on the ground. She drew her weapon and turned to the hallway, still crouched.

"Next!"

Lopez followed, his descent less acrobatic, his landing far heavier. While Lightfoote kept watch, he reached up and helped Houston down, softening the landing of her weak leg. Lightfoote moved toward a small booth. The window glass had been blown inward, a bloodied figure inside slumped over a security system. She reached in through the narrow doorway and pulled him off the chair, the corpse falling against the back wall.

The shattered remains of a panel of five monitors coated a long desk, only one still operating. It showed multiple camera views of the underground bunker. Lightfoote sat in the chair and put her pistol on the table surface, pulling a keyboard up from under the counter. Her hands flew over the keys, opening command line prompts, navigating her way through the system. A map of the structure's below-ground levels appeared, and Lightfoote had the video cameras zoom in on each room in succession.

"Only two floors," she said as Lopez and Houston looked on. "Look at this. It's like one giant server farm. Especially the second floor. Hundreds of computers stacked to the damn ceiling. The whole floor below is nothing but computers and this one room at the far end."

A plush office centered on the screen, three figures within it. A smaller shape moved arthritically but with authority. Beside him, two hulking men with wide stances stood at attention, one holding a weapon. The old man spoke on a telephone.

"If this were a video game," said Lightfoote, "he's the Big Boss."

Houston scoffed. "Camera's labeled *Director*."

"Other guards?" asked Lopez.

"Not finding any," said Lightfoote, racing through the feeds from different rooms. She paused on the stream from a large room, the space packed with office cubicles.

"Who are these guys?" asked Houston.

"Don't know," she said. "Room's right down the hall, though. We'll check it out." She squinted at the screen. "What are they doing?"

"Looks like they're hiding under their desks," said Lopez. "I don't think we'll need to worry about them."

"You were right about the security," said Houston as Lightfoote continued to roll through camera views of different rooms. "I don't think they had more than ten guards."

"For the seat of global power, this place is a little disappointing," said Lopez.

Lightfoote stood up and grabbed her gun. "I guess it's white collar crime. Push the banks, pull the politicians. Throw money around. All the dirty stuff happened outside these walls."

"Not anymore," said Houston. "Time to visit *The Director*."

Lightfoote nodded. "The map shows a stairwell in the middle of the hallway. Let's sweep this floor and make sure there are no surprises, then down."

"We should hurry," said Lopez. "Didn't see any other exits on the map, but the longer we wait, the longer they can plan for us below."

"Or bring in reinforcements," said Houston.

The three stepped back into the corridor. They formed a staggered line, spaced apart and giving room for each to react and maneuver. Lightfoote ran point, swinging into rooms in succession, verifying they were empty. Lopez took the middle, prepared to back Lightfoote if confronted by a hostile. He carried a pistol in his right hand, and with his left continued to spray the cameras along the way, cutting off any surveillance the Director might have from below. Houston brought up the rear, spending half her time pivoting to defend against an attack from behind.

The largest room on the floor waited at the end of the corridor. A sheet of glass took the place of a wall from waist high, revealing workers inside. As the camera had shown, they cowered in a packed office space littered with cubicles and desktop computers. Whiteboards full of scribbled equations lined the walls inside.

"What the hell is this place?" asked Houston from the hallway. "Some economics crisis center?"

The workers would not have appeared out of place in a Silicon Valley programming company or a mathematics department at an Ivy League school. Behind their cubicles, many flinched as Lightfoote entered.

"Who's in charge?" she barked, her weapon aimed slightly over their heads. Lopez stood behind her to increase the show of force as Houston continued to watch the hallway. "No one?" She fired a shot into the ceiling. People screamed.

"Gelieve, ons niet doden! Wij zijn slechts werknemers hier!" cried a man on her right.

"English! Who's in charge?"

"The Director!" came his accented voice. "The Director is in charge!"

She leveled her gaze at him. "And in this room?"

The man swallowed. "Ah, I am."

"What do you do here? Tell me now or I'll fucking end you!" She aimed her weapon at him.

The man began a high-pitched info download. "We run models! Economic models, world politics, national power and resources for the Director! We predict the nations, world economy!"

"Stop!" cried Lightfoote. "You run simulations on the servers? Models for Bilderberg?" He nodded. Lightfoote turned her head to Lopez and Houston. "This is it. These are the fucking Nash equations incarnate."

Lopez shook his head. "You mean the world's being run by a bunch of nerds crunching numbers?"

Houston laughed softly. "Plus the money and mercenaries."

Lightfoote turned back to the room. "Access codes, to all your systems."

"We can't give those—"

Lightfoote's pistol blasted an empty terminal beside the man.

"Godverdomme!" He screamed, his khaki slacks darkening around his crotch.

"I'm not asking. Last chance."

He grabbed a sheet of paper and scrawled madly on it. As he wrote Lightfoote walked up to him, keeping her gaze across the rest of the room, coming to a stop with her gun inches from his head. "Show me."

"Show you?"

"I see the codes. Log in. Show me what I'm getting. They better not fail."

The man sat down in front of a monitor and moused the screen saver away. He opened a series of windows, entering in usernames and pass-words for each.

"The first is the modeling system, *ja?* I have root access, I can access all inputs and results, all weights and fundamentals."

"The others?"

He swallowed, opening a window. "Bank access. National intelligence systems. Ah, other things." Sweat dripped from his face.

Lightfoote stared at the screen, her eyes wide. "Is there a terminal that gives me access below?"

"Yes, at the control desk for the farm."

"The backup power—how long will it last?"

The man looked like he wanted to cry. "I don't know. This has never happened."

Houston cried from the hallway. "Let's move, Angel. Seal them inside. I've rigged a little deterrent."

"One more thing," she called back to Houston. Lightfoote went to the main power strips, following several cables to sockets in the walls. She spoke over her shoulder to Lopez, "Watch them." Placing her gun on the ground, she removed a sharp knife from her belt. One by one, she removed the plugs and beheaded them, cutting off the pronged ends. A minute later all the monitors in the room were dark, the computers without power. She tossed the plugs out in the hallway.

"Your mobile devices. I want to see each of you bring me one. And I don't want to find out that even one was left out." She placed an empty box on a table and turned to the man in front of her. "Explain it to them."

He did. Eagerly, with terrified expressions, the workers brought smartphones and tablets and dropped them into the box. After the last, Lopez carried it into the hallway.

"We're going to go down this stairway, but I wouldn't recommend trying to follow us or go get help. Sara?"

Houston banged on the glass and the heads of those inside darted toward the window. Her muffled voice spoke from the hallway. "This is a *detonator*. It's tied to a block of explosives right there," she indicated, pointing behind the wall. "When we close the door, don't open it! It will trigger the bomb. *Boom.*" She paused for effect. "You'll all go home to mother in a bag."

"Now, under your desks! And stay there!"

The figures didn't need to be told twice. They scrambled to move chairs and fit themselves within the cubicles. Lightfoote closed the door and examined the wires Houston had rigged. The detonator didn't connect to anything.

"I thought so."

Houston raised an eyebrow. "You didn't think I'd risk sealing off our only exit?"

"And we might need the explosives below," said Lopez opening the door to the stairwell. "Here we go."

DECAPITATION STRIKE

The stairs opened to a dark room punctuated by thousands of blinking lights and a heavy hum. Seeing the server farm on the cameras was one thing, but standing in the midst of it like Theseus in the labyrinth plunged them into an electronic sea. The individual servers, their fans and hard drives, the electrical coils and transformers used in power supplies and motherboards, even the vibrations of the metal chassis, multiplied by thousands of units created a strong, constant wind modulated by a droning heartbeat.

A clear corridor through the server racks led straight ahead and Lightfoote followed the path toward the center of the room. They passed numerous rows fanning sideways, the passageways lined with rack after rack of processors, resembling a cybernetic public library. Overhead, air conditioning vents blasted air into the frigid space, as if the units funneled the wintery chill outside directly into the building.

The canyons of computer racks stopped abruptly and they stepped into an open space. A large table with numerous monitors greeted them. Uneaten food and coffee mugs sat perched at the sides, one still steaming.

"Looks like the techies made for the hills," said Houston.

Lopez scanned around them and up to the ceiling, moving quickly to spray-paint a camera above them. "This place is an electricity black hole. They have to have other generators somewhere."

"I'm going into their system. Keep an eye out." Lightfoote sat down in front of the keyboard. She placed the paper with the scrawled codes on her left and began to type furiously.

Lopez and Houston kept vigil, back-to-back with weapons out. In the white noise and hum, they began to lose their sense of time and space. Each found themselves anchoring their position on the other, the table beside them, and on the repetitive clacking of the keys.

"This is amazing," called out Lightfoote. "They have direct links to the major world financial centers, biggest banks, trading floors, the Federal Reserve. I mean superuser type privileges, complete access and control. Right here I could change money flow across continents, manipulate stocks and trading. It's all automated, the Nash equations steering everything to preset ends, but I could also go in manual, too."

"Chase Bank, account 5748395033. I'd like to be a billionaire please," said Houston, her eyes on the passageways in front of her.

Lopez mirrored her scanning. "Darling, don't you remember, Uncle Sam froze all your accounts last year?"

"Those bastards."

"Listen!" said Lightfoote. "It's not just the banks and exchanges. That neckbeard was right. They have access and control of intelligence, even *military* systems. It's a click away—Homeland Security, DOD, CIA. Records, accounts, agents in the field." The clacking continued. "Oh my God." She pushed the chair back from the table.

Houston turned toward her, lowering her sidearm. "What, Angel?"

"Holy shit. They're plugged into the fucking nuclear arsenal. NORAD, submarines, satellites. They have the president's *access codes*, complete targeting control. They could launch a nuclear war against anyone they wanted."

"That's about as bad as it gets," said Lopez.

"Actually, it isn't," said Lightfoote, back at the keyboard and squinting at the screen. "Because if I'm understanding this readout, they *are* launching a nuclear war. Right now."

"What?" said Houston, her face incredulous.

Lightfoote continued to type. "There's access to multiple silos in the US, upload of target coordinates. Some kind of timer waiting for a signal."

"What signal?"

Lightfoote shook her head. "I don't know. It's not clear. Waiting for some kind of communication inbound."

"Trigger what, exactly?" asked Lopez, leaning toward the screen, his face grim.

A list of names and numbers scrolled before them. "Armageddon," said Lightfoote. "New York, Washington, Chicago, LA, Houston, Philly." The list continued to scroll. "*Jesus,* it must be twenty or thirty sites. Key population centers, government, military targets, oil, gas, mineral deposits. It's a crippling strike. From within. With our *own* missiles. USA cluster*fucked*. Gone."

"For God's sake, why?" asked Lopez.

Lightfoote shook her head. "I don't know. Only, look. Something here in the modeling programs. See? Two networks of lines in this global map. The gray web looks like what we calculated in the hacker bunker—Bilderberg at the center, nodes at major centers of power. But look—here in color, like some new world order, the web is broken. The New York node is gone. *Nothing* connects to the US. The other nodes re-balance with different weights and connections."

"It's like they're cutting off the United States," said Houston. "Putting it in a coma."

"Which is exactly what you'd expect to happen if there were a nuclear decapitation strike," said Lightfoote.

Lopez looked around. "We don't have much time. We've got to get to the office and capture the Director, whoever he is."

"Agreed," said Houston. "We've given him too much time, already. And maybe he knows how to stop this. Come on!"

"No!" said Lightfoote glaring up at the pair. "You two go. This is too close. Once a signal is sent, whatever it is, there isn't much time to stop it. I've got to see what I can do here while I still have access. Before they lock me out or this server farm fails."

"Or before someone comes up and shoots you in the back of the head," said Houston.

"You think you can stop it?" asked Lopez.

"I don't know!" said Lightfoote.

Houston gestured around them. "You'll be blind here, Angel. Vulnerable."

"Gotta risk it," she said turning back to the screen, her fingers working the keyboard. "It really looks like these maniacs are serious."

Lopez stared at Houston, who reluctantly nodded. "If you think you've got a chance to interfere with an attack, do it," he said. "Sara and I will take care of the Director."

Lightfoote shot them a quick glance. "Be careful! I don't want to save the damn world again if you two aren't going to be in it."

60

CHARLIE FOXTROT

"We've lost twenty-three silos!" came a voice from the back of the Command Center.

Admiral Myers' thick hair danced in disarray, the gray like an explosion from a geyser. To exacerbate the chaos, he repeatedly grabbed chunks and yanked them mercilessly, glaring down at the terminals in front of him. "I can't believe this is happening. Morris—anything on the subs?"

Another voice called out from behind him. "Negative, sir. All the boats are quiet."

"Any targeting info?"

"No, sir. Not yet. We're getting the data now, but so far, just the silo readings. And things are definitely powering up."

"Sir, we've got a live stream from Montana."

"Put it up."

Myers glanced up to the giant monitors in the front of the Command Center. A grainy video appeared on one of them, the image of two men in a small room furiously working the control panels. Some panels had been torn out, wires dangling.

"These boys trying to sabotage the thing?" asked Myers.

A man below him at the desk looked up. "Believe so, Admiral."

Deputy Commander Duval walked into the Command Center trailed by three others. He headed straight for Myers.

"Any pattern?" he asked the Admiral.

"Nothing. Seems random. Silos here, silos there. Most of the arsenal is still under our control. These others—Christ Almighty. *Charlie Foxtrot.*"

Behind Duval were York, Savas, and Cohen. Filthy, clothes soiled and torn, scrapes and bruises covered their exposed arms and faces. Savas was the worst, a shattered nose red and swollen, dried blood caked around the nostrils, the entire middle of his face a violet patch. Myers turned to the trio and shook his head.

"You three look as bad as we feel. Sorry to welcome you here under these circumstances, Ms. President, but I'm glad you made it." He saluted.

York saluted back. "Duval tried to brief us on the way up. You've lost contact with several nuclear missile silos, I understand?"

"Not exactly," said Myers. "See there? We've still got video feeds and communications with the operators. But a lot of good it's doing us. The missiles are severed from their control. No presidential orders. No football bag with codes. No two-man rule. Someone else is running this show. The damn things are going into a pre-launch state, signals from the silos indicating they've been prepped and target coordinates uploaded."

"Impossible," whispered York, staring at the frantic efforts of the men on the screen.

"God knows I wish it were. It's spread all over our Minutemen locations, across multiple states simultaneously. Seemingly random except in each case the silos are also sealed off from the rest of the facility. We can't get anyone near, and we don't have the personnel to go after each one on the outside. Although we're putting it in motion."

"Hackers?" asked York.

"These systems are dinosaurs, Ms. President. Hell, they run off nine and a quarter inch disks. They're not even networked." He shook his head. "No, this has got to be far older."

Cohen whispered, "Bilderberg."

Myers and York turned to her, but a loud voice from in front interrupted.

"We've got coordinates on ten missiles! Going to the monitors."

Numbers rolled across the screen along with associated map names. Gasps vented across the Command Center.

"All the targets are internal," said York.

"All targets identified!" came the voice. The numbers and names continued to pass by on the screen.

"NORAD?" asked Myers as a map of the nation appeared, red circles indicating the missile targets.

The man at the station in front of him spoke. "No, sir. Doesn't seem so."

He shook his head. "I don't understand. If it's Bilderberg, why not us? We're the enemy, not the rest of the nation!"

Cohen spoke. "NORAD's a very hard target. Too buried. Too ready. The other targets are soft."

York turned to her. "It's *madness*. Why? And how?"

"I don't know how," said Cohen. She looked at Myers. "You said this wasn't hackers, it had to be something old. Probably something long in the planning and maintained. Think about what Bilderberg is, what they've been doing for decades: pulling all the strings at every level. Why would they leave control of the most powerful weapons on earth out of the equation?"

"And the why?" asked York. "This isn't Hastings trying to take me out. This is the end of the nation!"

"We need to reach Angel," said Cohen. "They're at Bilderberg. They might have found something out!"

"We've been trying to contact them for days," said Myers. "Nothing. Only static since they touched down." He turned back to the screen, staring at the soldiers in the silo. "Besides, it's not gonna matter much *why* if we don't find a way to stop it soon."

61

L-PILL

The Director screamed on the phone, his bodyguards flinching and tense, the air in the room stale and claustrophobic. He gestured to a computer screen in front of him, the emergency lights bathing the lush office in flashing bursts of red.

"There is no choice!" he screamed. "We're completely compromised, main power cut, security neutralized. Our computer system is infiltrated. I don't know how! But I'm locked out. They have access to everything. They could shut the entire program down!" A voice shouted indistinctly from the speaker. "Correct. We need to accelerate the launches. We need to amputate this node and transfer control to another. Yes, long term. Don't you understand? We're completely blown. Bilderberg is finished!"

One of the guards leaned toward the Director. "Sir, we've lost another camera." His gun was out, and he assumed a crouched position behind the desk. The other guard mirrored him.

"I've got invaders approaching as we speak, Alpha. We don't have time to argue. Yes, I *know* you and Zero are not out! So we spare the New York node, at least for now. Damn the simulations! We don't have time to check the repercussions." More shouts from the speaker. "And we don't have time to confirm or debate. If we don't launch now, we could lose the opportunity forever!"

The Director glanced at his screen. The monitor was tiled with squares. All of them were black but one, a camera looking toward the server farm. Two dark shapes sprinted toward the lens, one reaching a hand toward it. The last video feed went black.

"Damn!" He pulled out an ancient looking revolver. "They're standing outside my office door. This is it, Alpha. Transfer control to Maryam. Abort the New York warhead. Then launch the rest."

The guards aimed toward the door as the Director placed the receiver down on the phone. He checked the bullets in his revolver.

"We don't know their numbers, but if—"

His voice was swamped by a thundering roar, the door blasting inwards, debris and dust slamming the three men backward and against the wall.

"SHIT!" said Houston as the she turned toward the Director's office. The door was gone. Along with it a portion of the wall, an enormous dust-choked hole opening its maw toward them like a hungry beast. "I never get the damn yield right. We need him alive!"

The pair jogged forward cautiously, weapons raised in front of them. Darting into the wrecked room, they approached the three bodies behind the desk. It was as they had seen in the video feeds—the old man and two guards. Now coated in dust and pieces of rubble, their weapons flung against the wall and out of reach. The guards opened their eyes.

"Barrel on each of you!" yelled Houston. "Don't even—"

The men leapt at them, one throwing a large wooden plank at Lopez, forcing the former priest to deflect it, and preventing him from firing. Houston pulled the trigger twice as her target crashed into her and sent her sprawling. Dust kicked up in the scuffle. But her shots had flown true, and the assailant was badly wounded. The wind knocked out of her, she managed to pull herself to a crouch, gasping for air and steadying her aim as the guard in front of her rose clumsily. Her third shot struck him in the forehead, the body hanging in the air, paralyzed, then dropping like a rag doll.

Lopez had tried to reorient after deflecting the projectile, but he didn't have time to aim and the shot went wide. The guard slammed into him and they toppled backward. Lopez rolled with the motion, drawing his knees to his chest and propelling the attacker over his head and behind. The man's momentum did most of the work, hurling him against the wall, before crashing to the ground.

Lopez flipped to his feet and spun around, a fire in his eyes, his feet planted in a fighting stance. Disoriented, the man braced himself with one hand against the wall, and rose as well, turning with his fists raised to engage.

He never threw a punch.

Lopez darted forward, closing the distance with a step, nearly inside the reach of the guard. The first impact came from his knee into the man's groin. The guard's cry was stifled by the second blow, a double strike from each hand to the side of the head as Lopez swung his arms like a pair of short fighting sticks. The impacts were titanic. The man's jaw cracked loudly. He dropped to the floor unconscious.

"Leave the weapon!" cried Houston.

Lopez spun around. She pointed her gleaming Browning at the Director. The old man's arm was reaching up the desk to his handgun. Lopez walked toward him, bent and retrieved his own weapon, and took the revolver as well.

"What have you people done?" moaned the old man, silt crusting his lips and face, like macabre makeup for the dead.

Houston righted a fallen chair and sat across from him, careful to remain out of reach. Lopez trained his weapon on the Director.

"The question is what have *you* done, you crazy fuck. Nuclear war?"

"You understand nothing, nothing of what we have accomplished, what your dear president York had gone along with for years."

"She didn't have much of a choice, I'd bet. You people had your hands in every pot, on all the dirty laundry. Did you think you could try to control us all forever?" She brandished her weapon. "Now, we're going to have a little chat. About the nuclear silos and how to shut that shit down."

The man said nothing but brought his hand to his mouth.

"Sara! Stop him!" cried Lopez.

But it was too late. The heavy jowls bit down and a liquid flowed out from the sides. The Director swallowed as Houston rose, a grim smile on his face.

"Poison," said Lopez, a disgusted scowl on his face. "You son-of-a-bitch."

"It's a special blend," choked the Director, foam beginning to burble in his mouth. "High dose. Very...fast. Acid adjuvant."

He doubled over wheezing, the foam more prodigious. His body convulsing. Lopez and Houston watched in horror, powerless to stop the inevitable biochemistry. The convulsions continued for several minutes, increasing in severity, and the old man toppled over on his side beside Houston's feet, unmoving.

"Well, fuck." She turned to Lopez. "Now what?"

62

HAZARD BONUS

A voice called out over the loudspeaker system in the NORAD Command Center.

"Repeat, all silos restored to base control. Ten are non-operational due to damage. The remainder are responding to operator commands."

NORAD staff dashed around the center, data flying over the giant monitors, those at desks on the phone or working their computers furiously. The room stank of tension, men visibly sweating even in the air-conditioned environment.

Admiral Myers sat down and hung his head. "Jesus Christ. Thank God for deliverance."

York frowned at the screens. "You still don't know why we're back in control?"

Myers shook his head. "No idea. And *yes*, it worries me. But right now, with those birds shutting down, I'm going to take five minutes and count this as a win."

Cohen turned to York, her brown eyes sharp. "It's got to be Angel and the others. Too much a coincidence."

York nodded. "We need to reach them as soon as possible."

"We're on it," said Myers. "Still reaching out. Still nothing. They're either really busy—or dead, sorry to say." The old man closed his eyes and leaned back in the chair.

"Keep trying," said York. She put one hand on Savas and the other on Cohen and led them forward. "Meanwhile, you two come along. They've set out a little office for me down the hall, and we need to talk."

YORK CLOSED the door to the office, the noise and frenetic chaos of the crisis center muted behind the glass and wood. Photos of a man and his family decorated a desk in the center. Savas and Cohen rested in two chairs facing inward, and York moved behind the desk and took a seat, staring across the cluttered surface at the FBI agents.

"This may or may not be over," she began. "We may or may not contact your friends overseas. This war with Hastings might be ending or gearing up to another round. Either way, I've got to plan for our next steps." The pair watched her expectantly. "We need an anchor on the East Coast. The West is ours, and that won't change unless there's a dramatic shift in the balance of power or those nukes finally do fly. But the East is still enemy territory." She leaned forward, holding their gaze. "I've lost all my advisors, some also my close personal friends. After what you and I have gone through, after I've seen you in action, I trust you. I value your advice. Since Kansas City, you've been my road advisory council."

Cohen fidgeted uncomfortably. "An honor, Ms. President."

"What kind of anchor?" asked Savas.

York leaned back in the chair. "We need a second base of operations until this war is over. Something secure that's right in Hasting's side of the court, under his nose. A place we can store troops and equipment, launch guerrilla attacks. One that can be defended against anything but the most powerful assault."

"The Manhattan bunker," said Cohen.

"Exactly."

"But we abandoned it," said Savas. "It could be in Hastings's hands now."

"It could," agreed York, "but it isn't. You might remember we left a contingent to try and hold the base? Not many. They couldn't have held it if Hastings had gone after the bunker seriously. But he didn't. He figured the real war was out on the plains—and he was right. But he's been handed devastating losses and left himself open for an attack from within. We're going to be flying several secret missions to bring the fighting numbers up at the bunker. Personnel to make it a base of operations." She smiled. "What I need is someone to run the place. People who have shown the strength and character, creativity and courage under fire it will take to make that base work. People I trust."

Savas and Cohen glanced at each other, and back at the president.

"Elaine, if you're thinking to suggest—" began Savas.

"I'm not suggesting. This is an Executive Order. From this point, until I deem it no longer necessary, I hereby appoint both of you as the civilian heads of the Manhattan bunker. You will have authority over everyone there, including armed forces personnel. You will be charged with getting the location back up to speed, readied for an extended war campaign if necessary. I will of course provide you with military advisers, logistics support and a contingent of Special Forces troops."

"Ms. President!" began Cohen.

"Never interrupt the Commander in Chief," said York. "I know you both are tired. God knows, I am. Half the staff out there are ready for early retirement after this. But it's *not* over. I, this nation, needs our best people and everything they have."

"We aren't qualified to serve in a military capacity," protested Savas. "Whatever you think of us, we aren't ready to be put in charge of such an important operation and given the power over soldier's lives."

"Let me be the judge of who is ready for such duty," she said. "Your command there will violate a hundred regs and piss off a lot of people. But that will all go on the back-burner. Because right *now* we have a *Last Days* problem on our hands." She stood up and put her hands on the desk. "You'll leave within the hour."

"What?" said Cohen.

"Several Special Forces teams will accompany you. They're prepping a transport and fighter escort for you at Peterson right now. This can't wait. We have Hastings on the ropes. You're our left hook."

York walked to the door and opened it. The flood of noise swept over them again—calls on the loudspeakers, machinery, the incessant drone of the fans pumping air into the underground buildings.

"Take a few minutes to gather your thoughts. Then meet me back in the Command Center. Myers will have people ready for you." The president turned and strode down the hallway without looking back.

Cohen frowned at York's retreating back. "Well, John, I can't wait for the hazard bonus."

63

ZERO

"Don't you two know how to knock?"

Lightfoote stood inside the cavernous hole blown in the wall, her gaze tracking the circumference of it. She carried a black backpack with her.

Lopez stood over a body on the floor, wrapping the man's arms and legs in duct-tape. Houston sat on the edge of a damaged desk, padding her neck and chin with a bloody cloth. A long abrasion ran down her chest.

"The Director's dead," said Lopez. "Suicide. We'll get nothing from him to help stop the attacks."

Lightfoote walked in through the rubble and stared down at the crumpled body of the old man. She dropped the bag on the floor and turned to look behind Lopez. A soft moaning came from the floor beside him.

"You roped that calf?" she asked. Lopez nodded. "Okay, well, the good news is I managed to fry their controls on the silos. Irony! I used some of Fawkes's leftover code on their systems, subroutines my immune packets hadn't completely erased. I modified a few and set them loose on their command and control code. They're not going to be using it again for some time."

Houston cocked her head to one side. "I didn't think missile silos were networked like other things."

"They aren't," said Lightfoote. "Irony number two. To keep control of them, Bilderberg had to link them. So, Uncle Sam at NORAD was out of the loop and could do nothing while Bilderberg pulled the strings. But their links, on modern servers, exposed them to hacking."

Lopez clapped her on the back. Houston smiled broadly. "Damn, girl, you *did* just save the world again. Or maybe a hundred million lives."

"I think it was definitely a team effort," she said. "So, now, the bad news."

"I'm looking for the mission when we stop hearing that," said Lopez.

"Bilderberg—whatever this place is, or was—it's not what we thought. Not the whole beast, but just one part of it."

What do you mean?" asked Houston.

"Bilderberg has been the nexus for decades. Maybe centuries. Who knows? But whatever this organization is, it's a hydra. Many heads in different parts of the world."

"The nodes in the computer simulations?" asked Lopez.

She nodded. "The Nash equations were incredibly predictive. They've locked me out of the system now, totally wiped it, probably amputating this node. But not before I found connections to the other locations. They're subservient, taking orders from here, but active, focal points for local manipulations of markets and politics. Each had a different name, its own contact, its own infrastructure and power base. I was going to save all the data, transfer it, so we could chase them down and figure it out, but they trashed the server before I could."

"So, the New York cluster is real?" asked Houston.

"More than that," said Lightfoote. "It's the heart of it all."

"I thought this place was," said Lopez.

"Bilderberg was a *front*. It's so devious. For the simulations and string pulling, this served as a focal point. If anyone came looking—really came looking like us—they'd be drawn here. But it's *not* the puppet master. Bilderberg's strings, and the strings of the other nodes, are all being pulled from New York. By *Zero*."

Lopez furrowed his brow. "Zero?"

Lightfoote shrugged. "These guys like drama. But that's all I have. A name. *A handle*. The records didn't spell anything else out. Just Zero."

"What do we do with that?" asked Houston.

"Well, there *is* more," said Lightfoote. "More on the location, anyway. They set up the perfect facade to hide him. While the conspiracy theorists of the world had their eyes on Bilderberg, the real puppet master was hidden away, completely unsuspected, in a green, intellectual oasis in Manhattan. A place standing unimpeachable, working for the 'benefit of humanity,' while it served in the shadows as the beautiful mask to hide the hydra. Whoever Zero is, he's there, at a biomedical center called the Ramsey University."

"The what?" asked Houston.

"I didn't have much time to look it up. Little I got said it was founded by the Ramsey family in 1901 along with some other oligarchs. People thought it was a tax shelter with some 'give back to the world' guilt down payments for the tycoons. But it looks like the story was just social camouflage. The place was set up to hide something very different, much darker."

Lopez shook his head. "You mean Bilderberg *isn't* the center of power? But this Ramsey University is? How?"

"I don't know," said Lightfoote. "But that's where this Zero is. A place no one would think to examine, with Nobel Prize winners, disease cures, a research hospital. And it's been the center of power for over one hundred years."

"The name Ramsey raises some red flags," said Houston.

"More conspiracy theories," said Lightfoote. "But yes. It's all starting to feel very eerie." She shook her head as if to clear her thoughts. "Back to the nukes for a minute. We need to contact NORAD, get them to move on the silos to prevent this from happening again. I'll walk them through it."

"You can do that?" asked Houston.

"Should be able to. Their control system was all spelled out in the connections here. It's not magic. I think we can wall them out forever."

Lopez turned to the receiver on the old-style landline. Dust slid down the sides of the plastic handle as he raised it to his ear. A dial tone spilled from the speaker. "Still works."

"Good," said Lightfoote, retrieving her laptop from the bag and laying it beside the phone. "One more piece of critical intel. Zero is *still* in NYC.

The missile launch was only to be triggered by his command. The silos were prepping and on standby, firing once he bugged out."

"Wait, are you serious?" asked Houston.

Lightfoote nodded, opening her computer. "Probably who Mr. Cyanide here was talking to before he offed himself. We've wounded them terribly, but we didn't get the queen bee. But maybe we can. Zero is leaving NYC within the next twelve hours."

"What can we do about it?" asked Lopez "We're here. I doubt anyone has any available assets in the area after all the chaos. No one will get there in time."

"We have to try," said Lightfoote. "Another reason to get NORAD on the line." She scrolled her fingers on the trackpad. "Here's the protocol York gave us for calling in." She picked up the receiver and entered a sequence of numbers, followed by several pauses and three more number sequences. "This takes forever if I remember. They filter and trace the hell out of the calls."

Finally, there was an audible click.

"Yes, this is Angel Lightfoote. I'm here at the Bilderberg hotel with Gabriel, Mary, and a lot of dead guys. I need to speak to Admiral Myers."

64

HALO

"Agent Savas? Agent Cohen?"

A soldier peered into the back cabin, pulling back a makeshift privacy screen to see inside. Savas opened his eyes, rising on an elbow from the seat. Cohen slept unmoving in the chair beside him.

"I'm sorry to wake you, but there's an urgent call."

Savas shook his head. "Can barely breathe through this damn nose. Can't sleep."

The soldier motioned to him. "It's the president on the secure line."

A minute later both he and Cohen were huddled together in the chilly transport, Cohen yawning and still half asleep. Savas spoke to York on a video screen.

"Slow down, Elaine. One thing at a time. My team, they're alive, unharmed?"

York nodded. "They're worse for wear, but no major injuries."

"They really did it. The missile aborts, the silo shutdowns."

"Yes," said the president. "Lightfoote's fingerprints all over it, of course. But their team had to infiltrate the hotel underground. We don't have time, and I'm not clear on all the details, but it looks like Bilderberg was running some sort of science fiction population simulation, shape world events by using computer models."

"And this all had to do with this Nash figure? Fawkes's file was about some econ genius and his work?"

"Yes," said York. "Frankly, I'm skeptical until I've learned more. Sounds ridiculous. But they're sure. They're meeting with local CIA and US military representatives in the area now to lock the site down. But they saved our asses."

Savas bowed his head. He couldn't help but feel both relieved and proud. "Okay, so how does this relate to New York and this university?"

York sighed. "It's all moving so fast we can't hope to verify everything. So we're going on trust, John. Do you trust your people?"

"With my life. Looks like we all did."

"Well, what your people are saying is there is more to this than simply Bilderberg. Bilderberg was only a center of operations, but the organization is spread around the world. Most importantly, a key figure, maybe *the* key figure, is right in front of your plane in New York."

"At the Ramsey University," said Cohen.

"Yes. Angel Lightfoote was sure of it. She begged us to get someone there, to stop him."

"Stop who?"

"All they had was an alias. *Zero.*"

"Someone in New York at a biomedical institute running the damn world named Zero?" said Savas. "You know how this sounds?"

"Of course I do! So I ask again—do you trust your people? And do you trust us? Because there's more. We've done some of our own digging based on Angel's data. We think we know who this Zero is—Luc Osomer-Levitt, the president of the university."

"Wait, I've heard of him," said Cohen. "Big time pharmaceutical player. A scientist I think. Was embroiled in several financial controversies but nothing ever stuck."

"That's him," said York, static partially garbling her words. "But a little digging into government databases reveals some very interesting coincidences. Like invitations to the annual Bilderberg conference, to begin."

"Gets my attention," said Savas.

"How about the funneling of huge amounts of money from some of the most powerful families in the world to the university? Charitable donations on paper but the numbers don't add up. Finally, NSA data on communications between his corporate offices and seven of the Bilderberg nodes identified by Angel."

"That's no coincidence," said Cohen.

"Unlikely. Angel claimed she had information that Zero's on the move, bugging out of New York in a matter of hours. He might already be gone."

"Leaving from Ramsey?" asked Savas.

"Best intel we have."

Cohen nodded. "All right. Send in a strike force. Take him into custody."

"*You* are the strike force," said York, her expression grim. "We don't have the skill set in the staff left in the Manhattan bunker."

"Us?" said Savas incredulously.

"Your special ops teams are perfect for the job. This could be the kill shot to Bilderberg. You both *have* to be there." Her face stared unblinkingly at them through the screen. "We've uploaded what known schematics of the place are available—campus map, entrances and exits, buildings. But there's likely to be a hidden layer, like at the Bilderberg Hotel. There may be levels and structures buried in the bedrock we know nothing about."

"And we have no sense of how fortified they are. We could be walking into a shooting gallery," said Savas.

"Yes, you could."

He placed his hand on his bandaged face. "Okay, how do we get there? I didn't even think this through when we boarded the damn plane. Are the airports open? LGA is close."

"Negative. Hastings controls it. Or did. It's chaos on the ground still. Airport isn't operational as far as we can tell."

"Then what?" asked Savas, holding his arms in the air.

"Sergeant Williams, would you introduce yourself?" called out York loudly.

"Yes, ma'am," came an authoritative voice behind them. A tall black woman stepped toward the screen. "HALO specialist Aisha Williams."

"HALO?" asked Cohen.

"High Altitude Low Opening."

Savas looked at the video feed. "You aren't serious?"

Williams continued. "We'll jump about thirty-five miles out from the island, sir. At forty thousand feet and this airspeed, we'll need a good distance to land on target. Give it three to four minutes for the drop. But it keeps the aircraft out of SAM range and minimizes possible flak."

"In case Hastings is watching," added York over the speakers.

"Jump?" Cohen asked, her eyes widening.

"Three teams," said Williams. "You'll both have chaperones. They'll steer you with the groups until we touch down." Savas and Cohen simply stared at her. "We've only got an hour to the drop point, and we need to get you both on oh-two as soon as possible."

"Oxygen? Why?" asked Savas.

"Purge the nitrogen from your blood, sir. You can't just jump at forty-K. Pressure's too low. You'll get the bends."

Cohen turned an incredulous look to Savas. "Nitrogen bubbles in the blood," she said, swallowing.

"Hurts like hell, sir, and could kill you."

Savas stared at the soldier. "And assuming we survive this madness, where are you intending to put us down?"

"Central Park," said Williams. "Lots of open space there."

"Surrounded by skyscrapers," he said.

"We've done worse, sir," said Williams.

Savas stared toward the ceiling. "You've got to be kidding me."

York smiled on the screen. "Good hunting, all of you. Bring us back a trophy."

65

TERMINAL VELOCITY

The jumpsuits were ungainly, awkward for the untrained bodies of Cohen and Savas. They breathed deeply from the oxygen tanks, a helmet fitted over their heads and a fighter pilot style mask to their mouths. In theory, the enriched gas was slowly pushing the nitrogen out of their bloodstreams. A second tank of oxygen would accompany them on the way down. Savas struggled to breathe regularly through his bandages.

"Remember," said Williams, momentarily repositioning her own mouthpiece and shouting over the din in the aircraft, "you're jumping at commercial airline cruising altitude. It's minus sixty out there or worse. You can't breathe the air. Stay with your chaperone. Keep repeating the thumbs-up sign if all is good. Stay calm. They'll guide you through the jump at each step. The chutes will deploy toward the end of the jump, controlled by your chaperone. We'll steer you to the target site."

A sturdy Special Forces soldier crouched behind each agent, checking their suits and tanks. They were strapped lightly to their charge. Both reacted to the coming leap into the sky as a routine day at the office and treated the FBI agents as just another package they had to deliver. Savas couldn't decide if that was comforting or alarming.

A red light began to flash above them, signaling the approaching jump point. Williams motioned for them to stand, and together with their chaperone they moved to the back of the troop transport, the bay doors opening and the loading ramp pointing downward.

The early morning light spilled brightly into the aircraft, a waterfall of sound churning from the wind turbulence around the opening. An abstract patchwork of boxes and lines passed below, different colored shapes separated by highways and intermittent urban clusters. A deep red ball rose over the horizon.

Williams waved her arm several times. "Go, go, go!"

One by one the soldiers stepped to the edge of the ramp and toppled over calmly, performing a short somersault before zipping from view behind and below the aircraft. At the line's end, the FBI agents were positioned at the edge, Cohen briefly turning her helmet back to look at Savas, her eyes and face obscured by the tinted wind guard. The soldier pushed her forward, and she dropped, racing away toward the other members of the parachute team.

Soldiers guided Savas to the edge. He looked down, the height deceptive, the seven and one-half miles between him and the ground not registering to a mind utterly unused to such vertical distances. He felt a pat on the shoulder and gave the thumbs up. A push drove him forward into an explosion of white noise. He was flying.

Or falling. The sensations were overwhelming. First the noise hit him. The churning air racing against his plummeting form roared like an engine, nearly blocking out his ability to think. The vibrations were powerful, the air beating against the fabric of his suit and helmet, the invisible medium hardening into something powerful and tangible, slapping strongly across his body. The rising sun blinded him, even through the tinted visor. He could barely stare forward toward their destination and was forced to look straight to the onrushing earth.

He hardly noticed the soldier strapped to him above, his senses numb. Another series of hard pats on the shoulder reminded him he hadn't signaled. He put out his hand and did the thumbs-up. He felt no nausea, no dizziness, the pummeling he took from the battering wind and sound overpowering all other sensations.

A line of skydivers approached ahead. He had lost all sense of time. The divers maintained a separated distance. Williams had said it would create a low radar profile. An obese shape trailed the others ahead of him. He realized it must be Cohen and her chaperone, and that he likely presented a similar image. Considering the enemies lurking below, he hoped they were indeed as invisible as the soldier predicted.

Down they were yanked by earth's pull, their velocity now constant, the force from the air they pushed against equal to the force of gravity. *Terminal velocity*, thought Savas. Williams had said it would take only minutes to complete the jump, but it felt like they'd been falling for hours before he finally saw the jagged landscape of Manhattan. They plunged through a layer of clouds, momentarily blinding him, but he saw the chutes in front of him deploy. A second later, the soldier above him pulled the chord, and Savas was yanked upward harshly.

Their fall slowed dramatically, but the approaching skyscrapers only intensified the sense of plunging recklessly forward. The group of jumpers passed over the lower tip of Manhattan, the Statue of Liberty a flattened speck below, the Freedom Tower reaching upward toward their feet. Ahead the white, snow-covered rectangle of Central Park loomed, the chutes angling steadily toward it. Adrenaline coursed through him as they approached midtown, their height appearing to put them on a collision course for many of the taller buildings surrounding the park. But they skirted over them, the penthouse balconies a short drop below, the barren trees of the park rushing up to greet them.

The soldier slapped his shoulder three times. The signal for landing. Savas looked down and set his legs, the trees inches below. They exploded over a wide space, descending rapidly over a field of bright white. His feet slammed roughly into to the snow-covered grasses of the Great Lawn.

They maintained their balance, and the chute collapsed neatly behind them. Savas removed his helmet and exhaled deeply, relieved to be on the ground and to see Cohen disengaging from her chute. While cold, the air tasted fresh compared to the bottled gas from the tank. He squirmed out of the jumpsuit and let it fall to the ground. The Special Forces soldiers were grouping together. Savas and his chaperone jogged up and joined them.

Williams pulled out a GPS device. "We have the coordinates of the target here. We'll make as direct a course as possible through the park and city to that location."

"Don't bother," said Savas, interrupting her. The eyes of the other soldiers turned to him in surprise. "No need for GPS. This is my city. Follow me."

66

ROKNEGY

They stood at the bottom of a large hill, a twenty-foot arch with the university's name and logo engraved on the side. Towering metal rods barred the entrance, the gate locked in place. A gleaming set of turnstiles occupied the space on the right and left, refusing entrance without an activated ID card.

The young man stared intensely at Savas, his eyes nervously darting to the crowd of armed soldiers behind him. He licked his lips and grasped the security badge on his uniform.

"I'm sorry, sir, but I can't let you in the university unless you have an invitation. Now, we can try to call—"

"Let me repeat," said Savas. "This is a matter of *national security*."

"You have no ID, you're armed. I'm sorry, sir. Now, I'm going to call the police if you don't move on."

Savas laughed. "Seen much of the police these last few months?" The man said nothing. Savas motioned to the soldiers who stepped closer, their weapons aimed slightly over the head of the guard. "Now, look. We can do this easy," he growled, "or we can do it *real* easy."

The security guard stared at the soldiers, his eyes wide.

"Richard, what the hell is going on here?" A tall black man with a thick Jamaican accent rounded the security booth and stared through the gate's bars at the assembled teams. "Who the hell are you?"

The young gate guard spoke, wiping sweat from his forehead. "They claim they're sent from the *president*. President York. They don't have *any* clearance. No invite. *Nothing*. They have guns."

The older black man nodded. "Yes, son, I see those guns. Do you know what they do with those guns?" The young man swallowed. "Those are Special Forces. Look at those insignias. Rangers, Seals, Green Berets." He looked at Savas. "Why are you here?"

"A matter of national security. We have to see the president of this institution. Immediately."

The older guard nodded, a last look at the weapons removing all doubt. "Good enough for me." He punched in a code inside the booth and the mechanism for the large gate engaged, the two halves swinging back and in. "But you better hurry. Something strange is happening. All the docs running to the tunnels, following the president."

Savas turned to Cohen and the others. "He's rabbiting." The doors opened and the troops moved in. Savas turned back to the guards as he headed up the hill. "You made the right call. You have access to the security system?"

"I do."

"Shut it down. Shut every camera in this place down."

"Yes, sir," said the guard. He pointed up the hillside. "To Patron's Hall. Building at the top. Left stairs down to the tunnels."

Savas nodded and turned to sprint up the hill, catching up to Williams.

"Heard him, agent Savas, but slow it down. We're going to treat this as hostile territory. Move smart."

"We might not have much time!" he seethed.

"Better late than dead, sir. We can't do nothing if we're dead."

Cohen grabbed his arm and stared at him. Savas exhaled. The soldier was right. Given what Hastings and Bilderberg had at their disposal, a squad of mercenaries wouldn't be out of the picture. This invasion could end before it began.

They reached the hilltop, the Special Forces group moving cautiously, examining vulnerable angles and approaches. A six-story building from another era rose before them, a set of marble stairs leading to a set of glass doors. Around them, the campus was utterly deserted.

A different welcome greeted them in the foyer. The armed team of soldiers burst through the doors in tactical formation, weapons aimed forward, their posture aggressive. In front of them stood a buzzing crowd of older men and women, many in ill-fitting suits or lab coats, pacing the marbled room. At the sight of the soldiers, they fell backward, eyes wide and fearful, conversation extinguished.

"Where is the president?" asked Savas, stepping forward and acting as the group's spokesman. No one responded. "This is a matter of national security. Where is your president?"

A rotund man with a beard, resembling some baron in an Armani suit, stepped toward them authoritatively. "I'm Joac Ratkvetch, Full Professor and Head of Laboratory. We need some answers. Are you with the police?"

Savas motioned to Williams. "The stairway. See if it leads to the tunnels." Williams and several soldiers moved to their left and a doorway to a set of steps leading down.

"Tunnels," said Ratkvetch. "Yes, it most certainly does. Our president went that way, but seems to have lost his mind."

"Explain," said Savas.

"First tell me who you are? You wouldn't believe how we have been treated these last days. Herded, shouted at! Can you imagine—"

"*Explain,*" growled Savas.

The professor startled. "Well, he came here with *armed men*. They've destroyed the president's office, all the records. They've stolen important samples. The noise brought us all here. We know something terrible is happening. He's heading to the river campus access."

"And so?"

"To escape the island! The war is coming here, no? You have to get us out!"

Several heads nodded as the university professors crowded around Savas.

"We're important people!" cried one.

"I'm Michelle MacKinnon, Nobel Prize winner."

"Korgie Barfmour," cried a botoxed blonde.

Two men stepped forward. "Seth Burley and John Harrison. We need protection!"

Pandemonium erupted.

A burst of automatic gunfire exploded. Marble chips and dust rained from the ceiling. Williams stood at the stairwell, her weapon smoking. Savas nodded to her.

"Stairwell's clear," she said.

Savas motioned to the rest. "We move. To the tunnels."

The tall blonde grabbed his collar. "And what about *us?*"

Savas swiped her hand away and continued to the door. "Write your damn memoirs or something. Stay here and panic. I don't give a damn. Stay out of our way or you're going to get a bullet."

She gasped, and fell back with the others. Williams led the way down the stairs, Savas and Cohen behind her, the remaining soldiers following closely.

"Little harsh, John?" asked Cohen with a raised eyebrow as they rounded a turn in the steps.

"*I have a Nobel Prize*. What a bunch of self-important blowhards."

The stairs ended, the passageway opening to a broad tunnel leading down into the bowels of the island.

"Why does a university have a series of underground tunnels?" asked Cohen, staring in disbelief as the passageways plunged down in front of them.

"For something that needs to hide underground," he mumbled. He drew his sidearm and began to head down the tunnel. He felt a firm hand on his shoulder.

"No disrespect, agent Savas," said Williams. "We're all combat vets. Seen more tunnels than we'd like to think about. We'll take the lead here."

Savas nodded, stepping to the side. "You have point, Sergeant. We'll stay out of your way and watch your back."

"Glad you're not going to go alpha on me," she smiled, moving forward.

"Too damn tired for that, ma'am."

Williams turned around and motioned the soldiers forward. They swept into the tunnels.

67

IRON OXIDE

They did not get far. The group had been moving cautiously down the main tunnel passage, ignoring side branches and the many closed doors and hatches dotting the walls. Most of those were locked on examination, and the maps York had provided indicated none led to anything more interesting than storage or machinery rooms. The maps did not show where the main path ended, which was all the suspicion they needed to continue following its course.

The temperature within the tunnel spiked dramatically as they moved forward. Enormous steam pipes ran overhead and alongside the walls, the thermal energy radiating outward and noticeable from a few feet away. After less than ten minutes, having seen no one and no clues, the passage began to slope upward and a large opening to another building came into view.

"Damn," said Williams. The extended line of soldiers stopped along with Savas and Cohen in the back.

"The new research building," said another soldier, pointing to the map. "The tunnel connections fade out in the middle, but we've just gone from building to building. No secret lair. No escape route."

"He had to go somewhere!" Williams said. "What did we miss?"

"About fifty doorways that aren't on the maps," said Savas, moving toward the front of the group. "And that might have something else behind them the maps don't show."

"We go back over it, carefully this time," said Cohen. "There's got to be more to this than a simple passage between buildings."

"We're running out of time," said Savas.

Cohen nodded. "Then let's work fast."

Williams moved through her team and toward the FBI agents. Savas interrupted her.

"No disrespect, Sergeant, but this is where we take over."

Williams smiled. "Touché."

"Only Rebecca has point, and we give her some cover. She's the real sleuth."

Williams positioned men at the beginning and end of the tunnel, blanketing all entrances and exits. She and another soldier accompanied Savas as he followed behind Cohen while she meticulously swept along the tunnel walls. Her deliberateness was painful. Time was running through their hands, every second an hour. When she stopped in front of a rusted door, he checked his watch, surprised only five minutes had passed.

"This is it," she said, crouching and touching the ground.

Williams shook her head. "This is what? What do you see?"

Cohen held up a finger, a dull orange powder coating her skin. "Rust," she said and stood up, gesturing to the door. "This thing's been here a long time. The metal's built up a layer of rust ignored for years, maybe decades. But look. Around the handle and the hinges, the rust is disturbed. Some scratched, some cracked. It fell to the floor here," she pointed to a thin film of red on the rock below.

"There's a shoe print in it," said Savas.

Cohen nodded. "Not from your team," she said to Williams. "I got a lot of looks at the boots from behind. Not John or my shoes." She placed her hands on the door handle. "Someone's opened this door very recently."

Williams called the soldiers back from the tunnel extremities. They took positions near the doorway as Cohen yanked on the handle. It didn't move. Savas stepped up and together they forced the rusted hinges to yield, a screeching sound echoing around them.

The red glow of emergency bulbs lit an empty passage. The rank smell of sea and grime spilled outward, and the shoe prints continued into the thick muck coating the floor. But the prints were far more numerous, a confused stampede of footsteps preserved.

Savas checked the map. "Definitely not a machine room. And judging from all these prints, it looks like the president has a few friends."

Williams motioned to her team. "We move in separated pairs. Khyber spacing."

A soldier stepped forward and into the tunnels. "Back in the hellholes, snake-eaters," he said and disappeared. One by one they entered, and again, Savas and Cohen were relegated to the rear.

Moving through the hatchway Savas nearly struck his head on the low ceiling, the sounds of footfalls ahead of him echoing in the concrete tube. The red emergency lighting painted an infernal glare on the roughly hewn stone surrounding them.

The sounds of pounding metal reached his ears. The tight tunnel opened broadly to reveal a small chamber, a ladder racing upward, a four-way intersection of passages running from the focal point. The twelve soldiers were spaced to cover the passages, several training weapons on the ladder.

"Now what?" asked Cohen. "Four possibilities."

"This doesn't exist on the maps," said Williams. "We'll have to split up."

Savas felt his stomach drop. Too much time wasted, and now their forces thinned.

The soldiers conferred, pairs moving down the three new tunnels. Williams pointed to the ladder.

"We'll leave two here to guard against someone coming up our ass from the first tunnel. Leaves us four and you two to try this ladder. Here's what—"

Her words were cut off by gunfire. Echoes rang from the passageway in front of them. "Found them! Henson, Ripley, hold this point. The rest of you, with me!"

The automatic weapons discharge continued, and Williams and three other soldiers sprinted down the tunnel. Savas turned to Cohen.

"I guess we stay—"

Above him, metal screeched. Savas glanced up to see a hatch over the ladder open briefly, and momentarily caught a glimpse of a face. The man vanished, omitting to even seal the hatch, panic in his eyes.

"John, no!" cried Cohen.

Savas leapt onto the metal rungs and raced upward, thrusting his torso through the opening, weapon raised. A blurred shadow turned a corner down a narrow hallway, and Savas vaulted from the ladder to sprint down the passage. As it veered left, he spun quickly, gun raised, poised to engage.

He found himself in a claustrophobic space hewn carelessly out of the bedrock, a wall of guns aimed his way. Light poured from a broad opening behind the mercenaries. A brief glimpse showed Savas a short ramp leading down to the East River. An armored yacht approached on the water.

A thin man, in a suit, his hair graying, stepped forward. He held up a hand to the four bodyguards who had trained their weapons on Savas.

"A firefight at this juncture would be most unwise," he said to them, his eyes darting behind him.

"Luc Osomer-Levitt," said Savas, refusing to lower his weapon. He recognized the face of the Ramsey president from the last-minute dossiers York had sent them. The man appeared even more robotic in person than he did in the still photos, his face hardly displaying a flicker of emotion. "Or should I say: *Zero*."

"Agent Savas," he said. "I'm impressed, but please put your gun down before someone gets killed."

Savas heard the sound too late, distracted by the men in front of him. A heavy blow struck the back of his head as he tried to pivot. The ground raced up surreally. On his hands and knees, the world spinning, his gun kicked across the floor, powerful arms raised him to his feet.

"We wondered how you escaped," said Osomer-Levitt. "You live up to your reputation."

His head exploding, the figures around him only slowly returned to focus. The arms dragged Savas before the man. He winced as a gun pressed against his head.

"How do you know..."

"Who you are? Don't be coy, agent Savas. If you're here, you've clearly put together enough to know I have been involved in your capture and interrogation. I took a very personal interest in everything you and your Intel 1 group had to say."

"You bastard," Savas managed, his head pounding. "You have my people's blood on your hands."

"Collateral damage is such an unfortunate part of war. And this has been a war, agent Savas. Anonymous nearly destroyed us, and your cyber-crimes head had radioactive material we could not allow to be released. We had no choice."

"The Nash Criterion."

"Yes. That madman was a double-edged sword for all of us. Useful for his time, but it's over now. Your people have put the planet on a course of self-destruction. We may not be able to fix this."

His fogged head still couldn't process much of his surroundings, let alone rebut the man. Adding to the confusion, a new voice spoke from behind the phalanx of guards

"Bring him forward. Let me see him."

The voice rasped and carried a striking tone of authority. For the first time, Osomer-Levitt's mask cracked, and concern flickered briefly over his features. The guards instinctively shifted, opening a small wedge to what lay behind. Savas strained to focus, the blurred outlines of a short and squat figure refusing to clarify. A grotesque form rolled forward, the legs swollen beyond possibility. Unless...*wheels!* The figure sat in a wheelchair.

Osomer-Levitt spoke. "We don't have time. There may be others with him. At the least his agent wife."

A woman's voice came from behind him, and Savas flinched.

"Too late," said Cohen. "She's already here."

Savas's head throbbed as he looked over his shoulder. Cohen stood alone, an army-issue coat wrapped around her, eyes trained on Osomer-Levitt.

"Time for parlay," she said.

68

KINGFISH

"Parlay?" scoffed the Ramsey president. "I have your husband at the barrel of a gun. You are unarmed. What can you possibly bring to the table?"

"You're talking. You're hesitant. What are you afraid of, Luc?"

Osomer-Levitt licked his lips as Cohen stepped several paces closer. Savas looked on helplessly, trying to organize his thoughts for some sort of attack. Cohen simply stood there, her arms awkwardly out from her sides, her eyes fierce. *What is she doing?*

"It wouldn't be the figure behind you, in the wheelchair? Or the ship coming into dock?"

"You both should have never come looking."

Cohen stepped two more paces forward, now only feet from the group of men.

"Did you think we would simply turn our backs on what's going on? We stopped Anonymous, Luc. We saved your little plan."

"And then blew up our base of operations."

"None of our people."

Osomer-Levitt smirked. "Such coincidences do not happen. You have shadows we can't uncover. I commend you for that. But it has York's fingerprints all over it."

"The boat is about to dock!" cried out one of the mercenaries.

Osomer-Levitt shook his head. "You have no idea what you have done. You think you are saving the world, but you are dooming it to repeated cycles of dark ages."

"And only your tyranny could save us all from ourselves? That's why you nuked an entire city? Were about to nuke the entire country? This is your enlightened march to global civilization?"

"A *necessity* because of the terrorist Fawkes. Had we been left alone, the course of human history would have only been forward. But you are too trapped in your primitive tribal systems to see it." He pointed to one of the guards. "We'll take them with us. When we are secured, we'll deal with them in a controlled fashion."

"Don't count on it." Cohen smiled as the guard approached her. "A little trick I learned from a hacker frenemy."

Cohen raised her arms out from her body. Savas's blurred vision leapt back months to a warehouse in New Jersey, the motion and similarities triggering the deja vu. Two metal canisters clanked on the ground, rolling forward toward the group. The men instinctively looked down, their weapons aiming toward the floor. The gas bombs ignited.

Even without shrapnel, the compressed air blast stunned Savas and the guards. Then, the chemical concoction attacked. He felt his lungs and eyes burn, his breath hellfire. He fell to the floor coughing violently.

A short spurt of automatic weapons fire erupted behind Cohen. *The Special Forces soldiers? More mercenaries?* Time ticked languidly. His body heaving, he crawled blindly to find some escape from the gas. Someone grabbed his head. He couldn't resist. He felt a bag yanked over his face. No, *a mask*. A short blast of fresh air purged the toxic fumes. He breathed wildly like a drowning man.

"John! Slow down! Breathe slowly." *Rebecca*. He grabbed her arms, opening his eyes. A masked monster from World War I stared back at him. Inside the goggled eyes were brown irises, threads of brown hair. He staggered to his knees, leaning against the wall. A pair of strong arms helped him to his feet. *Sergeant Williams*.

"The boat!" she cried, darting past him into the room.

Weapons fire erupted again. He turned and limped through the dissipating gas, bodies of mercenaries littering the floor. Among them, the blood-stained suit of the powerful president of Ramsey University, Luc Osomer-Levitt. His eyes stared vacuously toward the ceiling.

Savas watched as Cohen holstered her Glock pistol. He looked between her and Osomer-Levitt. "You?"

She nodded. "Got it when I need it, John. Just next time, don't run off like an untrained monkey after the bad guys. Okay?"

He nodded, turning his head to the East River below them. Williams and the other soldiers returned from the ramp, their eerie masks still in place. She spoke loudly through the plastic.

"It's gone, dammit. We took out some windows and maybe punctured the fuel tank, but not enough. We need to get assets on the river and ocean before they disappear."

"The man in the wheelchair?" asked Cohen anxiously.

"What wheelchair?" said Williams.

"There wasn't an old man in a wheelchair? He's not in here. He got to the boat!"

"Who got to the boat?" Savas asked.

Cohen's shoulders slumped. "The kingfish. *Zero*."

Savas stared into her mask. "That old man was Zero? I thought it was Osomer-Levitt!"

"I don't think so, John. Osomer-Levitt was taking orders. One more facade in this cursed house of mirrors. And Zero escaped."

"All the more reason to get on the COM and call this in." Williams left them and consulted with her team, several of them accompanying her outside with a backpack.

"Let's get outside," said Savas, "and get some real air."

The pair walked outside. Already the soldiers had removed their masks, and Savas and Cohen followed suit. One of the men had placed a portable radio on the ground, quickly working the device. Savas bent over and coughed, breathing in the crisp winter air, the cloud of water vapor heavenly after the chemical fog.

"Jesus, John, you've got blood all over your neck." Cohen removed a scarf from inside the heavy coat she wore and pressed it to the back of his head.

"Easy!" said Savas, pulling away. "Damn, that hurts."

"Sit still. You always find a way to bleed on these missions." He sat down as Cohen applied pressure to the back of his head. She shook her head. "You need stitches."

"The old man—Zero?" he sighed. "Who was he?"

Cohen looked out over the water, a mist rising off the river, no sign of the boat or other activity. Across from the university, Roosevelt Island ran along the water like a thin canyon wall.

"I have a theory," she said.

"Yes?"

"There is one name that comes up over and over in all this. A key member and organizer of the Bilderberg group meetings. A well-known proponent of a one-world government, on the record as preferring it and that it be run by a small group of financially aware people. The key figure funding this university, selecting its leadership, and whose family set the entire project in motion."

Savas grimaced as he turned toward her. "You mean?"

"And of the right age and health to be trapped in the constraints of a wheelchair," she ended.

"Daniel Ramsey."

Cohen nodded. "I didn't get a good look at him, and I wouldn't likely recognize him anyway. Like the old Soviet leaders, he's been rumored to be dead fifty times. He's over one hundred years old."

"One hundred?" asked Savas. "How?"

"Through his nineties publicly active. I don't know how. Ramsey biomedical science miracles?"

"This is crazy."

"I agree. And I'm sure it's not over."

The heavy boots of Sergeant Williams tramped down the wooden ramp toward them. She crouched beside the water.

"Reached a relay. NORAD's in the know. New intel: Hastings is dead. The coup had its own coup. It's chaos over on this side of the country right now, but the president is moving fast to reassert authority. Looks like this might be over soon."

"The boat?" asked Savas.

Williams shook her head. "Not many assets in the area we can use. They'll do what they can." She fixed her eyes on them. "But I think it'll be long gone before they do."

69

GOING UNDERGROUND

"I like what you've done with the place." York sat down in a chair beside Cohen, the cluttered surface of a desk separating her from Savas. The newly outfitted office smelled of wood finish and plastics. "This is yours, John?"

Savas nodded. "Rebecca's is down the hall, next to the data centers. She wanted to be close to the raw intel."

"You two look a thousand percent better." The president smiled. "I think John's nose almost looks normal."

"We've all recovered a good bit since Ramsey," said Cohen.

"At least physically," said York.

Savas shifted uncomfortably. "Still nothing on our Zero?"

"No," said York. "Coincidentally, the Ramsey family has let it be known that Daniel passed away peacefully during the crisis. A funeral attended by big names will occur soon. By invitation only."

"Amazing," said Savas.

"Could be true," Cohen said. "He was over one hundred. Maybe the stress of what happened at the university? Or should I even call the place that?"

"A university?" asked York. "It certainly was a research institute handing out PhDs, did real science. But it was a golden facade over a skull. While you two were holding the East Coast together, I turned loose some less gifted detectives. Their job wasn't hard, once we knew where and what to look for. The place was a cesspool of corruption and fraud. Researchers bought like free agents, showered with insane amounts of money. Biotech and Big Pharma on their leash. Oligarchs laundering support for Bilderberg through the financial ledgers. Nobels bought and paid for. All to construct an unassailable reputation, one that would shield the university from all prying eyes."

"How on earth do you buy a Nobel prize?" asked Cohen.

"Like anything else. Meet the market price. You don't think the old farts in Sweden handing those things down are the Twelve Disciples?" York smiled ruefully. "They even had one poor researcher on ice for days, hiding his death from the world. Paying off the hospital and doctors for a week until the prize was announced."

"Why in the world?" asked Cohen.

"Nobel Prizes only go to the living. And Ramsey had put a substantial down payment on this one and wanted to get the return on his investment."

"I expected something more," she said. "A lot more. Science is supposed to be about truth."

"A hundred years ago, Alfred Nobel dumped a ton of money on the prize. Money spoke loudly then. It speaks loudly now. Always has, always will." York laughed. "You wouldn't believe the email exchanges the NSA dug up. The Nobel committee's a tired group of Swedish has-beens, mostly unknown in the world, even in the fields of science. Poor bastards are charged by history with the important yet unrewarding task of bestowing the ultimate scientific prestige on others. Think of the power they hold. Think of the *temptation* to make that job a little more *rewarding*. Many had their price. And Ramsey had the means to meet *any* price."

"This is science, not politics!" said Cohen.

"My dear, everything is politics. And with so much power and money involved, bring in the plumbers. Because you've got a nasty brew. Priests, senators, and scientists—dirty laundry all the same. Human nature."

"They should be held to higher standards."

"They are. Just means the price goes up. Ramsey had more than enough to shape things as he wanted. And those investments did bring a return, a shield of false honor. Behind it Bilderberg operated with impunity." She shook her head. "It's so ironic. Nobel and Ramsey were rivals for the world's oil supply before the Communist Revolution. Some accuse the Ramsey family of funding that coup. It blew up the oil region, and Nobel suffered a crippling loss while Ramsey locked in control of the world's petroleum supplies. Nobel actually had to sell his remaining shares in oil companies to Ramsey! *Humbling*."

"You know a lot about this," said Savas.

"Former law and history teacher, John. Also, it's been an eye-opening read of the intel reports the last few months."

"So, Daniel Ramsey inherited a Nobel Prize that owed his family deeply," said Cohen. "Zero had a lot to work with. A brilliant use of resources."

"Assuming Zero *is* Daniel Ramsey," said Savas. "With his disappearance, or perhaps death, we might never know. Meanwhile, with or without him, Bilderberg will be regrouping."

"With Angel's data, it's not going to be easy for them," said York. "We've busted four of the sites on her list, apprehended several powerful and shadowy figures. The others managed to make a getaway, but their organization is trashed, their web of influence shredded. They've got *a lot* of rebuilding ahead of them."

"And so do we," said Savas.

"We do." York looked them in eyes. "I won't forget what all of you went through for me, for this nation. I won't forget what you lost." She pulled out a set of papers and placed them on the desk. "Here are the orders for the Presidential Medal of Freedom. Frank Miller and Jean-Paul Rideout. Congress has too much on its plate with elections and reconstruction. Had to go executive order for the funerals."

"Without the bodies, it's a hollow ceremony," said Savas.

"Not at all," said York. "Funerals aren't for the dead. The dead get nothing from them. They're for us, the living. For grief and something even more important—for memory. It's what holds our society together. That's why we need them. And that's why I'm going to make sure these men are remembered well."

Savas didn't yield. "Even so, they deserved better."

"It's all very much appreciated, Elaine," said Cohen, reaching across the chair and squeezing the president's hand. "John never really lets go. It's why he's up at 3am too many nights. But he does appreciate what you're doing."

"I know he does," York said, smiling toward Savas. "It will be a beautiful service in DC. Many of the cherry orchards survived the riot fires. They're beginning to bloom. Colors everywhere."

"A rumor of spring," said Cohen wistfully. "This bunker has some strong downsides. Most of us don't get out for weeks at a time. It's a problem for morale. We need to schedule more frequent top-side rotations, even if it means some risk of exposure."

"You're the bosses," said York. "But I think you're right."

Savas shifted in his chair. "On that point, Elaine—the coup is over. The military and civilian leadership stabilized. We still have distribution problems, but beyond the function of this bunker. I think we've done our job in the crisis."

"Indeed you have, John. And it's been a critical one to getting things back on track quickly. You two have coordinated a truly remarkable East Coast intervention."

"Then we're wondering what the end game is. We need to get back to Intel 1, to the FBI. I know there's an interim leadership in place, but I'm anxious to make sure things are done right."

"Anxious to get your crime-fighting division back into the game?" asked York. "After all this, you're not looking for a break or early retirement? You could ask for a helluva severance package."

"You have to ask after Kansas City?" Savas shook his head. "I don't think I'll pass any emotional quotient tests or whatever they're called. My therapy is work, the only one I've known or will know. Work to protect this country. Over and over again I've seen how much needs to be done. What's happened hasn't changed that. It's only strengthened it. And I'm not done with Bilderberg quite yet."

"And you?" she asked Cohen.

"This is what we do, Elaine. This is what we love to do. At least when we're not getting shot or tortured for it."

York nodded. "Well, you're right. The need for this Manhattan bunker is coming to an end. Fawkes and his brand of Anonymous are gone. Bilderberg is on the run. The country is coming back online."

"I'm glad you agree," said Savas, relief evident in his voice.

"I do. And that's why I'm here today. Canceled some terribly important and boring meetings with Congress to make it." York stood up and looked through the window to the hive of activity outside the office. "You've taken a decayed infrastructure and turned this bunker into a formidable enterprise. Of course, you had ample funding and top personnel we supplied. But give people a mound of clay and only a few can turn it into a masterpiece." She pivoted back to them. "This site is too valuable to simply shut down. Our world has changed, my friends. Become too fragile, at the mercy of poorly secured systems and encircled by terrible weapons too easy to use. And we know too well that powerful forces want to control our destiny beyond the will of the people. After what's happened, after we nearly lost our nation—well, I think this place needs to go on functioning. But perhaps in a different guise."

Cohen arched an eyebrow. "What kind of guise?"

York sat down again, placing her fingertips together in front of her face. She stared intensely at the two agents.

"Well, that's what I really came to talk to you about."

THE CONSTRUCTION VEHICLES passed by the unusual military checkpoint, a wall of concrete slabs and scaffolding obscuring what lay behind. Alongside the checkpoint, cars continued to rumble through the Lincoln tunnel, traffic beginning to pick up again in the intervening months since the crisis ended. All was not back to normal, as the armored Army vehicles lining the toll booths testified. But for many, normal appeared to be on the horizon at last.

Lopez and Houston sat in the far back of one of the beat-up vans passing through the hidden entrance. They wore laborer's work gear—boots and blue jeans, yellow hats on their laps—distinguishable only by the looming bulk of Lopez behind the other workers.

They passed under the archway in the bedrock, the van rocketing down an orange-lit tunnel under the Hudson. The driver spoke. "Clear of the final checkpoint. We'll be at the facility in five." The passengers relaxed, some loosening and removing the hot costumes, revealing other clothing beneath.

"So, the bat cave?" said Lopez, his large hands spinning the hard hat. "Are we sure about this?"

Houston shook her head. "I don't think so."

"Good answer."

She whispered to him privately. "Look, Francisco, cons: we're disappearing again, giving up the hope of a pardon or vindication. Getting a new set of laundered identities."

"I love it when you talk dirty in my ear."

"Shut up." She smiled. "York was right. Her political situation is too fragile right now. The country is barely on its feet again. We're too radioactive. But the pros! We get to fight bad guys with people we trust and believe in, with ridiculous, *presidential* resources to conduct investigations."

"Doesn't this secret presidential force scare you a little?"

She looked out the window at the rock walls speeding by. "It does. Sounds a little too much like something Cheney would have done. *Or did.* Don't forget his secret assassination squads. But, I trust York. More than most, anyway."

"Maybe more than you should."

"Maybe. But she's proven to me where her heart lies. She could have *been* Hastings, held on to power, been Bilderberg's puppet." She exhaled, a smile on her face. "And Intel 1! John, Rebecca, and Angel—we've been through fire with them, more than once. I'm alive because of them."

"That I don't forget," said Lopez, running his hand through her hair.

"They're gold in my book. Besides—all of us, we did good. We did *damn* good. I don't know, but if we're gonna get the bang-bang toys and put on a fucking cape, who else would you pick for your team? I trust them. Not just to do the job, but to do it honorably."

The orange light began to fade, replaced slowly by a sterile fluorescent glow. Through the front windshield, they could see the opening in the tunnel and large underground lot that lay behind it, two monstrous metal doors swinging inward to allow their passage

"I hope you're right, Sara. Good intentions and the path to hell and all that."

Houston stared forward, the vehicle passing through the blast doors. She set her jaw. "You know, Francisco, so far every damn road we've been on has been to hell. We might as well do what we want while we're traveling."

Lopez grunted. "And Angel? You think it's wise to put it all in her hands?"

Houston sighed. "I don't know. Power for good or for evil. Crazy stuff. If you had sole control of the plans for the atomic bomb back in '45, what would you do? Turn the tech loose on the world? Destroy it? Either way you play God. I don't want that kind of responsibility. Do you?"

"No," said Lopez. "I'm glad I'm not able to make the choice. But two times she's held the fate of the world in her hands. Now a third. I hope she makes the right choice." The van pulled to a stop and the giant doors slammed shut behind them. "Whatever it might be."

70

GODS ANOTHER DAY

The setting sun burned a potent crimson through the glass, backlighting the explosions of spray from the massive waves pummeling the rocks below. Lightfoote stared out toward the craggy rocks and the expanse of the Pacific racing to the horizon. Her scalp was freshly shaved and gleaming, her bare arms like Greek marble against the dark fatigues she wore. One hand played with an eyebrow piercing while the other drummed along the thick glass. Around her, the floor-to-ceiling windows of the restaurant offered stunning panoramic views of the ocean, the Seal Rocks, Marin coastline, and the entry to the Golden Gate Bridge.

It had been a peaceful day, but she experienced it only as a bizarre and unnatural event in the context of the last six months. At dawn, she had begun at one end of the San Francisco Zoo, walking leisurely west toward the shore. No animal, no botanical arrangement was too inconsequential for her time. She lingered at each exhibit. Her eyes drank the miraculous life forms around her like balm poured over a burnt wound. By the time she reached the jutting outcrop of rocks thrusting the restaurant over the churning waves, the day had almost ended and the sun had begun to dive toward the water.

Her laptop was open on the table, an untouched plate of food and full cup of now cold coffee on either side of it. She refused to look at the screen again. Its contents were memorized, seared into her mind from hours of obsession. The final code was ready. Looking at it wouldn't change anything. Her problem now wasn't technical—it was moral, and she struggled to make a choice.

Press ENTER, and let loose a modified version of Fawkes's code, one that would leapfrog over the duct-taped patches placed across the world's computers to block it. Code that would take her still ranging immune worms weeks to recognize and erase. By then, the task would have been completed, every trace on the computers of the Bilderberg group wiped clean of the Nash equations. The power to scientifically model human populations and manipulate them would once again be relegated to science fiction, the can kicked down the road to some near future when the ideas were rediscovered. Gone would be that temptation to tyranny, to the godlike powers offered. Gone also would be the ability to correct societies that had gone wrong, to use reason to try and steer the mad human course on Earth toward something less self-destructive.

All she had to do was press a button.

Lightfoote had already erased the files Fawkes had sent to her, the images of the mad cork board she and Houston had reduced to ash. Gone too was the decoded text of Nash's paper. With the murder of Nash and Kaplan, the last human beings able to resurrect that work had perished as well. All that remained were the computer servers of the scattered Bilderberg group. As Fawkes had shown, they hadn't adapted to the new realities of the digital realm. Her code would hunt them down faster and more effectively than any governmental agency. It would complete the destruction of this terrible knowledge.

And all she had to do now was press a button.

"I'm sorry, ma'am, was there a problem with your meal?"

A young waitress looked down anxiously at Lightfoote and her plate, her bulging chest and tight clothing contrasting oddly with her customer's militarized appearance.

"That's all there are," said Lightfoote. "Problems."

The woman smiled weakly. "I can get the manager."

Lightfoote stared through the woman, turning her head in a slow arc, taking in the restaurant, the clientele of tourists and Silicon Valley entrepreneurs. She frowned.

"You know, we're just not ready. It's too soon."

"If you want us to bring it out later, I can have another—"

"Not *mature* enough. Monkeys just knocked out of trees."

The waitress took a step back, her eyes darting. "I'm sorry?"

Lightfoote raised her index finger and struck a key on her laptop. She stared at the screen, ignoring the waitress for several moments.

"There," she said at last. "Yup. It's all done. *Cleaned up*. We'll be gods another day." The waitress looked on in bewilderment. Lightfoote stuffed her laptop into a bag. "Can I have the check, please?"

"If Bilderberg meetings are just talking shops, why do the most powerful figures from around the world bother to attend? What other summit of world leaders in politics, finance and business would go completely unreported in the mainstream media such as the BBC? It's impossible not to reach the conclusion that the non-reporting of these events is anything other than a conspiracy between the [Bilderberg] organizers and the media. It merely confirms the belief of many that the hidden agenda and purpose of the Bilderberg Group is to bring about undemocratic world government. It's a disgrace that the European Commission is colluding in that."

— GERARD JOSEPH BATTEN, BRITISH REPRESENTATIVE TO
THE EUROPEAN PARLIAMENT, 12 SEPTEMBER 2011, AT THE
EUROPEAN PARLIAMENT IN STRASBOURG, FRANCE

"For more than a century, ideological extremists at either end of the political spectrum have seized upon well-publicized incidents such as my encounter with Castro to attack the Rockefeller family for the inordinate influence they claim we wield over American political and economic institutions. Some even believe we are part of a secret cabal working against the best interests of the United States, characterizing my family and me as 'internationalists' and of conspiring with others around the world to build a more integrated global political and economic structure — one world, if you will. If that is the charge, I stand guilty, and I am proud of it."

— DAVID ROCKEFELLER, MEMOIRS

"We are grateful to The Washington Post, The New York Times, Time magazine and other great publications whose directors have attended our meetings and respected their promises of discretion for almost forty years. It would have been impossible for us to develop our plan for the world if we had been subject to the bright lights of publicity during those years. But, the world is now much more sophisticated and prepared to march towards a world government. The supranational sovereignty of an intellectual elite and world bankers is surely

preferable to the national auto-determination practiced in past centuries."

— DAVID ROCKEFELLER

[*purported remarks at the Bilderberg Group meeting in Baden-Baden, Germany in June 1991 (published in* Hilaire du Berrier Reports*), considered apocryphal despite widespread dissemination, as no written or audio evidence has been presented from this meeting.*]

ANDROCIDE
5th Book in the INTEL 1 Series

Investigators in New York City link a series of gruesome murders to a serial killer targeting men. As they piece together the clues, they enter into a cat-and-mouse game of survival with stakes that escalate beyond what anyone could have imagined.

"THESE ARE WORKS THAT NURTURE WONDER AND
SOMETIMES BREAK HEARTS"
—Foreword Reviews

FOREWORD BOOK OF THE YEAR FINALIST

READER, WRITER, and MAKER: Speculative fiction trilogy
with time travel, aliens, metaphysical mysteries, action, adventure,
cosmology, cybernetics, religion, and romance!

"VISIONARY" and *"ENTHRALLING"*
—authors *Richard Bunning and Norm Hamilton*

HARD TIME ADVENTURE NOVELLAS
WHERE SURVIVAL IS THE MEANING OF LIFE

HARD TIME SCIFI Series

Where survival is the meaning of life. A speculative fiction serial of adventure novellas set in a strange and punishing world. In Book 1, **METAL** a woman finds herself in two different worlds, as two different people. In one she is a criminal, sentenced to a new and terrible punishment. In the other, she is a stranger and then a prophet, granted the visions of God.

ABOUT THE AUTHOR

Erec Stebbins is a biomedical researcher who writes thrillers, science fiction, mysteries, and more.

He was born in the Midwest. His mother worked as a clinical psychologist, and his father was a professor of Romance languages at the University of Nebraska in Lincoln. In fact, his father's specialty, old Romance languages and their literature, is the source of the strange spelling of his middle name: "Erec." It is an Old French spelling, taken from an Arthurian romance by Chrétien de Troyes written around 1170: *Érec et Énide*.

He has pursued diverse interests over the course of his life, including science, music, drama, and writing. His academic path focused on science, and he received a degree in physics from Oberlin College in 1992, and a PhD in biochemistry from Cornell University in 1999. He completed postdoctoral studies at Yale University. He has worked for several decades studying the atomic structure of biological macromolecules involved in disease.

For more information:
www.erecstebbinsbooks.com
erecstebbinsbooks@gmail.com

www.ingramcontent.com/pod-product-compliance
Lightning Source LLC
Chambersburg PA
CBHW020359260626
47156CB00007B/2177